Dawn of Wings & Wrath
Trinity Matthews

Copyright © 2024 by Trinity Matthews

All rights reserved.

No portion of this book may be reproduced in any form without written permission from the publisher or author, except as permitted by U.S. copyright law.

Cover art done by Artscandare

CONTENTS

Trigger Warnings	V
Treaty of the Inner Kingdom	1
1. Chapter 1	2
2. Chapter 2	17
3. Chapter 3	26
4. Chapter 4	36
5. Chapter 5	46
6. Chapter 6	54
7. Chapter 7	60
8. Chapter 8	71
9. Chapter 9	86
10. Chapter 10	101
11. Chapter 11	114
12. Chapter 12	124
13. Chapter 13	132
14. Chapter 14	142

15. Chapter 15 — 149
16. Chapter 16 — 162
17. Chapter 17 — 172
18. Chapter 18 — 187
19. Chapter 19 — 200
20. Chapter 20 — 215
21. Chapter 21 — 230
22. Chapter 22 — 246
23. Chapter 23 — 259
24. Chapter 24 — 272
25. Chapter 25 — 290

Trigger Warnings:

Your mental health matters to me so I've provided a list below of some triggers that are present in my book. It is possible that some could be missed and if that's the case, please feel free to message me on instagram, my handle is @authortrinitymatthews or email me, my email is authortrinitymatthews@gmail.com, so that I may update the list and do better in the future.

Triggers include:
-the FMC struggles with panic attacks
-sexual assault
-blood & violence
-light sexual content
-psychological torture that includes but not limited to - tampering with food, not allowing sleep & degradation
-abusive relationship that includes but not limited to - controlling the other person and lying
-alcohol abuse by main character

Treaty of the Inner Kingdom

1. **The Law of Non-Agression:** No kingdom may initiate war or violence against another kingdom protected under the Treaty, without just cause, which would be determined at an Inner Kingdom meeting.
2. **The Law of Free Movement:** All kingdoms must allow their citizens to move freely throughout the kingdoms.
3. **The Law of Cooperation:** All kingdoms must work together to address common threats, whether that be natural disasters or an overlooming threat.
4. **The Law of Peaceful Resolution:** All kingdoms must use peaceful means to resolve conflict
5. **The Law of Mateship:** All kingdoms must recognize all rulers' mates and will ensure cooperation in protecting their mate because a mating bond is sacred.
6. **The Law of Refuge & Asylum:** All kingdoms must provide refuge to anyone fleeing violence, war, or persecution.
7. **The Law of Mortality:** Humans are not to be harmed.
8. **The Law of Freedom:** All kingdoms must give their subjects free will when it comes to the choices of their lives.
9. **The Law of Diplomatic Relations:** The kingdom must maintain diplomatic relations with other kingdoms and nations promoting peaceful cooperation and understanding through diplomacy.
10. **The Law of Summons:** All kingdoms must recognize and adhere to Summons which are to be used in the direst of circumstances.

Chapter 1

Alethea

I would not be broken.
I would find a way to escape.

That was what I told myself every day. I had lost track of the amount of time I'd been here after forty-five days, if I had even tracked that correctly.

The stale, musty air of the dungeon filled my lungs with each labored breath. My body had weakened substantially since my capture. I could see the bones in my hands, and they constantly trembled. I knew it had to do with a lack of food and the cold, rigid temperature.

The last time I had been here, Eryx had rescued me before a full day had passed. But by now, my nostrils had become accustomed to the smell. At first, it reeked so badly that it caused my eyes to water.

That had stopped too.

I adjusted my hands; the chains scraped against my raw skin. As I huddled in the corner of the cell, my body trembled with exhaustion and fear. The flicker of hope in me that had once burned bright had been extinguished. I had thought that if the High Priest had left me alone, then it wouldn't diminish, but now I wasn't so sure.

I longed to smell fresh air or take a bath. I wanted nothing more than a hot meal or to feel the sun on my face. When I laid down, I would close my eyes and imagine Eryx and me dancing in the garden, or dancing with Freya at the tavern. I would dream of my family.

Anything to remind myself that my life previously hadn't been a dream, that I had been strong enough to conquer the Isle of Mirrors, or that my blood was somehow strong enough to change an ordinary man into a mage.

Eryx haunted my dreams. His dark cider eyes, the way the edges of his eyes crinkled when he laughed. I missed him so much that it felt like it made my physical condition worse. Not knowing if he survived the mating bond being ripped from us dug into my every waking moment. Without the warmth of the mating bond, it felt like there was a layer of skin that was missing. The bond was like being coated in a blanket, my mate being a constant presence. I hadn't noticed it until it had been taken from me.

Anger stirred through me anytime I thought of it. I had been so wrapped up in myself, in my own feelings, to even notice the bond, but once it had been pointed out to me, there was no way I couldn't recognize it.

Funny how that always worked.

I still hadn't seen my family. I thought they would be in the dungeons, but the High Priest must be keeping them elsewhere.

The sound of a door opening above stirred me. I pushed myself up slightly and squinted at the two guards who walked toward my cell. Surprise and fear flitted through me as they opened the door and swept into my cell without a word.

"What's going on?" I mumbled as they lifted me entirely.

They didn't answer.

"Please, just let me go," I gasped as my head fell limply to the side. "Please, just let me and my family go." Neither of the guards spoke. They only stared straight ahead numbly.

Guards lined the walls on either side. They didn't spare a glance my way, simply staring ahead with blank expressions. They carried me by my arms up a set of stairs before finally pushing open a door. Their fingers would surely bruise as they bit into my skin harshly.

My stomach dropped as a bed came into view. It was draped in a black silk comforter.

"The King wants her cleaned up and fed," one of the guards said to one of the ladies' maids standing at attention.

"Yes, sir," she said as she curtsied to him, and I was deposited onto the washroom floor. The guards shuffled out of the room. I heard the sound of running water, and then the maid knelt next to me.

"Are you able to stand?" she asked softly.

I nodded as I pushed myself up onto my elbows. She held her hands out for me and helped me up to my feet. My body swayed, but thankfully, I stayed upright. She helped strip off my dress then led me to the oversized tub. The steaming water lured me in, and I settled beneath it. The aroma of lavender caressed me as I let the warm water loosen my muscles. I closed my eyes and thanked the Gods for the maids who let me soak. My stomach roared, but the steaming water felt too good. I could fall asleep and never wake up.

"Sit up," one of the maids commanded, pulling me from my mind.

Sliding my eyes open, I met their gazes. "I can wash myself."

The two women held my gaze. I could see the challenge rise up in one of them, but finally, she nodded and handed me a bar of soap.

I scrubbed my body until my skin was pink. Then, once I managed to get the stink out of my hair, I scrubbed it again. My fingers were prunes by the time I felt clean enough to drain the water.

The red-haired maid helped pull me to my feet while the brunette wrapped a fluffy towel around me. As I stepped out of the tub, the red-haired maid grabbed another towel and began dabbing at my dripping hair. The other began lathering on a thin paste to help my dry and cracked skin.

"This was laid out for you," the brunette said as she held up a simple dress.

Nodding my thanks, I took the dress from her and slid it on. She moved behind me and gripped my elbow as she led me to the vanity with a plate of food. Taking a seat, she began brushing through my knotted hair, and I set on devouring the food in front of me. My stomach roared as I inhaled the cheese and fruits. It felt like I hadn't eaten in a lifetime. My mouth nearly watered as the scent of the roasted chicken filled my nostrils. Pairing that with the herb butter roll, I devoured that too.

By the time she had brushed through my hair, I had already finished my food and drank two full glasses of water. Energy surged through me for the first time in weeks.

"Thank you," I whispered.

"It's our pleasure, My Lady," they said in unison.

My Lady?

I wanted to laugh. They spoke as if I was a guest here.

"Mmm," a voice behind me purred.

My entire body stiffened as fear shot through my limbs. I hadn't heard that voice since I'd been tossed in the dungeons to be forgotten. That would have been a better fate.

I cringed as the hand traced my shoulder. "Beautiful."

I didn't answer as the High Priest ran the tip of his finger down the back of my neck. I squeezed my eyes shut as his lips skated the shell of my ear.

"Chain her to the bed," he commanded and withdrew his hands.

"What?" I gasped as two guards gripped my arms and dragged me backward off of the stool towards the bed. "No, please. Don't do this!" I screamed.

The High Priest shoved the robe draped over his shoulders. It tumbled to the ground, and he stepped out of it, leaving him in a tunic and trousers.

"Get out," he snapped at the ladies' maids.

Without sparing me a glance, they ducked their heads and scurried from the chambers.

The guards yanked me back onto the bed. I kicked my feet wildly, trying to get away from them. Two more guards surged forward to hold my legs still as they successfully chained my wrists, and then they all dropped their hands after making sure I was secured. I pulled myself up into a sitting position, and my chest heaved as the door slammed shut.

We were alone.

His face was set in a harsh glare as he stopped at the foot of the bed. Locking my jaw, I turned away from him and fisted my hands to hide the tremor in them. I heard more shuffling, and then the bed creaked. The bed shifted beneath his weight, and I felt his hands graze my ankles and calves. I squeezed my eyes shut as he settled on his knees before me. He had removed his shirt, but I hadn't looked below his waist before I closed my eyes.

"How are you feeling, my bride?" he whispered teasingly, and I flinched as the tips of his fingers brushed across my lips.

"Don't touch me," I managed to bite out between my clenched teeth.

He laughed harshly.

"No!" I screamed as he gripped my legs and forced them apart. His hands fisted in the layers of my dress, and he yanked it up, exposing my calves and my thighs. He growled as he gripped my ankle and lowered his face to the joint.

Forcing my eyes shut, I bit down on my tongue in an attempt to keep the tears at bay as he pressed his lips to the inside of my ankle. Bile burned the back of my throat as I twisted my wrists in the chains. I jerked slightly at the feel of his lips moving up my leg; they brushed against the back of my calf, then my knee. Then his lips were on my thigh. He paused, his face inches from where my legs met, inches from the place I'd only let Eryx touch me.

I tried to picture his face as the High Priest's tongue swirled against my skin. Instead of goosebumps, like I'd experienced with Eryx, I felt fear. I knew if I didn't cooperate, then he'd hurt me, maybe even kill me.

A sob slipped free as his hands slid up the outside of my thighs and then moved to glide up the insides of my thighs. "Please," I whispered, my voice trembling as I shook my head. "Please don't do this." I felt the first tear slip down my cheek.

His movements paused for a moment, and then I felt the sharp sting of his teeth. I cried out and ripped back, but he kept his teeth embedded in my leg. It was like he was marking me; there was nothing sensual about it. I could feel my skin tearing as he bit down deeper before pulling back. Blood pooled around the circular mark as he rose up on his knees. He didn't say a word as he leaned forward and unbuttoned the top buttons of my dress.

I cried out again as the cold air hit my chest, exposing my breasts to him. Another part of me only Eryx had seen.

I turned my face away as he dropped his face into my neck. My skin revolted as his tongue danced across it and moved down. My chest rose and fell quickly as fear latched onto my throat with a vice grip. His hands slid down my front, cupping my breasts. But unlike Eryx, whose hands were soft and gentle, they squeezed painfully until I cried out. Then his mouth moved down my collarbone, and once his mouth reached the swell of my breast, he bit down like he did with my thigh. But this skin was more sensitive, so I dropped my head back and screamed.

His hand snaked out and slammed over my lips. Like it mattered, he was the King and could do whatever he pleased. I cried out against his hand as he bit down harder, drawing more blood than he did before.

Tears streamed down my cheeks as I fought against him. Finally, he yanked away and wiped the blood from his mouth.

He pushed himself off the bed and picked up his robes. "One day, you'll give yourself to me."

"I would rather die," I croaked as I let my head fall back against the wooden headboard.

He growled in response but didn't say another word as he draped his robes over his shoulders and tied them. The sound of the door closing triggered the onslaught of tears. I couldn't breathe through them; they blurred my vision and clogged my throat. My chest heaved as I threw myself forward. The chains rattled off the headboard, but it didn't budge.

"Please let me out of here!" I screamed as I slammed back again.

I needed to get out of here. My chest swelled as my breaths became shorter. I tried to picture Lira as she combed her fingers through my hair, but it was too much. I focused on breathing in through my nose and out through my mouth.

I slammed back into the headboard, the chains rattling. I dropped my head back and let out another scream.

The door opened in response.

"Sister," Laney snapped.

I jerked my gaze towards the door in disbelief. My mouth gaped open as she stood before me, clean and whole. She was in a pristine pearl colored gown and donned matching gloves. Her shimmering hair was pulled into an elegant bun atop her head. Two pieces framed her face and curled away from her cheeks. Laney had always been beautiful, but she'd never been given the opportunity to dress up like royalty. Now that she did, she looked the part.

"Laney," I gasped as another stray tear slipped down my cheek. "What are you doing?"

"He sent me in here to tell you to calm down," she sighed, clearly exasperated.

She turned as she closed the double doors behind her and strode towards me. *He sent her in here?*

"What do you mean?" My voice trembled involuntarily.

She didn't look at my face as she reached over the bed and began doing up the buttons he had undone. Her face was set in a stoic expression, there wasn't an ounce of understanding that her sister was chained to a bed and was evidently being touched against her will.

"What are you doing?" I asked again.

"Compose yourself. I'm to escort you."

She pulled a set of keys from beneath her skirts and undid the left shackle and then walked around the bed to undo the other.

"Hurry up," she urged with raised eyebrows.

My fingers fumbled the remainder of the buttons as I slid off the bed.

"Follow me."

She strode towards the doors and threw them open. She didn't look at me as she waited for me to stop behind her. Her back was rigid, and it seemed like she stood taller.

"He's not going to hurt us," she said without looking at me.

"He cut off our father's finger!" I shouted.

"Because your *King*," she spit the word, "had spies sent in, and they were found."

I gaped at her, and my feet froze. "You're defending him? Where are you even taking me?"

"I'm taking you to see Father. He requested he see you."

"He's alright?" I breathed in relief.

"As well as he can be," was all she said as she continued down the hall.

I tried to do my best to memorize where I was. If I was going to escape, then I needed to learn the layout of the palace.

I didn't hear anything besides the padding of my feet on the floor and we didn't pass a single soul. It was like the castle was a ghost town. The hall we strolled down was unfamiliar to me. We passed closed door after closed door so I was forced to examine the walls as my only means. The walls were lined with paintings of Kirin, the previous King, and his bloodline. Each picture was framed in gold that stood out against the bright red of the walls, red like the blood he had forced down my throat.

"We're going to have those removed," Laney said as she noticed me glancing at them.

"Why does it matter?"

She shrugged as we stopped before a set of double doors. She turned the extravagant handle and stepped back as she shoved open the door. She didn't look at me as I swept around her and into the plain bedroom.

"Papa," I gasped as I rushed to the side of the bed.

I dropped to my knees and gripped the side of his face.

"Alethea." He smiled up at me. His skin was tinged gray, the skin on his lips were peeling, and his hands trembled as his fingers wrapped around my wrist.

"What happened?" I gasped as tears prickled behind my eyes. My chest felt like it was going to cave in on itself. The last time I had seen him he had been thriving and now - I couldn't form the words to describe how he looked.

His eyes were glassy and in them a hint of hysteria. His hands trembled, and his eyes jumped back and forth across the room, like something would lunge at him at any moment.

"Papa," I insisted. "Papa, please look at me."

"I'm sorry. I'm so sorry we never told you before. We knew we needed to, but we never knew when the right time was." His lips shook as tears threatened to claim him.

I frowned. "Tell me what?"

He huffed a breath as tears sprang forth in the corner of his eyes. "That I'm not your father," he whispered.

"What?" I gasped as I jerked my hands from his face. "What are you saying? What do you mean?"

"Your mother and father left you in our care to protect you. It wanted to claim you, and they wanted to keep you from it. They left you with us to keep you safe," he explained. "But we failed you, and I'm so, so sorry. We failed your parents. We promised them."

As he spoke, I saw flashes of our lives. Each of them confirmed what he was telling me. The difference in how Laney and I looked. Laney had been a spitting image of our mother, but I had never looked like her - even in the ways we were similar, like how the gold in our hair had different hues. I had always thought it was because of how much time I spent in the sun, but so had Laney. Her hair had always resembled honey, but mine was much lighter, and my father had deep brown eyes with his matching brown hair. My eyes were brown but with speckles of green, making them more of a hazel.

"But," I stuttered as I tried to wrap my mind around it.

"We still love you. We love you so much." His eyes widened. "Your mother, Alethea, I'm so sorry."

"I know, Papa," I whispered as I placed a hand on his cheek.

"She fought. She fought so hard." He chuckled as tears flooded his eyes. "They said that if we didn't fight, they wouldn't hurt us. But she had fought. She didn't want them to find out about you once word spread of you being taken by the fae."

"Shhhh," I hushed as I felt his forehead. "You're burning up." He gulped and nodded. "My finger got infected after they removed it. The King refused to give me bandages, and once he did, it was too late. The infection had already spread."

"No," I gasped as I shook my head.

"The King said your time is up," Laney said from the doorway.

I didn't spare her a glance as I stroked the side of my father's face. "He's not my *King*." I spit the words.

"Have it your way," Laney said passively, and I gasped as a guard gripped each of my arms.

"Alethea!" My father exclaimed as I was pulled away from him.

"No! Papa! Please, let me go to him!" I screamed as I lunged forward.

He reached a hand towards me, but he was too weak to sit up. "I love you, Alethea, no matter what. You are still my daughter, and I love you so much."

Tears stung my eyes as I tried to reach him but failed. "I love you, Papa," I cried right before the door slammed.

The guards didn't release their grip as they continued dragging me down the halls. I screamed for them to let me go. Maids hurried by us with wide eyes. Perhaps I looked feral to them.

"Please, he's dying! He needs me!" I pleaded.

Laney appeared beside me, and the guards kept me from lunging at her. Her eyes widened, the first show of emotion on her face, as she stumbled back a step. My fingers hooked as I tried reaching for her again. I wanted to gouge her eyeballs out. She had barely even looked at him.

"Why are you doing this?" I screamed.

After a moment, she composed herself. The disbelief was wiped from her face. "The King wants to see you."

"He's not my King!" My voice echoed off the halls as they dragged me.

I recognized the halls; they were bringing me back to his chambers. The guards threw the doors open, and the first thing I saw was the High Priest lounging. His robes were gone, and he was in a pair of trousers lounging on a chase before the open set of double windows. My time spent in the dungeon had made me lose track of night and day.

The sky was a deep maroon, signaling the setting of the sun.

"Chain her up," the High Priest commanded without sparing us a glance.

My heart plummeted as they yanked me into the room. The doors thudded shut behind me with Laney still outside. How could she do this? How could she let her sister go through this? She hadn't even batted an eye at our father's condition or that he looked like he might keel over at any moment.

The guards dragged me to the side of the bed. A hint of relief coursed through me as I realized that the chain he was referring to was in the middle of the floor. One of the guards dropped to his knees and secured the iron shackle around my ankle. He tested out the sturdiness of the chain as he yanked against it. The bolt that secured it to the floor didn't budge. They released me once I was restrained.

"Get out," The High Priest's voice commanded.

The guards slithered out of the room without another word. Slowly, I lowered myself to the ground and pulled my knees to my chest.

"Are you comfortable?" the High Priest asked after several minutes of silence.

I gritted my teeth, keeping my mouth shut.

He chuckled. "You might as well be polite, considering you're going to be stuck here for a while."

"Why did you choose me?"

The High Priest's beady gaze moved over me once before settling on the fireplace.

"I needed someone filled with hate," he answered as he tipped the glass back and downed it in one gulp. "When you were dragged in, your eyes were burning with disgust. You looked like you wanted to gut Kirin on the spot." He laughed darkly.

"He was ogling young women," I growled in response.

The High Priest laughed again as he stood and stretched his arms over his head. "I suppose."

"There will be an uprising once word spreads of the new King being a mage," I warned.

He merely laughed again as he twisted towards me. "Let them," he mocked. "I don't care for them. They will be slaughtered."

"You would murder your own people?" I demanded.

"I don't care about ruling," he answered.

"Then why kill Kirin?"

"I was just as human as he was. I needed him to lead me to you. I didn't have the means or resources."

So many questions spiraled in my mind as I stared at him. The cold air that blew through the curtains caused a chill to spread down my spine.

"How did my blood turn you into a mage?"

He shrugged as he placed his glass down on the small table and stood. The muscles in his back popped as he stretched his arms over his head. Now that he was a mage, he looked dozens of years younger. The first time I'd seen him, his blonde hair had been buzzed close to his scalp. But now it had grown. It fell around his face in waves. His skin was deeper than before, more olive, and his brown eyes glittered.

"I'm not entirely sure," he admitted.

"Why still keep me?" I tightened my arms around my legs.

His heavy gaze settled on me as he contemplated answering. Placing his glass down, he turned. My heart sped up as he prowled towards me. He lowered himself onto one knee before me. My breath caught as he stroked the back of his finger down my cheek and leaned into me. I turned my head away from him as he trailed his nose across the bridge of my shoulder. My eye twitched as he stopped just below my jaw.

"Do you not want to be made a queen?" he whispered against my skin.

The feeling of his breath across my skin made me want to vomit. I shook my head.

"There would be nothing worse on this earth than being your Queen," I warned.

His hand struck out without warning. It bounced off my cheek. I cried out as the slap resonated through the room around us. My cheek stung as I fell to my side. I managed to catch myself before my other cheek hit the ground.

He tsked his tongue as he lowered back beside me while I gripped my throbbing face. I flinched as he reached towards me and cupped my chin. His eyes scoured my face before his brows turned down.

"Enjoy sleeping on the ground like a dog," he bit out in disgust as he threw my head back.

I glared at him as he turned and headed towards his bed.

Chapter 2

Eryx

"*Please don't let them take me!*" *Alethea begged as she was dragged backward. Three men dragging one tiny innocent girl. How disgusting and pathetic. "Please, Eryx, don't let them take me!"*

I could see the tears shimmering in her eyes as the door to the carriage was thrown open. But I couldn't get to her. Shame built inside of my chest as she too realized that I wasn't going to be able to save her. I grunted as another sword pierced through my side; if I couldn't get away, they were going to kill me. I was losing the ability to keep my eyes open; I was losing blood too quickly.

Understanding dawned in her eyes, and she offered me the tiniest of smiles. The kind of smile that gutted me from the inside out and forever imprinted itself upon my soul.

"It's okay," she said as the fight began to leave her body. "It's okay. I'll be okay."

I shook my head as I tried wrenching away from this damned tree. "I'll come for you, Alethea. I promise."

She nodded at me, tears flooding her eyes as another man came up behind her. Her eyes widened in panic just before a sack was tugged over her head. She screamed again as she was lifted off the ground. I screamed her name as another sword pierced my side. My breath whooshed out of me as I slumped forward. I heard her scream my name again as my consciousness faded.

Gasping, I bolted upright with a single thought. I needed to find her.

"Eryx!" Merdrina gasped as she shot up from her stool. "Send for Cadmus," she told the guard stationed at the door.

"Where is she?" I growled as I swung my legs off the cot.

I was shirtless with bandages stuck across my chest. There was a fire roaring in the fireplace, and the sky outside had darkened.

"You need to sit down." Medrina ignored my question as she pushed me down by my shoulders.

"I need to get her," I argued.

Her brows drew down, and I groaned as her powers wrapped around me. The airy feeling tightened around me as I lowered onto my back.

"Please, please don't. She needs me," I pleaded, but I had no choice but to obey.

"You need to heal first." Her voice was soft as her powers lulled my racing heart.

"I need to find her. I need to find her," I whispered over and over again as my eyes slid shut.

Medrina's humming woke me some time later. I groaned as I pushed myself up slower this time.

"Eryx," Cadmus said.

My head snapped towards him. He was resting in an armchair beside my cot. He looked rested, not a scratch on him like the last time I had seen him.

"How long was I out?" I croaked.

My throat felt like I'd swallowed a box of sand.

"Twelve days," Medrina answered from the other side of the room. She was hunched over the table messing with vials. "How are you feeling?"

"Exhausted."

She nodded. "That's to be expected. You were in bad shape when they brought you here."

"Where is she?" I growled in response.

Cadmus heaved a sigh. "Kirin has her."

I shot to my feet. "Then I need to go get her."

"We can't! Not yet, anyway!" Cadmus argued but I shoved past him.

I threw open the door and stormed through the hall. I could feel my powers roiling beneath my skin, ready to pounce.

"Eryx, we can't go. Not yet!"

"They took her!" I roared as I spun on him.

"I know that," Cadmus said lightly as he stepped towards me. "I know they did, and we will get her back. But we will be of no use to her if we get slaughtered."

"We are fae," I bite back. "We can easily overpower them."

"We have sent men to Kirin's borders, and we have lost them all. Whatever is going on, there are powers at work we are unaware of." Cadmus reached his hand towards me and placed it on my shoulder. "You have always said that you trusted me as if I was your own brother. Now let me prove it to you."

I paused as I took in the sincerity in his gaze. I trusted him with my life and in turn, Alethea's. My shoulders dropped as I nodded.

He breathed out a sigh of relief. "Let's go to your office."

I followed behind him, passing guards that had been stationed at every door. Opening the door, I headed straight for the wardrobe tucked in the corner of the room. I pulled out a tunic and began to button it as Cadmus sat down.

"Fill me in on everything," I commanded.

"We sent troops to their borders after she was taken, and they were met head-on with Kirin's men," Cadmus paused as he ran a hand through his hair. "We lost every one of our troops."

Everyone? Full-grown fae?

My mouth dropped open as I sat back in my chair. "These men were all fae?" I asked as I glanced at the bookcase along the wall. "Something's not right, Cadmus."

"Hear me out," he responded as he sat on the other side of the desk. I leaned forward, waiting to hear what he had to say. "I have a few theories, first starting with Kirin and his kingdom. I think that they're meddling in black magic."

"Black magic? Like a mage?"

Cadmus nodded. "That would explain how his human troops were able to overcome and slaughter three dozen fae males."

I sighed as I ran a hand down my face. "Okay, what's your next theory?" With Cadmus, I knew by the look on his face that there was more. He looked too distressed.

He let out a deep sigh and leaned forward, propping his elbows on his knees. "I think Alethea has fae in her."

I wanted to feel shocked, but even Medrina had already mentioned the possibility.

"It would explain our mating bond," I nodded.

"I did some digging," he responded. "I can't find records of Alethea's parents giving birth to a second child."

My mouth dried, and I nodded numbly. My skin yearned for her, needing to feel her safe against me. It was enough to distract me. My thoughts flickered back to our last night together before she had left with Freya. That night had been perfect. We had drifted to sleep in each other's arms, then I had awoken the next morning later than I normally did. That's when I felt the effects of the sleeping herbs. They made my limbs feel like they were weighed down with lead, and it was like walking through quicksand.

Medrina had given me the herbs after my father's death.

My heart twinged as I thought of the fear and betrayal that had racked me when I found her letter on the pillow.

"Any word on Freya?" I asked. Cadmus shook his head. "Keep searching for her. She has the Eye."

"We've gone through her entire quarters. Nothing hints at why she betrayed us."

"There has to be something. Was there anyone tracking her movements before she and Alethea set off for the Eye?"

"There were guards who saw her coming and going a lot, but that was normal for her," he answered.

I groaned and scrubbed a hand down my face. "Damn it."

"We'll find her," Cadmus assured me. He was referring to Freya, but I couldn't bring myself to care entirely, even if she was my little sister. She had betrayed us and almost killed Alethea.

"We bring Alethea back first." My hands clenched in my lap. "She's our first priority. Build up numbers, try and get some spies inside to report back to us if she's okay and if they can find out what Kirin wants with her."

Cadmus nodded. "We're training batches of warriors from the city. The Barren have been a problem since she was taken. They've been pillaging the outskirts of the city. They're taking people."

I frowned. "Taking people? Where?"

"We're not sure. They are just disappearing with them. We're not finding bodies drained of blood. Just sightings of Barren and then reports of missing fae."

Worry settled in my bones. "Set up more patrols on the borders. Tell Harn I want to meet with him about the security around the perimeter tomorrow morning."

I pushed up from my seat as he nodded.

"I need to bathe," I said. "I'll find you when I'm done."

Cadmus merely nodded, and I slipped through the halls quickly. My chest tightened as I felt my control slowly slipping. The guards all must have sensed it too because no one approached me or nodded in my direction.

Closing the door behind me, my body shook as I approached the unmade bed. As I pulled the blanket back, I stumbled away as her scent assaulted me. My knees gave out from beneath me, and I lowered myself to the floor. My entire body shook.

More flashes of the night before she had left danced behind my closed lids. It was serene, but now thinking back on it, I could see the secretiveness. I could see the nervousness as she fidgeted. I had seen it several times before then, but I thought it may have been because she was nervous around me. Gods, how I was wrong.

I should be angry at her, at her deceit. If she had only trusted me, then maybe we wouldn't be in this mess in the first place. She'd have been here, safe with me. But I knew part of it had been my fault, I had her treated like a frail flower that could be blown away in the wind. *Blossom.* I had named her that because it was what she had reminded me of, but she had evolved. She looked like a soft petal on the outside with her round, rosy cheeks and doe eyes, but inside was someone willing to do whatever she needed for her family.

I had underestimated her. If only I had seen that tenacious spirit lurking beneath, if only I had paid more attention. I had let the Barren and Cador's death distract me.

My hands shook as I lifted off the ground. I waved a hand towards the bed, the sheets making themselves.

I needed to find her and bring her home. I wouldn't make the same mistake of treating her like a fragile vase again. I had told her she was my equal, but I hadn't treated her as such. We were mated, which meant that whatever magic ran in her veins rivaled mine, and there were few who were as powerful as me.

Heading into the washroom, I stripped off my shirt and stopped to look in the mirror hung on the wall adorned with two golden lion heads. There were thin marks that were duller than the rest of my skin. They were scars from the swords that had held me back from saving her. I needed to circle back with Medrina; they shouldn't have scarred over, and I shouldn't have been out that long.

I ran my fingers over one of the scars. The skin was slightly raised.

It had to be the result of some poison of some kind. That was the only thing I could think of to explain the scarring.

Bathing quickly, I changed into a fresh set of clothes and immediately felt more like myself. I needed to keep a clear head and think things through clearly if I was going to bring her home safely. I didn't look at the bed as I passed by and gripped the door handle. I paused as I breathed in her fresh scent once more before yanking the door open.

"Refreshed?" Cadmus asked as I closed the door behind me. He pushed up off the wall and strode to my side.

I nodded. "I need to speak with Medrina. Have her come to my office."

"She has actually already requested to meet with you," he answered as we descended the stairs. "She's already waiting in your office."

I nodded as we moved quickly through the halls. Even the space around me seemed duller without her here. Cadmus must have stationed more guards because we passed by some every turn. There were two guards stationed on either side of my office.

"My King," Medrina bowed as I threw open the door.

I waved for her to sit as I took my seat on the other side of the desk. "Were the blades poisoned?" I asked immediately, abandoning all pleasantries.

Cadmus closed the door and stood behind her with a grim expression as he crossed his arms over his chest.

Medrina nodded. "Yes. I'm not sure what the poison was yet; I'm still working on it. But I was able to extract it from you, which is why you finally regained consciousness."

"Okay, let me know when you manage to find out what it is."

She nodded again. "I may take it to a healer in the city, Madam Varley. She may know more about it."

"Fine, just try and find out quickly what it is so we can find out where it came from," I commanded and waved my hand, dismissing her.

She bowed her head as she rose. "Yes, sire."

Cadmus opened the door for her, allowing her to exit.

"We're not able to take on Kirin's men on our own," Cadmus said as he closed the door behind her.

Sighing, I leaned forward and scrubbed my face. "What should we do then?"

"We can ask for reinforcements. Mykill is the closest to us."

I groaned. "I fucking hate him."

"I know, but he won't have a choice. She's your mate, so she's protected under the Treaty."

"The Treaty," I rolled my eyes. "That bastard couldn't care less about the treaty. I say we just go in on our own."

"That would be suicide."

I nodded as I stared down at my desk. He was right. *Damn it*, I knew he was right. "We'll send a letter," I said as I yanked open the top drawer and pulled out a parchment, pen, and a wax seal.

After scribbling down a letter, I addressed it to Mykill and handed it to Cadmus. "I'll have this delivered right away." He bowed before leaving me alone with my raging thoughts.

Chapter 3

Alethea

I was woken up by one of the maids the next morning. They quickly helped me bathe and provided me with a fresh set of clothes. They said the High Priest was waiting for me to join him for breakfast in the dining room. I made sure to take my time bathing and dressing before guards forcibly escorted me to the dining room.

The High Priest was seated at the head of the long table. The table was bare except for two place settings for him and me. There weren't candles to adorn the center of the table or any other centerpiece. It made the already uninviting room unapproachable entirely. My heart raced the second I crossed the threshold. The guards acted as if they couldn't get away faster. I hadn't seen him engage with the guards, but I was sure he wasn't kind to them either.

"Please, sit." He waved at me.

My hands trembled at my sides as I stopped behind the highback chair. I knew I should move, pull it out, and sit down. I wasn't supposed to show fear. But even if I schooled my face, he'd hear the rapid beating of my heart.

His eyes narrowed much like that of a predator as he leaned forward. He leaned his elbows on the table and intertwined his fingers. "Sit." His voice was low, commanding.

Sit or be sat.

Breathing in deeply through my nostrils, I reached for the chair and pulled it out. The feet scraped off the floor, heightening my nerves. Sitting down, I went to pull myself in but yelped when the chair moved on its own. I felt my eyes widen as I gripped the arms of the chair. My gaze lifted to the High Priest's, who was merely smiling at me with a raised brow.

"Eat." He motioned to the already prepared plate before me.

I stared at him a moment longer before I reached for the fork resting beside the plate.

"No," he clipped. "You use your hands."

My eyes widened as I looked back up at him in disbelief. Then I looked back down at the plate of food. Mashed potatoes, a slice of chicken smeared in gravy, and soupy green beans. I glanced back up at him expecting him to say he was kidding, but he merely stared at me.

Nodding, I turned my attention back to the plate before me. My stomach roared, and I knew if I didn't eat now, then I didn't know when I would get another chance. My trembling hand paused above the mound of mashed potatoes. He was humiliating me, degrading me, making sure that I knew that I was beneath him.

"Eat."

Glancing up once more at him, I mustered every ounce of courage I had and hooked my finger into the mound. I ignored the runny texture of it and leaned over the plate as I brought some to my mouth. I could feel his cruel smile as I shoveled the food into my mouth the best I could. The food ran down the side of my hands, the butter greasing my skin.

I felt like a dog. It was like eating through a veil of shame. It made it worse that he not only watched me but enjoyed humiliating me. I felt tears rush my eyes as I shoveled another bite into my mouth.

"Eat faster," he commanded.

With tear-struck eyes, I glanced up at him. Much to my mortification, he was smiling at me. He looked psychotic; his grin stretched ear to ear. My body felt paralyzed as I stared at him. I had never felt this amount of fear as I stared at him. I could see what becoming a mage had taken from him. His eyes were dark and vacant. Becoming a mage had stripped him of his humanity. The eyes staring back at me were devoid of emotion, and I needed to fear him. Because he didn't care what was done to me. He didn't care what I'd feel; he would use me to amuse himself. I wasn't a human to him. I wasn't a being. I was merely a toy.

His smile turned into a scowl, and he shoved his chair out. I jumped as the legs squealed heinously off the tiled floor. I tried shoving my seat out, but the chair didn't move. He had trapped me in the seat. He dove for me and gripped my hair in his fist. I cried out as he ripped my head back, my neck craned so far it felt like it was going to crack.

I tried to scream as he shoved a handful of chicken into my mouth. Instinctively, I gagged, but he shoved the mashed potatoes into my mouth next. I tried to talk around the food, to beg him to stop, but he continued shoving it into my mouth until I coughed it up. Mashed potatoes flew into his face, and he cringed. He released the hold on my hair and threw my head back. Curling over my plate, I coughed up the food. My appetite instantly vanished as I stared at the pile of food mixed with vomit.

"Disgusting," he said as he plopped back down in his seat. "You got potatoes on my boots."

Tears flooded my eyes as I met his hateful gaze. "I-I'm sorry," I muttered as I picked up the napkin resting beside my plate.

His gaze was unflinching as he said, "Lick it off."

"What?" I croaked in disbelief.

His eyes darkened, and he launched forward. I yelped as he fisted his hand in my hair again, and he wrenched me forward. My knees slapped off the ground and he shoved my face towards the floor.

"Lick. It. Off," he bit out.

I could feel my face burning as the tears flowed freely down my cheeks. My knees ached, and I braced myself on my hands. My limbs felt like they locked as the reality of my situation crashed onto me. All control of my life had been relinquished to *him*. I was trapped under his mercy, and currently his mercy was to degrade and humiliate me.

My limbs trembled as I lowered my face. Disbelief coursed through me as I stared at the shiny tip of his pointed boot. This was all one sick, twisted game. He was trying to break me down.

Beside the pile of gooey potatoes, I could see the faint outline of my face. My eyes were wide with tears streaming out of them. My hair was now a wild mane around my face. My skin was flushed, but the most prominent thing was the fear written across my features.

I was stronger than this, I thought to myself. I knew that. Eryx had told me that. I had conquered the Isle of Mirrors.

Closing my eyes, I willed all of my emotions down as I stuck out my tongue. The boot was cold beneath my tongue as I ran across the bridge of it. Shame radiated through me as I pushed myself up and rested on my feet. Taking a deep breath, I squared my shoulders and opened my eyes. I forced myself to meet his gaze. His gaze was mocking. He leaned forward and took my jaw in his hand.

"Good girl," he breathed, and I fought the urge to cringe as his breath skated across my nose. "Now clean yourself up." He tossed a napkin at me as he rose. "Bring her to the throne room," he commanded the guards.

Scrambling to my feet, I wiped off my face of any remains of food and grease. The guards waited for me by the door, thank the Gods, and didn't come after me. I placed the napkin back on the table as I stood, and I moved towards them. I waited for them to grab my arms, but they merely stepped aside and waved me through the doors. Neither of them looked at me as I passed. They didn't need to lead me. I knew where the throne room was.

I ignored the crude, vulgar paintings on the walls as I headed for the throne room. The guards' boots scuffed off the ground, the sound heightening my nerves. The double doors were already open, and the High Priest was lounging on his throne. There were two guards standing next to him, and on their knees in between them was a man in worn clothing - a villager.

"Come forward." He rolled his eyes as my steps faltered.

One of the guards clasped my elbow as he passed and pulled me along with him.

"This young man will be the first to be given the opportunity to use your blood and turn into a mage," the High Priest explained. "Your blood turned me, so your blood can turn him."

"What? No!" I exclaimed as I paused before the steps.

The High Priest waved me forward, but I remained rooted where I was. His glittery gaze moved up to mine as he quirked an eyebrow at me.

"You can move up here on your own, or they will move you." He leaned forward and gripped the arms of his throne as he threatened.

My hands fisted at my sides as my jaw clenched. My teeth rubbed together painfully as I forced my feet to move. The ground was cold beneath my bare feet.

He reached for me as I settled in front of him. A knife produced out of the air and floated to his hand. He snatched it out of the air and gripped my wrist. I gasped as he yanked me forward. His fingers tightened around my wrist, and he dragged the tip of the blade across my skin. I winced and shut my eyes as my blood trailed down the sides of my wrist. I flinched as I felt his tongue stroked across the gash. My eyes flew open, and I stared down at him in disgust. My blood gleamed on his tongue, and he smiled wickedly at me. He grasped the goblet resting on the arm of his throne and held it beneath my arm. I winced as he squeezed, trying to force more blood as it splattered into the goblet.

"Come forward." He waved at the man and released my hand. I scooted back several steps and covered the cut with my hand.

The peasant man stood to his feet. His eyes were worried as he looked at the High Priest before stepping towards him.

"Take this and drink it," he commanded the man, who nodded and took the goblet from him.

There couldn't be more than a mouthful in the goblet as he raised it to his lips and drank. My stomach wanted to revolt at the thought of him drinking my blood. It reminded me of the Barren. They survived off of blood.

He handed the empty goblet back to the High Priest, who waved his hand. It went tumbling through the air. The sound of it clanging across the floor echoed in the almost empty throne room before it finally rolled to a stop.

I watched as the man began to tremble. His eyes widened in fear, and he began to convulse. He dropped to the ground like a sack of potatoes and shrieked as he curled in on himself. With wide eyes, I fell back a step. The man's golden skin began to pale, like the blood was being drained from his body. His mouth fell open as he screamed again and rolled onto his back. I watched in astonishment as his teeth began to lengthen into points. His fingernails lengthened until they were talons. His skin turned almost translucent. He looked almost like a Barren but worse. His mouth dropped open in a silent scream, and his back bowed off the floor. The High Priest rose from his seat, his eyes wide in disbelief as blood began to drip from the corners of his eyes. Terror coated my limbs as I stepped back again.

He is going to kill me, I thought as his gaze fixated on me.

The man shrieked once more before his back bent at an unnatural angle and fell limp. My mouth dropped open in disbelief as I stared down at the man's broken body.

"It should have worked. It worked on me." The High Priest's voice sounded breathless.

My eyes snapped back up to him, and his eyes seemed like they were on fire as he stared at me. His gaze burned right through me. His anger was palpable in the air; even the guards remained behind me, almost like they were using me as a shield.

"What happened? What did you do?" the High Priest demanded.

I shook my head and held up my hands. "I didn't do anything! I don't even know how it worked the first time!" I argued.

"You did something!" I flinched as he shouted.

I shook my head. "No, no, no, I didn't! I swear!"

"Bring her to my quarters," the High Priest demanded. "Now!"

"This isn't my fault," I stammered as guards clamped their hands on my arms.

He threw his hands, and the doors thudded open. They bounced off the walls, booming down the halls. I could feel his anger radiating off of him as he stormed down the hall. The guards dragged me after him. I fought against their hands, but they were stronger than me. Anger swelled in my chest; everyone was always stronger than me.

Why hadn't I trained more?

Even the sessions I'd done with Cadmus seemed to have done nothing. I was no stronger than I was before. If I made it out of this, I would be sure to train.

The High Priest trailed before us as the guards' grips on each arm tightened. I squirmed in their grasp, but they simply lifted me as they quickened their pace. I could sense they wanted away from the High Priest's anger as much as I did. Luckily for them, they could leave. They were simply leaving me with him.

The doors burst open to his bedroom, and heat rolled through the room, a manifestation of his anger. My heart thundered in my ears as they drug me over to the chain on the floor and secured me there.

"Get out!" the High Priest shouted.

I resisted the urge to flinch as glass shattered. Wind kicked up from outside, filtering in through the room.

The curtains whipped around as the High Priest shed his robes. He stepped out of them as they pooled around his ankles, leaving him in his trousers.

The doors thudded shut behind the guards, and he whipped his fiery gaze on me. I stumbled backwards as he strode towards me.

"Please, please," I stammered and held up my hands in surrender. "I don't know what happened. We did exactly what we did last time!"

His eyes darkened as he reached for me, smashed his lips against mine, and fisted his hand in the back of my hair. I squealed as his teeth hooked onto my bottom lip. His other hand gripped my backside and pulled me into him. My hands were trapped between our bodies as I struggled against him.

"Please," I tried to murmur, but instead his tongue slipped into my mouth.

I fought the urge to gag as his tongue brushed the roof of my mouth.

"Get off!" I shouted.

I managed to get one hand free, and without thinking, I fisted my hand and slammed it into his cheek. He yelped in surprise but removed his hand as he stumbled back a step. One of his hands shot up to grip his jaw, and his eyes widened in surprise. His eyes darkened as he leveled me with his hateful gaze.

"Did you just hit me?" His voice was low, menacing as he took a threatening step towards me.

I shook my head as I stepped back. The chain tangled around my ankle, and I wailed as I tripped. I landed on my backside as he towered over me.

"You will learn what made your blood turn on him." He glowered as he lowered himself to one knee. "Hopefully, this will help you learn your lesson."

As he stood, a shadowy figure floated out from behind him. The shadows were scattered, but I watched as they pulled together and formed a being taller than the High Priest.

"What are you doing?" I didn't even feel shame as my voice trembled.

He turned away from me as the shadow figure circled around me. A low growl emanated from its chest. If it had eyes, I knew they would be trained on me. I screamed as it lunged at me. Its arms wrapped around me, chilling me to the bone.

This wasn't real. This wasn't real. I kept telling myself over and over again, but it felt real. I could hear the High Priest laughing at me, but I couldn't see him. All I could see and feel was unending terror clawing at me. It clawed through my chest and seared my flesh. My scream pierced my ears and carried through the room. The terror felt endless and all-consuming as I curled in on myself to try and do my best to block it out.

Chapter 4

Eryx

"Do you think he'll come?" Cadmus asked as we exited the dining room.

I hadn't been able to bring myself to eat much. I hadn't slept much either. It didn't feel right without her here. I yearned to know that she was safe and away from harm.

"I don't know," I sighed as we pivoted down the hall towards my office.

I had felt anxious all day. I worried about the treatment Alethea was enduring. The longer we were apart, the more noticeable the lack of our mate bond had become. Where our bond had once been was now a gaping hole. I had Medrina searching for any way to repair a broken bond, but no one had ever lived through one to our knowledge and she had come up with nothing. The bond had been noticeable the moment I had met her, and I never thought I would live without it. I was still astounded that I had lived through the bond being shattered. The fates must have been on my side in a way and then against me in another way.

Shoving the door open, I made my way over to my chair and hunched down. My skin prickled with the need to feel her again, just to touch her. The longer we were apart, the angrier I was. I was doing my best not to lash out at people unnecessarily. But part of me felt like it was earned; we may not have been prepared when we were attacked in the woods, but we should've been able to overpower some mere humans.

"I've been thinking about something actually," Cadmus said as he closed the door behind him.

Raising an impatient brow at him, I waved for him to sit down. "Please, elaborate."

"You said that there was something haunting her?" Cadmus frowned at me as I nodded. He sat in the empty seat before my desk.

"She said that there was this *being* that would haunt her dreams and pull her into trances. It had wanted the Eye, and in exchange, it would release her mother to the land of the living," I explained with a sigh and scrubbed a hand down my face. We were facing problem after problem.

"That's impossible," Cadmus answered.

I nodded. "I know."

"Did she say where she was pulled into these trances?"

"No, but it would be somewhere where she was alone. I'd assume her bedroom."

"Magic like that will leave an imprint on the space around it. If she was pulled into a trance in her bedroom, then there would be evidence of it. We could trace where the magic came from."

"Can you do it?" I asked. I rose before he finished nodding. "Let's go."

Quickly, we hurried to her bedroom. I hadn't visited it since she'd been taken, but the thought of being in her space made my heart clench.

Slipping open the door, her scent hit me like a club to the chest. For a moment, my feet faltered, and my chest ached.

I would not think of her as if she were dead. I would bring her back if it was the last thing I did, and the things I'd do to ensure she never experienced pain again would make the Gods themselves fear me.

I watched as Cadmus lowered to one knee. He turned his head, taking in the space around us. I didn't want him to see this space; it was hers. I didn't want her to feel like we were intruding on that, but I willed myself to remain still. Cadmus whispered something beneath his breath and placed his palm flat on the floor.

My body stiffened as the apparition of her appeared and closed the door. Pain spiked in my chest as she brushed past me to head towards the washroom. Her smile faltered as she placed her hand on her stomach. Her feet then tripped over the other, and she collapsed into the wardrobe. Her eyes were wide as she placed the back of her hand to her forehead, checking if she was feverish.

Then she whispered my name. My heart nearly stopped dead in my chest. It was a plea, a terrified cry, and I hadn't been there for her. I had just been on the other side of the door. How could our wards have been so weak to let something get to her? How had I not sensed it? The questions spiraled inside of me as she collapsed fully to the floor.

Every instinct in my body wanted to reach for her, to help her, but this was in the past. I stiffened as a veil draped over the room, shielding her from the outside. If they wanted, they could've done anything to her, and we would have never known.

Her eyes fluttered open, and she groaned as she slowly pushed herself up.

"You need to offer to go," the voice commanded.

"To retrieve the map?" she frowned. *"If that's what Eryx was talking about, then I already have. It's been decided."*

"You must not fail me, for something valuable lies in the midst of your success."

Her body stiffened as she raised to her feet. *"What does that mean?"*

"It means if you ever want to see your mother again, you'll make sure that you succeed in retrieving the map and bring me the Eye."

"How do you know of my mother?" she snapped. *"My mother is dead."*

"Your mother lies in the in-between," it answered. *"She hasn't crossed over to the other side, and if you retrieve the map and Eye for me, I can make sure she doesn't."*

"You can return her to the land of the living?" she gaped.

It was a trick. Whoever this was, they were playing a cruel trick on her.

"Only if you do what I ask." The voice paused. *"Do we have a deal?"*

I knew Alethea couldn't say no. I had seen how badly her mothers' death had wounded her. She missed her. No matter how long she had been here, the death of her mother had left a shadow over her otherwise bright eyes.

"Deal," she answered, and as she did, the veil lifted, and the entity was gone.

"What is it?" I asked as Cadmus rose.

His eyes were wide in what looked like fear as his mouth gaped. "It's a mage." His voice was riddled with disbelief.

Now I was gaping.

"What?" I clarified. "That can't be right. They're all dead."

"It is dead, whoever it is. They're reaching out to her from the deadlands."

"How did we not sense it? How did it get through our wards?"

"Mages are more powerful than fae," Cadmus answered as he shook his head.

I nodded. He was right. I had never encountered a mage in my lifetime, but I had known others older than me who had. They were vicious, bloodthirsty creatures. If they hadn't been killed off, they would have destroyed every species besides their own. Slaughtering them had nearly made fae go extinct. Our numbers had dwindled for a long time after the mage war.

"Is there a way to reach out to it?" I asked as I sat down at the foot of her bed.

Cadmus shook his head as he leaned against the wall and crossed his arms. "I'm not sure. I'll talk to Medrina, but I'm sure there has to be a way."

Nodding, I pushed off the bed and moved for the door. "Tell her to meet me in my office."

"Of course," Cadmus said as he followed me out of her room. "There was another attack this morning."

My throat dried as the words hit me. "How many casualties?"

"We're not sure yet, they've taken some but it seems as if they're more intent on destroying the city." I frowned at his words as he sighed. "We have a new watch set up and there are stations through out the city to feed those displaced from their homes."

"Open up the Estate to those displaced," I told him.

The Estate was where my father's council had stayed when he had ruled. But once I was crowned, I disbanded the council. I hadn't felt like I needed them.

Cadmus merely nodded and bowed before we split up, him heading to find Medrina and me to my office. I desperately needed the silent reprieve as I stalked down the halls. None of the guards spoke to me; none of them even looked at me. They hadn't since she'd been taken; they knew better. We had all failed her. Even if they didn't care about her, they knew what she meant to me. They knew I was disappointed in them, in us all.

I threw my hand and the door to my office flew open. I stalked inside and plopped down at my desk. I scrubbed a hand down my face as I waited for Cadmus.

"Where's Medrina?" I frowned as Cadmus shoved open the door and stormed in.

"Mykill's here," Cadmus said as he entered. "He insisted he get his own wing, and he brought his own set of guards. It was the only way I could get him to agree."

I resisted the urge to roll my eyes. Mykill had always been a pestering child. "Where is he?"

"You called, Your Majesty," Mykill mocked as he stepped in behind Cadmus.

My senses went on alert as I took in the size of him. He'd always towered over me in height and build, but I could take him down if I needed to. His harsh white eyes met mine, and I felt the challenge rise in him as his wings folded behind him. The corner of his mouth pulled into a smile as I glared.

"Mykill," I greeted and nodded my head. I wouldn't stand to greet him. I wouldn't give him the satisfaction.

It was a minor relief in some way that Alethea wasn't here because I didn't need to worry about him. She would be here soon enough, but I'd worry about that when the time came. Mykill wouldn't harm her; she was protected under the treaty, but I still didn't trust him entirely.

Him and his kingdom, Asgaith, had always kept to themselves. They never negotiated with others. They were never at odds with other kingdoms; they merely existed in their kingdom in the mountains. All of his people were winged as he was, and their kingdom wasn't laid out traditionally. There had been rumors that they had houses and markets in the clouds. Even their powers and strengths were surrounded by rumors. His people kept to themselves and never put any of them to rest. It was partly why they hadn't been involved in a battle since the Mage War, the only time they had proven themselves useful.

"What is this about a stolen mate?" Mykill said as he sauntered towards the seat across from me.

I steeled a sigh as I intertwined my hands behind my head and leaned back. "The King of the human lands has stolen my mate."

"The human?" He raised an eyebrow at me. I nodded. "So, the rumors are true then. The prophecy speaks of this."

I nodded again. "They broke our mating bond. I'm not sure how I'm not dead, but I thank the Gods that I'm not. She's being held prisoner there along with her sister and father. I'm not sure what kind of condition they are in, but they all need to be retrieved."

"Our men can attack in the air on their dragons, and we can get your men horses if needed." Cadmus spoke.

His wings flared as he stood. "My men won't need horses."

That was merely another way he and his kingdom had thought they were above us. Most of them were gifted with wings. It made them think they were superior to other fae. They considered themselves High Fae; they had always thought they were descendants of the Divine.

My head snapped to the side as the door banged open. It bounced off a wall, and a breathless guard stared at me with wide eyes.

"Sir, our spies have confirmed that Kirin is dead." The guard was breathless as he bowed his head.

"What?" I demanded as I rose from my chair. "What do you mean Kirin's dead?"

"His High Priest turned into a mage and murdered him." The soldier tensed, as if sensing my fury that boiled beneath my skin. "He took the throne."

A roar ripped out of me involuntarily, and as I spun, I drove my fist into the wall. Splinters of the wall flew around me, and I heard a dark laugh behind me.

Mykill chuckled. "Your mate may already be dead."

I swung my gaze on him and resisted the urge to bury my blade in the side of his neck. "She is alive. I can feel it."

"I thought you said your bond was taken from you?" He raised a brow.

"It was," I confirmed. "But I know she's alive."

Mykill shrugged and turned away from me. "I will get my men ready for battle."

"Do the same," I commanded Cadmus, who bowed his head and fled.

Moving quickly down the halls, I moved into the war room and began loading myself with weapons. I had two swords crossed over my back in an X and sheaths around each of my thighs. My men filtered in behind me, all doing the same. I fought to keep the tremble from my hands as I thought of her being in the hands of a mage.

"Move! Move! Move!" Cadmus shouted as he came into the room. He stopped before me, already armed, as he waited for me to finish.

"I'm ready." I nodded to him as I slid the last dagger into a sheath, and together, we rushed outside.

"We need to give them a plan once we get outside." I nodded as Cadmus spoke. "With the combination of our men and Mykill's men, we should be able to take them easily. Let's just hope that the mage is occupied."

"Let's also hope that he hasn't done the unthinkable to your mate," Mykill spoke from behind us as we stepped outside.

Groaning, I turned to Cadmus as Mykill began addressing his men. Cadmus gave me a look of sympathy before I turned and mounted Adruis. The orange dragon shook his head, readying himself as I patted the base of his long neck. He was sleeker than Cador but still just as strong and fast, if not a little faster. My heart clenched at the thought of my old companion. I had been there when he had hatched, and we became inseparable. My relationship with Adruis wasn't entirely the same, but he would protect me with his life.

"We take to the skies and surround them. A small group of you will go to the stables and burn them. Don't give them any way that they can come after us. If you encounter the mage, do your best to flee; he cannot be taken on his own," Cadmus explained.

"Our only priority is rescuing Alethea and her family." My voice rose, and all heads turned towards me. "She must be brought back alive. We take no prisoners. Start by burning the men that will be on the battlements. The humans won't expect us to come with reinforcements. Without the power of the mage, they won't stand a chance. May the Gods lead us."

"May the Gods lead us," all voices rang out in agreement.

"We burn them! Move out!" I shouted as I raised my sword in the air. Adrius followed my command, raised his long, slender neck in the air, and released a mighty roar. The ground shook as dozens of dragons took to the skies. Mykill's men followed behind them. Man and dragon, flying beside each other. We didn't have a lot, but this would have to be enough.

Chapter 5

Alethea

My entire body trembled as the cold leached into my skin and bones, taking permanent residency in me. I felt like I hadn't slept; the monsters plagued me throughout the night. They showed me visions of my worst fears, tormenting me, and when my fear heightened, they increased. My heart had been overbeating to the point I felt like it was going to beat out of my chest.

My limbs locked as I heard a deep voice say my name. I whimpered as I covered my face with my hands. I knew trying to hide was useless, but I couldn't help it. They had plagued me for what had felt like an eternity. They showed me visions of my worst fears. Laney and my father being beheaded before me, my mother bleeding out before me as she asks me how I could do this to her. Eryx's life slowly slipping away in my arms.

"Wake up," the voice growled, making me curl further into myself. "My Lady, please."

I screamed as hands gripped my shoulders and yanked me onto my back. "Don't touch me!"

"We were sent to help you bathe," the voice spoke, but the growl was gone. Instead the voice was soft, feminine.

I felt the tremors racking my body as I forced my eyes to open. One of the maids was sitting above me. Her eyes were concerned as she scanned me from head to toe.

"We were sent to help you bathe," she said softly and placed a tentative hand on my shoulder.

I tried not to flinch, but I was unsuccessful. Her face fell in response, and she pulled her hand away. "I'm sorry. It's not you. He-"

"We know what he did," the red-haired maid responded. Her round emerald eyes were sympathetic. "You have our greatest sympathy. Now let us help you up so we can help you bathe."

My hands shook as I grabbed her outstretched hands, and she pulled me to my feet. My entire body felt shaky and unsteady, but I managed to get to the washroom. After I stripped, I slid into the bubbling tub. I stared at the bubbling surface.

I was a prisoner here and in my own mind with fear and uncertainty surrounding me. I closed my eyes as despair washed over me. I missed Eryx so much my chest hurt. When I closed my eyes, I could hear his deep laugh, and I could see his eyes crinkling in the corners, the way they only did for me. I had never seen him smile at anyone else the way he smiled at me.

"Is there any way you can help me?" I whispered as I opened my eyes.

"There is nothing we can do," the brunette said softly as she gripped my hand. "We're very sorry."

"Please," I begged her as I clutched her hand to my chest. "He intends to keep me and torture me for the remainder of my life. If you won't help, then just kill me, please!"

Death would be better than being his prisoner.

"Please!" I cried as I dropped my forehead to her palm. "Please, you have to help me."

"We'll do it," the other maid behind her said. The maid holding my hand snapped her head in her direction. Surprise flitted across her face as her brows drew down. She looked like she was going to argue, but finally, she nodded.

"We'll think of something," she spoke softly as she turned back towards me.

I nodded as she released my hand. "Thank you," I croaked. "Thank you so much."

"You mustn't give us away, or we will lie. You have to understand; we have our own families. We will lie to protect ourselves," she warned.

"I understand. Thank you."

They both bowed their heads before they slipped silently from the room. Guards entered immediately after.

"The King is waiting for you," one of them said.

Nodding, I reluctantly stepped towards them. One of the guards reached for me, and I fought the urge to shrivel from his touch. This was my life now. I had to do what was commanded of me.

I felt numb as the guards led me to the dining room again. The High Priest was already waiting for me, and he was seated like he was before. I could tell by the hard set of his jaw that he was in a foul mood. He didn't look at me as I seated myself. My plate, much like the day before, was already made with an egg scramble with peppers and squash and a serving of berries. My stomach growled as I reached for the fork. As my fingers wrapped around the metal, I yelped as a shock moved through the fork to my hand. I dropped the utensil, and as I gaped down at it, it smoked. The High Priest chuckled and placed his fork down beside his brimming plate.

"Try again," he shrugged.

I knew I shouldn't touch it. He was goading me. The fork would do the same thing, but like the imbecile I was, I picked up the damn fork. The shock moved through my hand again, and I dropped the fork.

"Again," he commanded.

"What?" I gaped at him. "No!"

"I said, again!" His voice echoed in the space.

I stared down at the fork in disbelief. I didn't have a choice, and if I didn't pick up the fork, then he would hurt me. So I chose the fork. Over and over again, I picked up the fork and dropped it as it shocked me. It eventually left a burn on the inside of my palm.

"Eat," the High Priest finally waved at me and lounged back in his chair.

His plate was now empty, and he stared down at my full plate. Doubt gnawed at me as I stared back at him but his face remained impassive, revealing nothing. With a trembling hand, I reached towards the fork and nearly groaned in relief when it didn't shock me. My stomach was nearly howling as I shoveled up some eggs and brought them to my mouth. But I didn't expect the taste of rot to invade my senses.

Gagging, I spit the eggs back out. The eggs that had remained on my plate had wilted. They were a light gray with small maggots crawling through them. My stomach churned as I stared at the partially chewed eggs. Shoving out of my seat, I leaned over and vomited. My stomach was empty, but I couldn't help it. Tears streamed down my cheeks as the taste of rotten food and vomit mingled.

"You either be thankful and eat this, or you get nothing." I heard his chair scrape along the floor and then his footsteps as he passed me. "Bring her to the throne room when she's finished."

The doors thudded closed behind him, and I glanced at the two guards at the doors. As I pushed my chair out, my stomach roared in disapproval, but I wouldn't eat the rotten food. The guards stepped back and motioned for me to move past them. I followed the same path to the throne room and found a line of three men standing beside the throne. These men weren't peasants like the one before; they were soldiers. All of them were built like warriors with thick bodies and rugged faces.

"You already know what's expected of you," the High Priest spoke as he seated himself upon his throne.

I stopped at the foot of his dais and merely nodded. Fighting was pointless. He would take my blood if I denied him.

"This time you must offer up your blood to them."

"But I didn't offer my blood to you," I countered as I stared back at him.

"There's not a science to this kind of magic," he clipped, and I saw his hand fist. "Get her a knife."

I turned as one of the guards pulled a dagger from the sheath at their waist and outstretched it towards me.

"I should warn you that the punishment for using that knife foully will be agonizing." I glanced up at the High Priest as he threatened.

Nodding, I took the knife, stepped up the dais, and stopped before the first man. He was at least Eryx's height and just as thick as him. He had stringy blonde hair that was pulled back in a bun and dead brown eyes. He stared down at me with his brutal expression.

Taking a deep breath, I looked down at my hand and held the tip of the blood to my palm. Wincing,

I dragged the blade across my palm and blood immediately pooled over the side of my hand. The man snatched my wrist, twisted my hand, and brought it to his mouth. His lips wrapped around my palm as he sucked the blood in his mouth. I wanted to gag. I couldn't believe these men had no problem with drinking someone else's blood, even if it was under the premise that they would become a mage.

After a few moments, he discarded my hand and breathed a deep breath. "I feel the magic," he sighed with a smile on his face.

The next man snatched my hand and did the same. I watched the first man with dread as his skin turned translucent and veins began darkening. The darkness spread through his veins as he extended his arms on either side of him and dropped his head back, smiling.

The second man dropped my hand after it felt like he sucked me dry. The third man yanked me towards him. "Slice your other hand," he commanded.

Nodding, I cut my other palm with a shaking hand. He snatched my wrist greedily and pulled my hand to his mouth. After several moments, he shoved me back, and I grunted as I fell back on my ass. I scooted away from the cluster of men as the second one gripped his head and began screaming.

Two guards surged forward and pulled me to my feet, away from the men. Blood pooled beneath the second man's eyes as he dropped to his knees, threw his head back, and bellowed. The first man looked over at him in disgust and laughed. He outstretched his hand towards him and fisted his hand. As he did, the second man's neck twisted at an unnatural angle, and he collapsed to the ground in a heap. The third man watched; his skin had already turned translucent, his veins darkening.

Two were successful.

I frowned as I turned to the High Priest, who was staring at the two in wonder.

"Amazing," he breathed as his gaze slid over to me. "With your blood, I will create my own army."

I shook my head as dread settled over me. An army of mages would be disastrous. "You can't."

"I can, and I will," he responded as he stepped down the dais and gripped the back of my neck. "Move." His voice was a growl as he began leading me out of the throne room.

"Where are we going?" I asked fearfully as I tried to dislodge his hand.

He didn't answer as we turned down the hall. We passed the dining room and several sitting rooms before entering a room with a single chair resting in the center of the room. There were stains littering the ground that I didn't think too long on what they were or I'd faint. There was a single crackling fireplace in the corner, illuminating the small space. I could smell the terror of every person who had been held captive in this room.

He led me over to the chair and tossed me into the seat. My arms and legs involuntarily moved and shackles clamped down on my wrists and ankles, shackling me to the chair. The shackles were covered in a dried, crusty brown substance, and I nearly choked on my own heart.

"What are you doing?" I demanded as I yanked against the iron.

I hissed as it irritated my already raw and broken skin. He dropped a bucket on either side of me beneath my wrists and pulled a blade from his robes.

"If I'm going to make an army, I will need lots of your blood," he said without looking at me.

I didn't have the chance to respond as he dragged the blade across my arm. The cut went from my elbow all the way down to my wrist. I cried out as he pulled away, admiring the blood as it oozed out of the gash and dripped down on either side of my forearm. He raised up and moved around me. He crouched down on the other side of me and pressed the tip of the blade to my skin.

"If you kill me, you won't get an endless supply of blood!" I shouted as my blood seeped over the sides of my arm, and I heard it begin splattering into the metal buckets.

He laughed. "I'm not going to kill you. I'm going to drain your blood, heal you, and drain you again." His look was one of pure malice as he dragged the tip of the blade across my second arm. Blood pooled around it before spilling over the sides. Not even a minute passed before my head began to sway and my vision began to double. My head fell back against the back of the seat, and the High Priest's gruesome face was the last thing I saw before my eyes closed.

Chapter 6

Eryx

Adruis' wings beat at the air around us as we flew above the city. Humans pointed up at us in fear and screamed as they fled into their houses. Four dragons broke off to the right, heading towards the stables. We needed to make sure that they couldn't follow us back for some time. Two dragons led up front and swooped down as we approached the castle. A horn went off in the distance, signaling that we had been spotted.

At once, every dragon swooped down in unison. The two up front went towards the front gate and let out bursts of flames. Bodies of burning men fell from the battlekeeps, and the others either ran in fear or aimed arrows at them. The arrows bounced uselessly off the dragon's scales as the two dragons opened their talons, ripping the gate off its hinges entirely. We broke apart as the gate swung backwards. It sailed through the air and landed on a group of men. Mykill and his men swooped lower, diving through the open gate, and my men and their dragons took to the sky once more, over the walls of the castle. Men hollered out below us, and just as I was cresting the battle keep, one of the soldiers outstretched his hand and a wave of wind blew me back.

I frowned. I thought they said the High Priest was a mage? This man didn't look to be anything more than a footsoldier. High Priests were normally adorned with robes of purple.

He pulled his hand back again, pointed at us, and a faint glow started in his hands. "Disperse!" I shouted as fire flew from his hands.

Adrius reared back as a stream of fire hit his chest. He shrieked as he flew back and then shot towards the sky. The flames extinguished, and as they did, he angled forward and nose-dived towards the battlekeep. As we got lower, he reared back and rammed his talons into the side of the battlekeep. Men somersaulted through the air as bricks exploded inwards, burying soldiers. The soldiers recovered quickly, forming their ranks again

"Eryx!" Cadmus screamed my name.

I glanced up as men poured out along the walkway above us and all aimed arrows at us.

"The arrows have Chrono Crystals!" he warned.

I felt the blood drain from my face. "Take shelter!" I tried roaring over the battle.

The ones who heard me all shielded themselves. I watched in dismay as the arrows flew towards my men. The ones who hadn't heard me kept fighting, and as the tip of the arrows touched them, their bodies went hurling through the sky. Light exploded around them, and I could see the gaping holes in their armor and bodies as they fell. Their dragons all bellowed in distress as their riders tumbled to the ground.

We would give them a proper good-bye, even if we weren't able to retrieve their bodies. "May the Gods guide you." I whispered the prayer and held my fist over my heart.

"Take up your shields!" Cadmus shouted, and I felt the air shift as they all shielded themselves.

Ducking low, I signaled for Adrius to take to the sky, and as he did, I outstretched my hand. Pulling the power from within me, I threw a wave of air that sent several of the archers tumbling over the side. Their bodies plummeted to the ground, and the riderless dragons swooped in with their streams of fire. Men screamed as their bodies fell over the sides, but the heat of the fire took them out before they even hit the ground.

Remorse filled me as I stared at the riderless dragons. Losing men was imminent in battle, but the guilt of their lost lives still sat heavy on my chest. I was responsible for every single one of them, just as I was for Alethea, and I had failed them. Their families would be compensated immensely, but I knew no amount of gold could bring back a loved one. I had learned that when my father had been murdered.

I turned as Cadmus' dragon, Prior, swept down with his talons extended and scooped up dozens of soldiers in each claw. Prior shot straight up towards the sky, higher and higher, and as he raised above the highest point of the castle, he opened his talons and let them fall. Their screams were like a sweet chorus as I watched their tumbling bodies. I couldn't keep the sadistic smile from my face as their bodies collided with the ground. They were all responsible for taking Alethea from me. They were responsible for every painful moment of her life, and they all deserved to pay.

My head snapped to the side as lightning erupted across the sky. Mykill was flying above soldiers, and as he threw his hands down, the lightning followed his command. It struck down several soldiers, and he passed by their crisped corpses without a second glance. He touched down on the ground and threw his hand back. A clap of thunder sounded above us, and power exploded out of him. Men screamed as water bubbled out of their mouths. Their eyes bulged as they gripped at their throats and crumbled in heaps. I watched as he stepped over their corpses and threw his hands open. He glanced up at me and then started inside the doors.

I needed to follow him. He didn't know what Alethea looked like and could kill her in the process.

I signaled for Adrius to swoop down, and two of my men descended down with me. The ground shook as our three dragons landed. Some of the soldiers had the gall to run away in terror as Adrius yanked his head back and let out a mighty burst of flames. I could feel the heat on my skin, even with it directed away from me. My two soldiers' dragons did the same. Flame erupted around us, and we all raised our shields. The flames bounced harmlessly off my shield as the three dragons obliterated the men in the courtyard around us.

When the flames died, all that remained was scorched grass and the burnt remains of the soldiers. Two more dragons landed behind me as men poured out from inside. As I dismounted Adrius, I pulled my swords from the sheath at my back. Raising my sword, I charged towards the men, engaging them head on. They were merely human; they moved slower and less graceful than fae. I sliced my blade across one of their stomachs, spilling his guts, before spinning to face the other.

He was better. He was light on his feet, but I moved quicker than he did. Our swords clashed together like thunder. I kicked my boot into his chest and sent him stumbling back as another man attacked me. I grunted as I absorbed the blow of his fist to my cheek.

"Adrius!" I shouted. "Shields up!"

My ward went up again, and Adrius bellowed before releasing more flames. Within moments, their scorching bodies dropped like flies.

"You've come for the girl," a deep voice spoke.

I turned as a man broke through the flame. His tunic was on fire, but he didn't pay it any attention as he strode towards me. His hair was tied back in a ratty bun, and his face was set in a permanent scowl. The air around him breathed arrogance, and as he raised his hand towards me, I realized why. He was the mage who wielded flames.

I jumped to the side as he released a current of power. Throwing up my wards, I turned back towards where I had been standing. The ground was merely a black splotch.

"I've got to say, she is rather beautiful, and her blood was tasty." He threw his head back as he laughed. "Maybe once the King has had his fill of her, I can convince him to let me wed her."

I glared, not giving into his banter. He was trying to goad a reaction out of me. I knew better; it was childish.

"I like them unwilling," he growled, and I felt my entire body stiffen.

I threw a hand towards him in an attempt to throw him backwards, but he charged me. His arms went around my middle as we went rolling. I aimed a blow for his face and felt the splatter of blood across my face as I got him square beneath the jaw. He grunted and drove a knee into my stomach as we rolled to the side. I kicked both legs out, sending him flying backwards, and rose fluidly. As I did, I pulled my daggers from my thigh sheaths and hurled them at him. Each one embedded in each shoulder as he rose. He smiled sinisterly at me as he motioned with his hands, and the blades yanked themselves out. His gaze met mine as he moved his hand again, and the blades turned and flew towards me.

I threw up my arm, my ward following it, and the blades both fell uselessly to the ground.

"You're no match for me, and you know it." He smiled as we circled one another. "You don't know how many of us there are now." He smiled at me, but it looked like more of a grimace.

I watched as Cadmus and another guard both slid silently behind Adrius. I noticed the bows they both held in their hands and the arrows with Chrono Crystals embedded in the tips. My gaze slid back to the man as he stopped and frowned. He spun just as Cadmus and the other solider released the arrows. He laughed as he held up his hands, but they cut through his defenses. The crystals exploded as they collided with his body, and I watched as his body exploded in two separate directions. Blood streaked across the grass as we all stared down at the littered remains.

"He was a mage." Cadmus' chest heaved as he stared back at me.

"Yes," I confirmed.

"There must be others," he breathed. "Her blood was used to turn him. I can sense it."

I nodded again. That meant Alethea was alive. There was no way the High Priest would dispose of her if her blood was turning ordinary men into mages.

The ground shook as more dragons landed, some with riders, others without. I bent to retrieve my daggers, then both of my swords, and sheathed them all.

"Find her," I commanded.

Chapter 7

Alethea

I groaned as I forced my eyes open. The surface below me was soft, cushioned. A bed. I took in the space around me, recalling my surroundings. I wasn't in that dingy room anymore. I was in the High Priest's bedroom.

My limbs felt exhausted as I pushed myself up onto my elbows. I didn't hear him in the washroom or see him in the room.

Fear shot through my body as I recalled the events previous to him draining my blood. I had turned two mages. One of them had died. I shoved myself off the bed. I needed something, anything I could use for a weapon. I knew it would do little good against three powerful mages, but having something would give me a little piece of mind. I yanked open the drawer to his nightstand and riffled through the notepads and sleeping tonic before slamming it shut. Pausing, I looked around in search of anywhere he could have hidden a weapon. Although he didn't need one; I hadn't seen him use his powers much.

Heading over to the dresser, I looked through every drawer and came up with nothing. He had done a great job making sure I couldn't use something against him. I was shoving the door closed and rising as the door burst open.

Anxiety shot through me as I flipped towards the door, but I breathed out a sigh of relief as the two maids stepped in.

"We were sent to help you get ready for bed." The red-haired maid bowed her head as they shut the door behind them.

"Hurry," the brunette said as she shoved her forward. "Into the washroom!"

Following behind them, the red-haired maid turned to the brunette and pulled out a small velvet bag no bigger than my palm. "This powder will put him to sleep, and you will have a chance to run. We were not able to assist with the guards or anything else. You are on your own," the brunette maid explained.

The red-haired maid moved behind me as she undid the straps of my dress. Quickly, I slipped it off and took the nightgown they offered. It had pockets and thick ruffles, which made it easy to conceal the powder.

I let them braid my hair down my back after I finished dressing.

"We were instructed to bring you to his bed," the brunette maid said solemnly. I merely nodded, knowing that I didn't have much of a choice.

Anxiety spiraled through me as they led me to his bed. They gripped a chain wrapped around the post and circled it around my wrist.

I could tell what the High Priest intended to do when he came in here by the outfit they had bestowed me with. They had dressed me in a light violet top with thin straps, a deep v, and a ruffled ankle length skirt. They both were nearly see-through, keeping little to the imagination, but the matching robe concealed my form and tied above my breasts. The powder was in the pocket hidden behind the ruffles, giving me easy access to it if I should need.

"Good luck," the red-haired maid bowed her head.

"Thank you," I whispered as I gripped her hand and glanced at the brunette. "I appreciate you both risking so much for me."

"We hope you make it out of here," the brunette whispered and stepped away.

The doors creaked open, and my entire body stiffened as the High Priest stepped inside. "Leave us."

The maids both bowed their heads in respect and slipped from the room without another word.

"Good evening," The High Priest said as the doors closed behind him.

"Good evening," I said in response, willing my voice to remain neutral.

Waving his hand towards me, the chain undid itself and fell at my feet. I stared in disbelief at the piled chain and then back up at him. This was my chance. Sliding off the bed, I straightened out my clothes. I knew this was going to be one of my only chances to try and escape, and I would rather he kill me than stay here for the remainder of my life.

"Do you like my sleepwear?" I tried to sound alluring as I moved towards him.

Turning, he raised a prim eyebrow at me as I pushed the robe off my shoulders. Goosebumps spread across my skin from the chill in the air. His eyes followed down my bare arm. I had to swallow back the bile as his eyes slid down my barely concealed form. The skirt hung low on my hips, and his beady eyes focused on the strip of skin exposed between my top and skirt.

I willed my breathing to remain even as I sauntered towards him. His eyes trailed down my front to my swaying hips. They narrowed as I ran the tips of my fingers up his bare arm. His entire body remained stiff as he waited, watching for what I'd do next. I knew he could hear my heart rate, and I willed myself to calm down.

"Pleasure me," I whispered as his hands landed on my shoulders.

I met his gaze, and he leaned into me. Our breaths mingled as his nose brushed mine. I fought the urge to cringe as one of his hands slid around my throat. He yanked me forward and up onto my toes as his lips crashed to mine. I gasped, giving him perfect access to slip his tongue between my lips. Bile rose in the back of my throat, but I pushed it down. I forced myself to move my mouth against his, to kiss him back.

His other hand cupped the back of my head and threaded through my hair, loosening my braid. He held me close to him as his lips moved against mine. My body wanted to reject him, to shove him away. He felt nothing like Eryx; he wasn't as tall or as built as he was but beneath that, there wasn't the tender touch of love I felt whenever Eryx touched me.

Grief spiked through me as I recalled Eryx and his face, his hands, his scent. I remembered how gently he touched me and how gently he loved me. It was so different to how the High Priest handled me as he tightened his hand around my throat. He growled as he bit down on my lower lip and tugged me closer. My body stiffened as he slipped his hand beneath my shirt and brushed up my bare body. I broke off contact with his lips and kissed my way down his jaw. He let out a sound of approval, and his head fell back as I moved my lips down the front of his chest.

Slipping my hand into my pocket, my fingers curled around the powder. I felt most of it collect in my palm, and I pulled it out. I knew this was the only chance I would get, and I needed to use it wisely.

Collecting every ounce of courage I possessed, I yanked my hand up. I flattened my palm over his mouth and nose. His eyes widened as he inhaled. Panic spread across his face as he stumbled away from me. I stepped towards him again as I pulled out more powder.

I released a breath as his back hit the dresser. Objects clattered to the floor as he fought to remain upright. He opened his mouth to shout for guards, but his words were slurred. His knees gave out, and he collapsed to the floor in a heap.

I stepped back from him, my heart thundering in my chest. Anxiety shot through me as I glanced around. I couldn't kill him. I hadn't thought of them sneaking me a weapon. But I knew I needed to run. He'd kill me if he caught me again.

Running into the washroom, I found my discarded dress and changed quickly. By the time I came out, the High Priest was slumped against the wall, and his eyes were closed. His chest rose and fell, and his heavy breaths sounded throughout the room. My hands shook as I rushed towards the door and turned the knob. As I did, I prayed to every known God and Goddess that they would bestow their favor upon me. I breathed out a sigh of relief when the handle turned, and I yanked the door open. Sticking my head out into the hall, I noticed a group of guards with their backs to me who were rushing down the end of the hall. I watched as they rounded a corner, leaving the hall empty.

Slipping out of the room entirely, I pulled the door closed and moved down the opposite end of the hall. I wasn't sure where the entrance to the palace was, but I followed the path back to the dining room. I encountered no guards there either as I poked my head inside. Frowning, I turned and stumbled forward as the walls shook. A roar reverberated through the halls. My head snapped up. *It couldn't be.* Hope settled over my limbs as another followed.

Dragons.

That hope built up in my throat.

Eryx.

He had to be alive.

Shoving myself to my feet, I began running through the halls. I didn't know where I was going, but I was determined to find him and put as much distance between the High Priest and me. I stumbled to a stop as the sound of rattling armor and men shouting sounded from further down the halls. My heart launched into my throat as half a dozen men turned the corner, and their eyes all landed on me.

"Grab her!" one of them shouted.

Yelping, I flipped around and barrelled down the hall. If they caught me, they would find the High Priest unconscious in his bedroom. Either way, I was going to die. I cried out as the dining room doors exploded open. Splintered wood flew through the air, colliding with my body and sending me tumbling backwards. I landed on my back but quickly shoved myself up and froze as a man stepped out of the clearing smoke and debris.

My mouth dropped open as he threw his hand out and lightning erupted from his palm, arching straight for the group of men. I heard a chorus of screams and then silence. I didn't need to turn around to confirm that they were dead.

The man stalking towards me shot fear with a heady mix of curiosity up my throat. He towered a whole head over Eryx with identical, albeit shorter, black hair that parted down the middle of his scalp and rested in waves around his forehead. His eyes were a startling blue as they latched onto me. They were so blue they almost looked white. They stood out sharply against his dark tan skin. But what stood out most were the black feathered wings that flared behind him. They spread out at least six feet on each side of him and made him look even more menacing.

He looked godly, like he belonged in a painting.

My breath stalled as he stopped before me. My head craned as far back as it could to stare up at him.

"You're the stolen mate," the man spoke.

His deep voice vibrated through my entire body, kicking up my heart and soothing my frayed nerves. I nodded.

His brows furrowed, and his nostrils flared. "What are you?"

I stuttered. "What do you mean?"

He watched me with an intensity I'd never experienced before. His forehead creased as he stepped towards me. My breath stalled as our chests brushed, and he gripped my chin roughly. "What. Are. You?" He bit out again, his grip on my chin tightening.

"I-I'm human," I gasped.

"Hmmm." He inhaled deeply and frowned again. "Your mate is looking for you," he said as he threw my head back.

"Eryx is here?" I gasped as he turned.

He only nodded as he started back down the hall.

"Where is he?" I asked as I hurried to keep pace with him.

"If you follow me," he said, annoyance heavily lacing his tone, "then I'm sure you'd find him."

I glared but didn't respond as I followed behind him. I struggled to keep up with his heavy strides. Two men in familiar armor flanked the exit door, each with a sword in each hand.

There he was. His back was to me, but he was standing; he was breathing. Cadmus met my gaze, and his eyes widened.

Eryx's steps faltered as he turned towards me. Relief spread across his face as his sword slipped from his hand. My feet moved quickly as I ran for him. I didn't care about anything else but making sure he was truly here, alive. His arms opened as I threw myself at him. I wrapped my arms and legs around him as he pulled me to him. His arms tightened around my waist as he cried my name. One of his hands cupped the back of my head, shaking.

"Eryx," I whispered as tears wet my upper lip. "Gods, I thought you had died when he broke the bond! I felt you slipping away!"

He pulled away, and his trembling hands grasped my face.

"Blossom." He gasped as his thumbs swept beneath my eyes. "I'm so sorry, Blossom. I'm going to take you home. I'm so sorry."

My vision blurred as tears leaked down my cheeks. "You came for me," I whispered as my fingers tightened around his wrists.

"Of course." He breathed as he leaned in and placed his forehead to mine. His eyes closed momentarily before opening again. His eyes darkened as he noticed the bruise beneath my eye. "Oh, Alethea," he whispered.

His hand cupped the side of my face, and his thumb brushed across my cheekbone.

"I'm so sorry, Alethea." Guilt clouded his features.

"I'm okay," I lied as I wrapped my fingers around his wrist.

His touch was so soft, so tender, just like he always had been. A sob ripped free of me as I launched myself at him again. His arms circled my waist as I molded my front to his. "Gods, Alethea, I'm so sorry," he whispered against my hair. "I should've been able to protect you."

"It wasn't your fault," I breathed, desperate for him to believe me.

"Let go of me!" I turned at Laney's shout.

"Who's this?" Cadmus asked as Laney yanked her arm away from one of Eryx's men.

"She claims she's her sister," the guard spoke as he released her arm.

Everyone's heads shot to me. "She is," I confirmed.

Laney watched me wearily as I stepped back from Eryx. He placed a hand on my back as he stepped closer. We just held each other's gaze for several moments.

"Where's your father?" Eryx asked.

"Dead." Laney's gaze slid over to Eryx's, and I could see the hatred as she stared at him.

I clenched my teeth as my hands fisted. My sister was looking at me with so much hatred as I slid my hand into Eryx's. My gaze caught on the winged man as he stepped out from behind her. My throat dried at the intensity of his gaze.

"We need to go, Eryx," the man spoke with annoyance lacing his tone as he stared at me.

I glanced at Eryx as he nodded. "Let's head out." Eryx glanced back down to me, then to my sister, and frowned. "Get her sister," he commanded the winged man.

The man nodded and stepped up to my sister, whose eyes widened. She held her hands up as she stumbled away. "No, I don't want to go. You can leave me."

"Laney, don't do this," I pleaded.

"No!" she nearly shrieked as she spun on me. "Alethea, you need to go now. Leave me. I'm already dead anyway."

"What?" I gasped as I stepped towards her. "What are you talking about?"

"You need to leave, now!" She glared at me, but beneath her cold exterior, I could see the fear in her gaze. She turned her eyes on Eryx. "Go, now. He's coming."

"Come on, Alethea." Eryx tugged me gently towards him, and a dragon settled behind us. He slipped an arm around my waist and began pulling me up onto the dragon.

The winged man took to the sky, as did several dragons.

"Go!" Laney urged as she shoved me after Eryx. He wrapped an arm around my waist and settled me draped across his lap.

"Come with us!" I urged as I gripped her hands. "Please, come with me."

She shook her head as Eryx reached down for her. "I'm going to kill him."

"What? No, please just come with us. He will kill you; he's too strong."

Laney opened her mouth to speak but her mouth fell open. A trickle of blood slipped out of the corner of her lip. Her wide eyes met mine, and in them, I saw the love that only a sister could share. I saw every happy memory, every moment of laughter. I saw everything.

"Laney?" I gasped as I reached for her shoulder. "Laney, what is it?" I panicked.

She gaped, her mouth opened and closed as she tried to form words. She stumbled back a step and angled her body to the side, trying to look over her shoulder. I gasped at the sight of the arrow protruding from her back.

"Laney!" I screamed as her body fell to the side.

Snapping my head up, there were two guards. One of them had an arrow notched and aimed, but the other had already loosed his arrow. I cried out as another arrow embedded into her back. The High Priest stepped between the two guards with arrows notched and aimed at Eryx.

"I'm so sorry, but we can't stay, Blossom," Eryx said, and I realized all too late what he was doing as I reached for Laney.

His dragon extended his wings, and with a mighty roar that shook the castle, the beast took to the sky.

"I will find her!" The High Priest roared after us.

He threw a hand out, and a flame licked at the sky around us. The heat caused my skin to tingle. The guards released their arrows, but they bounced harmlessly off the dragon's scales.

"Laney!" I screamed as the High Priest stepped over her fallen body.

Her eyes were wide, staring unseeing at the sky. Blood pooled beneath her, the puddle growing bigger.

"I'm sorry, Blossom," Eryx said as they disappeared below us. "I'm so sorry, Alethea." He shook his head over and over.

I couldn't breathe. My chest and throat tightened simultaneously. I squeezed my eyes shut as a sob racked through me. I whispered her name over and over again as I clutched onto the front of Eryx's shirt. Eryx wrapped an arm around my shoulders and pulled me into him. He whispered words of comfort, but I heard none of it.

I thought before that my heart had been broken, but she was all I had left.

Chapter 8

Alethea

My mouth dropped open as I took in the damage beneath us. Streets were reduced to nothing but ashes and rubble. My heart launched into my throat as I watched fires in the furthest part of the kingdom. I could hear shouting, and in the distance, I could see people rushing to put out the fires.

"The city has been on fire for the last week," Eryx said, drawing my attention from the burning streets.

"What happened?" I gasped.

"The Barren," he answered. "After you were taken, we had to recoup. I was severely injured. I don't remember them bringing me back here. It took Medrina two weeks to heal my body, and right after I healed, they attacked."

"But why? We don't have the Eye anymore," I pointed out.

Eryx's dragon dropped, and I suppressed a squeal as I latched onto Eryx. I heard his chuckle, and before I had been taken, that would have made me throttle him, but now, the sound warmed my insides. I held on a little tighter until the dragon's feet hit the ground.

Glancing over Eryx's shoulder, I watched in astonishment as the man who found me in the halls landed. A dozen more winged men landed behind him. He strode towards us as we slipped off the dragon, his steps unfaltering and sure of himself. The air around him brimmed with confidence and disdain, like he wanted others around him to think he cared nothing for them. I didn't know what it was about him, but I could see the false wall around him as he stopped before us.

His gaze slid down to mine, and I inhaled sharply. His salt colored eyes were both startling and mesmerizing; they were the color of what I imagined seafoam looked like as the waves rolled in.

"Missing mate," he addressed me with a bow of his head.

"My name's Alethea," I snapped in annoyance, and his eyes widened, clearly startled.

"My apologies, *Alethea*." He tucked an arm across his torso and bowed dramatically. "I'm Mykill."

I merely nodded at him and gripped onto Eryx's arm. Eryx glanced down at me and then back at Mykill. "I'm taking her to our healer, Medrina. Are any of your men injured?"

"No," Mykill shook his head and finally met Eryx's gaze. "We will see ourselves to our wing." He bowed his head and pivoted on his heel.

"Let's get you to Medrina," Eryx said as he turned towards me.

His hand slid down my arm until our fingers intertwined. The motion calmed my racing heart, as did the familiarity of the castle. The glass ceilings gave the halls an openness about them, unlike Kirin's castle, where obscene images were painted.

Eryx pulled me from my thoughts as he knocked on Medrina's door, and she opened before he pulled his hand away.

"Alethea." She sighed in relief and stepped aside, rushing us in. "Please, sit. Let me look at you."

Eryx led me to the stool at her workbench. The room smelled of herbs, and her honey eyes lulled my racing thoughts as she settled before me.

"Can you talk through what happened? Is there anything I need to look at specifically?" she asked.

I merely stared at her as my thoughts started crashing together incoherently in an array of voices and images. My heart rate kicked up, and my lungs felt like they were deprived of breath. A tremor worked its way through my hands, but I willed them to remain still, planted in my lap.

"Alethea," Medrina said softly as she placed a hand on my thigh. I felt the tendrils of her magic circle around me, calming my racing heart. "That's alright. We don't have to. Let's just look you over."

"Alethea," Eryx spoke next as he stepped up beside the bench. "Did he touch you? Did he -" I could sense what he was asking beneath the intensity of his stare.

"He didn't," I paused and held his gaze, communicating to him. "He kissed me and bit me, twice. But that's all."

I could see the visible fall of his shoulders as he breathed a sigh of relief. "Where did he bite you?" Medrina asked.

My insides wanted to shrivel up and hide. Heat bloomed across my cheeks as I ducked my face.

"Answer her, Blossom," Eryx prompted softly.

"They're healed over," I whispered numbly. "They have already scarred over; they don't need to be looked at."

"Are you sure?" Medrina asked softly.

I couldn't look at her as I nodded.

"Alright," she said softly as she stood. "She's alright. She needs to eat. She's severely malnourished and dehydrated, but she will be okay."

"Thank you, Medrina," Eryx said, and I stilled as his hand slid across my shoulders. "Come on, Alethea. Let's get you cleaned up."

"I'm glad to have you back, girl." I only smiled at Medrina before we slipped from the room.

Eryx's steps were the only things I could hear as we moved through the halls. None of the guards looked at me as we passed, and if they did, I was sure they'd sneer. They had never liked me; they thought of me below them, simply human trash.

We hurried up the steps before we reached Eryx's wing. He opened the door for me, and I slipped inside. I stopped in the center of the room as the door clicked shut behind me. His scent hit me as I closed my eyes. Everything rushed back to me at once, and the grief surged to the forefront of my mind.

I was now an orphan, and the only sister I had was gone.

The weight of my grief settled on my shoulders. My knees buckled, and I swayed, not able to catch myself. Eryx's arms wrapped around me from behind, catching me before I hit the floor. My heart caved in on itself, but it continued to beat.

My mother, my father and my sister - all gone.

"They're all gone," I sobbed as I covered my face with my hands. "My family is gone."

I didn't hear Eryx's response as my heart thundered in my ears. Each thud of my heart became a painful reminder of the hole that was left in it.

My sister was my best friend and my rock. Each moment I'd spent with her played through my mind with piercing clarity. The sound of her laugh echoed in my ears; her smile was etched into my memory like a brand. The realization that I would never hear her laugh, never sense her comforting presence again, settled over me like a wet blanket, suffocating me.

My tears flowed freely, my chest heaved, and I wrapped myself around Eryx. He was the only thing I had left in this world. He held me back just as fiercely. He cradled the back of my head with tenderness as my cries shook us.

"I'm so sorry," he repeated as he rocked me.

My sweet, sweet father, who had never raised his voice or hand at me, was gone as well. He'd always loved me and protected me, even if I wasn't his in the end. But he had raised me like I was. He had never shown Laney more favor; he had treated us as equals, loved us like equals.

I'd never hear him call me 'Biscuit' again and pat my head. I'd never encounter his bear hugs that nearly crushed my lungs but had always comforted me and made me giggle.

I would never get to see my parents dance in the kitchen, whispering to each other as if Laney and I couldn't see or hear them. We had always teased them and chided them. But, now the memory sat at the bottom of my stomach, searing into me. Longing filled me. I would give almost anything to go back in time and cuddle up with Laney in the bed we shared, or sneak out the back door when our father would start peppering kisses along our mother's shoulder. She would always blush fiercely, and Laney and I would run through the city exploring until our heads were heavy with exhaustion.

"My necklace," I cried as I burrowed my face into Eryx's shoulder. "He took my necklace."

I didn't hear Eryx's response as another dam broke in me. The last remaining piece of my family had been taken by the High Priest. He was responsible for ripping my entire family from me, and he had taken the last reminder of them I had.

***

I watched with swollen eyes as Eryx closed the door behind him. He strode towards me with a glass of water, his steps light. After I had cried until my eyes had no more tears, he brought me to his bed and offered to get me some water.

"I need to tell you something," I whispered as I fiddled with the hem of my skirt.

He paused momentarily before placing the glass on the night table. "What is it, Blossom?"

Ducking my head, I stared down at the comforter beneath me. I felt my cheeks heating as shame emanated through me. "I kissed the High Priest." My voice was barely above a breathless whisper. "I had my ladies' maids bring me a powder that would put him to sleep so I could try and escape. In order to get close enough to him, I pretended that I wanted him. I *touched* him." My voice wobbled as I recalled the memories of his lips on mine. "Please don't think any less of me." My voice broke on a sob as tears rushed my eyes again.

I thought my eyes were out of tears, but I'd been wrong.

"Alethea," Eryx gasped as gripped my chin and pulled my face up. "I could never think any less of you, Blossom. You did what you needed to survive."

"But -" I tried to turn my head away, but he would have none of it as he forced me to look at him.

"No," he said forcefully. "I mean it. You were a *prisoner*, Alethea. He hurt you, and you did what you needed to escape. If you hadn't gotten away from him, then I may not have been able to get to you."

His eyes gleamed nothing but the truth as he stared down at me. One of his hands rested on my cheek, and his thumb swept across my skin. I blew out a breath and leaned into him until my forehead rested on his shoulder. Ever so slowly, his arms tightened around me, and he held me against him. His touch soothed something in me, and I closed my eyes, relishing in his strength.

Although I still reveled in his touch, I couldn't deny the lack of our mating bond. Every touch didn't feel like it reached the same depth as before.

"Can you feel the lack of the mating bond?" I whispered.

"Yes." The tremble of his deep voice vibrated through his chest. "But I still love you nonetheless."

I smiled as he ran a hand down my hair. We still had love without the mating bond. I had started falling for him before I had been acquainted with his touch. I had fallen for his deep laugh and how he tenderly cared for me. He had never pushed me; he had always wanted me to decide what we were, and I admired him for that. He could so easily overpower me - not just physically. He could easily press his wants onto me, but he hadn't.

"Let's get you into the bath." His quiet voice broke the silence.

Pulling away, I nodded and then gasped in surprise as he slipped his arms beneath me. I slid an arm around his neck as he carried me into the washroom and placed me down on the fluffy mat in front of the tub. As he leaned down to fill the tub, I slipped off the horrid nightgown and into the bath.

"Here, Blossom."

I turned as Eryx knelt beside the tub with a bar of soap in his hand. He leaned forward and reached behind me. I felt his hand splash water across my back before he started gently massaging the soap into my skin. I nearly groaned as he began working out the tension that lingered. His fingers worked firmly, kneading out the knots in my muscles.

"Thank you," I whispered as I pulled my knees to my chest.

He didn't answer as he continued working the soap into my skin. He used his hand to wash it off and then nudged my head backwards. After he wet my hair, he began massaging the soap into my scalp. My eyes slid closed on their own accord, and I rested my chin on my knee. The water ran down the sides of my face as he poured water on my head.

While he did that, I remained focused on the sound of his breathing. The sound of it grounded me here, to reality. It reminded me that I was safe.

"I'm done," Eryx's deep voice said softly.

I leaned forward and pulled the stopper up so the water could drain. As it did, Eryx held out a towel for me as I stepped out of the tub. He patted my body dry and offered me another towel to help dry my hair. I twisted it around my hair, squeezing all the excess water out of it. Wrapping the towel around me, I knotted it and stood before Eryx. His brows were drawn down. His eyes were dark and vacant, guilt looming in his gaze as he stood before me. He had removed his shirt because it had gotten soaked, and his abdomen was on display. My mouth dried at the sight of the masculine beauty of him.

"Thank you for caring for me," I said as I pushed up onto my toes and placed my hands on either side of his face.

I pressed my lips to his gently. He placed his hands on my hips as I kissed him again. My hands slid across his bare sides, slipping over every muscle and every curve. My arms slid all the way around him, and his arms curled around me, securing me to him. I laid my head down on his chest and let out a sigh as I closed my eyes.

"I want you to make love to me," I whispered as I tightened my arms around him.

His entire body tensed before his arms fell away and moved to cup my face. "I want to. Gods, Alethea, I want to. But I don't want to do something you're not ready for."

His words made my stomach flutter and made me fall even harder for him.

"Please," I croaked as I gripped his sides, keeping him against me. "Please, I need this. I want this," I confirmed.

His gaze was uncertain as he took in my face and features. I could see the uncertainty written across his face, like he was going to push me too far. I ran my palms across his bare back and felt his muscles shift. Finally, he nodded and leaned towards me.

"I can deny you nothing," he breathed before pressing his lips to mine.

My head dropped back as his lips traveled down the front of my throat. His hands pushed the robe off my shoulders, letting it pool at my feet. His skin was warm and burned into mine as he gripped my hips and then slid an arm around me. I wrapped my arms around his neck as he lifted me. My legs instinctively wrapped around his waist, and we moved back towards the bed.

His lips found mine again as we fell back together. My legs tightened around him as his hands skimmed down the sides of my body. His fingers undid the knot of the towel and laid it out on either side of me. My bare skin burned into his. The feel of him heated my core.

I bit down on my lip as his mouth moved down between my breasts. I couldn't help but groan as his tongue continued down my stomach.

My entire body froze as he hissed out a breath. I swung my eyes open. Eryx had spread my legs, and his gaze was trained on the inside of my thigh. A low growl was emanating from his chest, and he brushed his thumb across the scar.

I inhaled sharply. My legs trembled as he lowered his face to the scar, and with the tenderness I had come to associate with him, he kissed the center of it. Then, his tongue stroked across it.

I settled back down on the bed as his lips continued up the inside of my thigh. Fire followed his lips as he settled above the center of my legs. He let out a heavy breath, and I pressed my lips together as my eyes drifted closed.

His tongue lit me on fire, the heat pooling in my belly as my back arched off the bed. My fingers gripped the sheets as he tugged me closer to him. I cried out as the tension between my legs built and built until I felt like I was going to shatter.

Only then did he pull away. I whined in protest, and he chuckled softly as he climbed up my body. His fingers skated over my skin lightly, almost teasingly, before he settled above me.

"You will forever be mine, Alethea."

I cried out as he moved into me, filling me before I could respond. My head fell back against the pillow as my fingers dug into his skin. Every broken piece in me seemed to mend back together as we joined. Even through all the loss I had endured, he remained my light at the end of the tunnel.

He dropped his forehead to mine as he breathed raggedly. I couldn't do anything other than grip onto him. My limbs locked as the feeling like I was going to shatter heightened again. I groaned as Eryx's lips brushed my ear, then his tongue. His pace quickened, and sweat broke out across my forehead.

"Eryx," I gasped in desire as I dropped my head back, and with a final thrust, I shattered with a shout. He followed behind me as he quickened his pace momentarily.

I breathed heavily as I ran a hand down his back. It had been too long since I'd felt his skin against mine.

"Promise me that we will do everything we can to never be separated again," I breathed as I gripped his face.

His eyes shined earnestly as he nodded and ran a hand across my jaw. "I swear it on my life, Alethea."

"I love you," I whispered as I pressed my lips to his again. But this time, it didn't ignite the fire of need in my belly - but a fire of adoration. I had missed him so much, and being near him again was physically invigorating.

"I love you so much more." He kissed me back passionately, his lips lingering on mine before he spoke again. "We need to go to the dining room. You need to eat something."

I nodded as I placed my palm on the side of his face. "Thank you," I whispered.

He leaned forward and placed a kiss on my forehead. I smiled. "Thank *you*, Alethea."

He pushed up off me and rolled off the bed fluidly. I blushed and averted my eyes as he strode across the room naked. I stared at the ceiling as I listened to the sound of rustling clothes as he dressed himself.

"Here, Blossom." I glanced at him as he held a dress in his hands for me.

"Thank you," I said as I slipped off the bed. I managed to keep the sheet around me as I took the dress and shimmied into the washroom.

Eryx's deep laugh followed me, and I couldn't help but smile. I had missed his light, almost teasing manner when we were alone. That light and carefree side of him only revealed itself around me when he wasn't worrying about his responsibilities.

After composing myself, I slipped the dress on quickly and braided my hair down my shoulder. I looked so different from the last time I had stood in front of this mirror. My cheeks were hollow, and my skin was duller. My hair looked like straw, and my lips contained almost no color. I looked sickly. I forced myself to turn away from my reflection. I couldn't look at myself without recalling every horrible thing, and if I did, I didn't think I would be able to hold it together. It was all too raw and fresh.

"Ready?" Eryx asked as I stepped out of the washroom.

He offered me a tentative smile, took my hand in his, and led me through the halls. I heard brief conversations as we approached the doors, and Eryx flicked a wrist, pushing them open with invisible hands.

My hand slipped from Eryx's as we stepped into the dining room. Mykill and Cadmus were both already seated, picking at the food before them. My heart began to pick up pace as I took in the room before me. The image of the High Priest replaced Cadmus and

Mykill, and I felt like I couldn't breathe. Flashes of the electrified utensils, the rotten food, and every other horrifying detail rushed back to me in a mighty wave. I inhaled sharply as I stumbled back a step and shook my head. I couldn't be here. I needed to get outside. I needed fresh air.

"Alethea, what's wrong?" Eryx asked as he placed a hand on my back.

I shook my head as I tried to shove his hand away. My vision blurred as my knees gave out beneath me. He cursed as he reached around me and helped lower me to the floor.

"Please don't touch me," I gasped as I shook my head again.

"Alethea," Eryx prompted as he tried pushing my hair away from my face.

Tears clouded my vision. I knew these were his hands, but I could only feel the High Priest as he brushed his hands across my cheek.

"She's having a panic attack." Mykill's cool voice broke through my panic. "I would advise you to stop touching her like she requested."

"I didn't ask you!" Eryx snapped.

"Please!" I cried as I wrapped my arms around my middle. "*Please*, don't touch me."

Eryx's hands disappeared.

"Just focus on breathing in through your nose and out through your mouth," a cool voice said.

I nodded and breathed in deeply before exhaling between my lips.

"Good. Now, do it again," the voice commanded.

I obeyed. Breath after breath, my lungs filled more and more. The breathlessness vanished, and I was able to see the room around me more clearly. I wasn't in the High Priest's dining room. Unlike his dining room, this space was decorated with paintings of flowers, oceans, and gardens, and the glass ceiling let in the bright sun. The High Priest wasn't here. I was protected, and I was safe. They had rescued me.

"Alethea?" Eryx's tentative voice asked. "Can you stand?"

Nodding, I gripped his outstretched hand and let him pull me to my feet. Cadmus was standing beside Mykill, who stared down at me with intrigue. I frowned at him before turning back to Eryx. "I'm alright, I promise." I dropped Eryx's hand and stepped away from him. I needed the distance to clear my mind.

Moving around Cadmus and Mykill, I headed toward the table and took the seat beside Eryx's. Everyone slowly made their way over to the table and took their seats. I could see Cadmus' eyes flicker over to me every few moments, worry lingering in his gaze. There was a delicious array of foods lining the center of the table. I could smell rosemary butter rolls and peppered chicken, as well as boiled potatoes. There was a teapot before my place setting, and a glass of tea was already steeping for me.

I picked up the bag by the string, pulled it from the cup, and placed it on the edge of my plate. The chair beside me slid out, and my entire body stiffened as Mykill sat down. My head snapped to him, and he paused, as if he was aware I was looking at him. Then, ever so slowly, his head turned towards me. I was shocked again by the almost white color of his eyes; they reminded me of salt. As I looked at him, I could picture peaceful waves crashing onto the shore and smell the salty breeze. It was serene. His eyes narrowed as he held my gaze, his eyes just as questioning as mine. Eryx cleared his throat, snapping my attention back to him. His dark brows were pulled down, and his cider eyes were wary as he stared at Mykill. Then his gaze slid over to me.

"Please eat, Alethea." His voice was soft as he spoke.

I noticed the way his hand clenched as he gripped his wineglass. Nodding, I stared down at my plate as Eryx loaded food onto it. He piled the meat on heavily, and as I stared at the brimming plate, I thought that there was no way I could eat it all.

CHAPTER 9

Alethea

Dinner was strained. No one spoke as we all ate. The only sound was our breathing and silverware scratching off the plates. The food was filling, and just like I thought, I wasn't able to eat everything. Eryx glared at the pile of food on my plate as I set my fork down.

"You need to eat more," he said gruffly.

I shook my head at him as I glanced back down at my plate. "I can't."

"Please," he begged as he reached across my plate and picked up half of my discarded roll. "Just finish this roll, please." His eyes were pleading.

"She probably can't," Mykill said, and I stiffened as he did. Realization dawned over me as I slowly turned to him. He was the one who had told me to breathe. "When your body gets used to malnourishment, you aren't able to eat in excess amounts without making yourself sick. She could continue eating, but I'm sure she would vomit it back up. I'm not too privy to seeing that. Are you?" He quirked an eyebrow at Eryx.

As I glanced back at Eryx, his jaw clenched. He looked back at me before muttering, "Alright." His eyes slid over to me. "But you will eat more in the morning."

I nodded. "I'm going to take a walk before going back to bed. I just want some fresh air and to clear my head a little."

Concern grew across his face. "Would you like me to come with you?"

I shook my head. "I'd actually like to go on my own." I pushed out my chair and stood. "But I'll come to bed soon." I leaned into Eryx and placed a kiss to his cheek before I hurried from the dining room.

Not only was I glad to be alone for a bit and get a hold of my bearings, but it was also relieving to be away from such a strained environment. I needed to ask Eryx what the tension between him and Mykill was. They had barely spoken to each other, but I could feel Eryx's hatred for Mykill. It coated my skin. I could sense Mykill was the taunting type. He clearly liked to get on people's nerves, and Eryx was the perfect person for that.

First, I wandered to my old bedroom. Surprisingly, the room didn't smell musty like I would have thought. Everything was left as it was. Even the book I had been in the middle of reading still rested on the stand beside the armchair. That armchair and the one in the library were my two favorite places in the whole castle. My makeshift bookmark stuck out oddly, and I picked up the book and riffled through it for a moment. I smiled before placing it back down.

Eryx's scent lingered as I walked about, and then I noticed the indent in the bed. My steps faltered before I veered towards the bed. The closer I got, the stronger his scent became.

I ran my hand over the comforter. I had missed the elegant feeling of it. Flashes of what had happened before Kirin had sent his men for me played across my mind. The trances, collapsing into the wardrobe gasping for Eryx, the note on my pillow from Freya.

I made such a mistake trusting her. I would have given anything to take it back. I knew when I had decided to trust Freya that I should've trusted Eryx and that there would be consequences to my decisions, but I had never envisioned such drastic consequences. I replayed the moment we had been separated in my mind. The Whispering Winds were closing in all around us and Eryx's men were slaughtered. Cadmus dragged me out of the shadows as we fought the Wind.

I had thought of it regularly when I had been in the dungeons. I had thought of it not only as a way to keep myself busy but to remind myself that it all hadn't been some dream. I had spent days recalling my time in the Isle of Mirrors just to remind myself that I was strong when I had felt anything but. Even now, I felt like a fragment of the girl I had been before I had been taken, before I had experienced starvation and abuse.

Thoughts of the High Priest nearly made me frenzy with bloodlust. I wanted him to die. I saw him commanding his men to shoot my sister as she helped me onto the dragon. He had taken my last living relative as punishment for running. First my mother, then my father, and then my sister. He wanted me alone and isolated.

I would give my soul to feel his blood run between my fingers.

I stopped at the foot of the bed, and I froze as realization crashed over me. I wasn't the same girl I was before Kirin had taken me. My heart was harder, colder. I wanted my enemies to burn for what they took from me. Part of me wished I was still the same girl. I feared Eryx would find the new me less lovable.

Taking a deep breath, I slipped from the room. My lungs were in desperate need of fresh air. They needed the reminder that I wasn't there. I wasn't trapped anymore.

I followed the familiar path out to the gardens. My steps quickened as the need for fresh air heightened. I felt my breath quicken as my feet flew over the marbled floors. Pushing open the door, I stepped out onto the balcony. The cool night air hit me, spreading goosebumps across my arms. I breathed in deeply and closed my eyes as I closed the door, remaining frozen for a moment.

"That was an intriguing turn of events," a voice behind me said.

My shoulders stiffened, and my steps faltered. I turned at the waist to look at Mykill. He was seated in one of the lounge chairs with his feet propped up on the table in front of him.

"What does it matter to you?" I snapped as I turned towards him fully.

His cool gaze moved over to me. "It doesn't. I just know the signs of someone who has been tortured. Why didn't you mention it to Eryx?"

"It doesn't matter," I whispered.

Mykill shrugged as he dropped his feet to the ground and stood. He moved fluidly towards me, and his wide frame stopped before me. I had to crane my head all the way back to look up at him.

"It will pass," he whispered as his brows furrowed. He watched me for another beat before he headed inside, brushing past me without another word. The scent of the warm sea breeze lingered behind, cloaking itself around me until it was all I could smell. I closed my eyes and breathed deeply. The scent calmed my racing heart. I heard the door shut behind him, but my feet were frozen.

Fisting my hands by my side, I forced my feet to move. I scurried down the balcony steps and out to the grass behind the garden. I sighed as I sat down in the grass. Crickets chirped, creating their own melody with the swaying branches. The wind rustled my hair and cast a chill over my skin. Pulling my knees to my chest, I wrapped my arms around them and rested my cheek against them.

My heart clenched as I closed my eyes. If I pictured it long enough, I could see Laney sitting beside me. She would smile up at the sky and tell me how beautiful it was. Then she'd persuade me into sneaking off into the forest on an adventure. I would always follow, and we'd run through the trees as if we were being chased and laugh until we collapsed.

I sniffled as warmth ran down my cheeks. I squeezed my eyes and pushed the thought of her from my mind. It hurt too bad. I missed her too much.

I could still see the hatred in her eyes when she looked at Eryx, then at me. She had been taught horrible things about the fae too. But, I found after Eryx had brought me here that I had begun questioning everything I had been taught.

Finally, I pushed myself to head back inside. If I stayed out too much longer, Eryx would worry and come find me.

I walked numbly through the halls back to Eryx's bedroom. My thoughts strayed, but I couldn't keep focus on a single one for too long before I began to stray again.

"Alethea." Eryx immediately jumped up from the armchair before his fireplace as I pushed open the door.

I offered him a small smile as the door clicked closed behind him, and I stood frozen for a moment. The dragon we had ridden earlier was draped across the balcony. He was much different than Cador. He was longer and leaner. His neck was thin and lengthy. I didn't know much about dragons and their different breeds, but Cador and this dragon couldn't have looked more different. Sadness yanked in my chest as I thought of Cador. He had given his life for me and had cared for me.

He had also been Eryx's best friend. Even now, I still felt guilty over his death. He was another name to add to the list of people who had died for me.

"I have a sleep gown in the washroom for you," he said as he remained frozen at the foot of the bed.

Nodding, I slipped past the sleeping dragon and ran to the sink to splash some cold water on my face. There was a slip on the counter beside the sink, as well as Eryx's discarded tunic. Grabbing the slip, I stripped before sliding on the sleep gown and grabbed the robe hanging for me. I wrapped it around myself as I padded back out into the bedroom and took up residence on the armchair besides the fireplace. I pulled my legs up beneath me and watched as he settled in the seat across from me.

"How are you feeling?" he asked softly as he stretched out and crossed his legs.

I paused, contemplating my answer as I turned to look at the crackling fire. *How was I feeling?* So many thoughts and emotions tumbled through me as I tried to recall an answer. I fingered with the end of my braid as I watched the mixture of reds, yellows, and oranges.

"I'm glad to be back," I whispered as I dropped my braid.

Eryx was silent, but I could sense the questions tumbling about inside him.

"You can ask me anything you want to know." I slid my gaze over to him and met his dark stare. His cider eyes glimmered in the firelight, and they matched the deep hues of the orange in the flames.

"What happened when they first took you?" he asked softly.

My eyes moved back to the fire. "They kept me in the dungeons for a while, at least 45 days. But that could also be wrong, I lost track of time eventually." I shrugged. "Then, the High Priest had me brought up to his room." I didn't miss the way Eryx's entire body stiffened as I mentioned his name.

"You told me he didn't before, but let me be more clear. Did he violate you? Did he force himself on you?" I could hear the hidden tremble beneath his voice.

"He kissed me, and you saw the scar." I paused. "But no he didn't violate me further."

Eryx was silent for several beats, surely taking in what I said. I'm sure it eased something in him to know that the High Priest hadn't raped me. He wouldn't have been able to live with himself if the High Priest had.

"I'm so sorry Alethea," he said softly, and I heard him shift forward.

"I would do anything to take it back." I interrupted him and began fingering the end of my braid again. My cheeks heated, making me not able to meet his gaze. "I would give anything to take back trusting Freya. There's a part of me that knows that if I hadn't, if I had told you, then things may have turned out dramatically differently. But you kept things from me. I trust you with my life, but you have to trust me back."

"I know," he answered.

"Why did you want the Eye? What were you doing at Kirin's kingdom to begin with?"

"Alethea," he sighed. "You don't understand. I want to share with you, but there are things I'm not permitted to share as King."

I merely stared at the carpet beneath my seat. There was a part of me that had figured that would have been his answer.

"I also found out that my parents didn't give birth to me."

"Cadmus did some digging and found the same thing," he confirmed.

"Do you know where I came from?"

"Not yet, but we're still looking. We will find your real parents."

I dropped my braid and lifted my head to meet his gaze. His face softened as he sat forward and propped his elbows on his knees. "Let's get to bed," he said softly.

I nodded as I rose from the sofa. He stepped up beside me and gripped my hand as he led me to the bed. I slid beneath the luxurious comforter and felt the bed shift behind me as he laid beside me. His arms secured around me, and he brought my body flush to his. His warmth wrapped around me, enshrouding me and grounding me in reality, where I was safe and free.

Sleep felt empty, unrefreshing. As I opened my eyes, it felt like I hadn't slept for a minute, but also like I slept for an eternity. It was unfulfilling.

"Good morning," Eryx said as he stepped out of the washroom in only a towel.

"Good morning." I rubbed my eyes as I yawned and sat up.

"I have a meeting with Mykill and Cadmus, and you're welcome to come." I watched as he dropped the towel and began to dress.

My mouth instantly dried as I averted my eyes. I swallowed past the heavy lump in my throat and pushed myself out of bed. I scurried past his very naked form into the washroom and washed my face and readied quickly. He was fully dressed by the time I came out of the washroom dressed in a simple rose colored gown with long sleeves. I was delighted by the length of the sleeves. Medrina had healed most of my body, but the shackle marks around my wrists had become more permanent. I double checked to make sure they were covering the marks before nodding. "I'm ready."

"Come." Eryx waved to me as he opened the door. I brushed by him and out into the hall. "Just remain quiet. Mykill can be unruly," he said. I could hear the annoyance in his tone, but he didn't say anything else as we descended the stairs in his wing until we got to his office.

Mykill and Cadmus were both already seated on the opposite side of his desk. Behind Mykill was a woman in battle attire with her arms crossed. She was stunning with waist length, pin straight black hair that was pulled into a ponytail. Her eyes were pointed, much like a cat's, and were the color of emeralds. She glared at Eryx and I as we entered the room, and he tugged me behind his desk with him. He waved his hand and another chair appeared beside him. Taking my seat beside him, I placed my hands in my lap and waited.

"What would you like to meet about?" Eryx asked as he folded his hands in front of him on the desk.

"Well, for starters, I'd like to discuss what you plan to do. You've started a war with the human lands who have several mages in their arsenal." Mykill's cool voice slithered over us, coating us in his disdain.

I wasn't sure, but there had to be some sort of history between the two. I made a note to ask about it later.

"For now, we plan on waiting it out. We will do nothing. My only objective was retrieving her, and now I will keep her safe behind our fortified walls."

"She needs to be trained," Mykill said as he picked at his fingernails.

He crossed his feet as he propped them up on Eryx's desk. A growl rumbled from Eryx's chest, and he raised his hand. As he flicked his finger, an invisible wind pushed Mykill's feet over the edge. Mykill scowled but didn't say anything as he extended his legs and crossed his ankles.

"She will not be trained. She's human and won't do much good in battle," Eryx bit out.

"And this is coming from a warrior?" Mykill's head fell back as he laughed. "Has all the time you spent between her legs befuddled your mind? That mindset will ensure that she winds up dead."

My cheeks heated, and my mouth fell open at his vulgarity.

"You do not speak of her in such a manner." Eryx's hands fisted, and he clenched his jaw so tightly I thought his teeth would snap. "She will not be trained."

I fisted my hands in my lap, but I bit my tongue. Eryx had told me to remain quiet. Mykill glanced over at me, almost as if he sensed the shift of my emotions.

"I think she has some unexpressed emotions." Mykill waved at me. "Speak, human."

I glanced at Eryx, and his gaze didn't let on to how he was feeling. Still, his jaw was clenched.

"I want to train," I voiced.

Eryx shook his head. "Absolutely not."

Mykill raised an impressed brow at me before turning his annoyed stare onto Eryx. "It's no concern of mine. I just thought I'd mention the obvious. We will stay a month to ensure that the humans don't attack. But after that, you're on your own."

"But the Tre- "

"The Treaty," Mykill bit out, interrupting him. "The Treaty in no way obligates me to help you in a war you started. From my knowledge, she was betrothed to the King of the human lands, and you stole her away. They merely took back what you stole, and you stole her *again*."

"She's my mate!" Eryx argued.

"May I point out that I don't smell a mating bond." Mykill glanced between the two of us before continuing. "But, I helped you retrieve your mate. Anything I choose to do from this point on is out of the goodness of my heart."

I could practically hear Eryx's molars grinding together as a muscle in his cheek jumped in response to Mykill's words. "Thank you for your assistance," he finally said, but his voice was pained. "Now, let's go to breakfast, Alethea."

With that, he rose from his seat and took my hand. I followed closely behind him as we exited the room, but, much to my surprise, we didn't turn right down the hall towards the dining hall. We took a left instead.

"Where are we going?" I frowned.

"We're having breakfast on my balcony." His voice was clipped, and he didn't say anything else as we ascended the stairs to his wing.

He threw open the bedroom door with a wave of his hand.

"I want to talk about this," I said as he closed the door behind us.

I walked over to the balcony table. "Blossom." His voice was low behind me.

I spun towards him.

"I want to train!" I argued as Eryx began unbuttoning his shirt.

"We'll talk about it later, Blossom," he said as he discarded his shirt and stepped up to me.

My mind seemed to wander as I took in his powerful body. My mouth dried again as he lowered his lips to mine. His hands traveled around my waist, pulling me into his warm body.

"You're distracting me, but I still won't change my mind," I said against his lips as he nudged me onto the bed.

"We'll talk about it later," he said again as his hands traveled beneath my dress and up.

But there was a part of me that knew I wasn't going to like our conversation later.

Eryx was already gone by the time I awoke the next morning. We hadn't seen Mykill or Cadmus for the remainder of the day. Instead, we spent our time either tangled in his sheets or lounging on the balcony. Now, I realized that it was a distraction to keep me from pestering him about training, but I wasn't going to relent today.

Bathing quickly, I dressed in the silk burgundy gown that had been left for me on the washroom counter. I stared at myself in the full length mirror and made a note to go back to my room to bring some more clothes. This dress did not suit me. The color stood out harshly against my lightened skin.

I desperately need to spend some time out in the sun, I thought to myself as I exited the bedroom.

I noticed the guards that flanked the door and followed me down the stairs. I resisted a groan and an eye roll because I knew why he did it.

I was approaching the dining hall when Eryx and Cadmus were leaving. They spoke in a hushed tone and paused when they saw me.

"Alethea," Eryx said as he stepped towards me. "I didn't expect you to be up this early."

I nodded my head at Cadmus in greeting before I turned to Eryx. "Can I speak with you?" I asked.

Eryx nodded and glanced at Cadmus. "Give us a few minutes." Cadmus nodded as he slipped back into the dining hall, and when he disappeared, Eryx turned towards me. "I was walking to my office."

I followed behind him. "I want to talk about my training."

"I already said no, Alethea," Eryx sighed.

Anger stirred through me as I stormed after Eryx. "You can't just tell me no and expect me to listen. I'm not a child."

Eryx didn't look at me as he opened his office door and sighed again. "I just don't see a reason for you to train, Alethea. I want you to focus on healing. I can see the shift in your eyes." My feet faltered as he sat on the other side of his desk.

My heart rate kicked up, and my hands went slack at my sides.

"I can see the haunted look in your eyes," he said again, this time his voice softer. "I can see it as you check around every room we enter as if something's going to come out of the walls. I don't know what he did to you, but I can only imagine. What I want most for you is to heal."

I merely nodded. *But what if training would help me heal?* I hadn't been in control of my life when the High Priest took me. I had been on his schedule entirely. I couldn't eat unless he said so, and I couldn't sleep most nights because he didn't want it. I hadn't been in control of anything, and now Eryx was taking more control from me.

I stepped back again, my back hitting the door frame as I shook my head.

"Alethea," he sighed and placed his hands on his desk as if he was going to rise.

"No," I shook my head. "No."

I stormed out of the office as disbelief coursed through me. I needed to get out of the castle. I stumbled backwards as the walls around me seemed to close in on me again. My chest began to heave, and a tremor worked its way up my hands. My feet moved quickly over the tiled floor, but it felt like I was in a maze, and the halls kept getting thinner and thinner. The walls were suffocating me, and the paintings on the walls were getting closer to me until they loomed over me. They reeked of their joy and peace. They reeked of everything that had been taken from me.

A cold hand briefly touched my shoulder, and I yelped as I jerked away from the contact. "I'm just going to grab your elbow and get you outside."

"Outside," I gasped as I searched for the origin of the voice, but I couldn't see anything around me. It was like a dark storm cloud was descending on me, inducing hysteria. "Outside," I repeated almost breathlessly.

The cool hand touched my elbow, and the steely fingers wrapped around my arm. The sound of thunder broke out around me, and then the ground fell out from beneath my feet. I would've screamed if I had the air in my lungs to do so. The ground returned a moment later, and as I took a deep breath, I breathed in fresh air.

The sound of chirping birds and swaying trees thrust through the shroud around me.

"That's a hideous dress," an even, cool voice said.

Whipping around towards the voice, I halted as Mykill stood before me. His wings were tucked neatly behind him, and he was dressed in a tight black top that hugged his muscled frame. He donned them with matching black pants that were tucked into knee high riding boots. His jacket reached the tip of his boots, and the cloud-gray sash around his waist was the only pop of color he adorned himself with.

"You took me outside?" I asked, but I knew the answer already as he nodded.

"You seemed like you needed fresh air." He shrugged as he walked around me.

"You said you knew the signs of someone being tortured?" I asked as I followed after him as he casually strolled away.

The air around him reeked of disdain and dominance. His footsteps were nearly silent as we entered the gardens.

"Yes," was all he said in response.

My eyes followed his long fingers as they reached out and plucked a rose from one of the thriving bushes. Each finger was adorned in an array of rings - some shaped like skulls, others like daggers, but they all glimmered in the morning sun.

"I find fresh air helps me as well." He turned towards me and bowed at the waist. "Enjoy your day, Alethea." He was gone with a stroke of lightning before he fully rose.

Chapter 10

Eryx

"Eryx, please don't let them take me!" Alethea sobbed as she placed a shaking hand on my cheek.

"Alethea, I'm so, so sorry," I whispered as I placed my hand atop hers.

"Why did you let them take me?" She sobbed as her cheeks reddened and tears poured down them.

She shook her head as she dropped her hand and took a step away from me. Betrayal flashed across her features.

"You said you would always protect me," she cried out as she stepped further away from me.

"Alethea, please forgive me," I begged as I tried reaching for her hand.

She shook her head again and side-stepped me. "You promised," was all she said.

I dropped my head and pushed my fists into my eye sockets. "I'm so sorry," I said as my body slumped.

I let out a startled gasp as my eyes flew open. Sweat beaded my brow, and my chest labored.

It was a dream. It had been a dream.

I breathed in deeply as I took in my bedroom around me, the open balcony, and the light sun that now poured into the room. A cool breeze blew, and I could hear the sound of birds chirping as they fluttered about. Adrius was draped across the balcony with his long neck hanging over the railing. His eyes were closed, and smoke blew out of his nose with every heavy breath he took.

Turning my attention back to the bed, Alethea was tucked against my body with my arm beneath her head, much like how we'd woken up the first time we had laid together. Her eyes were open this time, but the innocence, joyfulness, and light they had once possessed was gone as she stared at the ceiling.

"Good morning," she whispered as those eyes slid over to me.

I leaned in and kissed her temple. When I pulled away, her eyes were closed, and she was softly smiling. "Good morning, Blossom," I said as I pulled her further against me, and she turned into me. "How did you sleep?"

Her eyes flickered away from me, darkening before she answered. "I slept well." It was a lie. I could sense it. "I'm starving," she said as she rolled away from me and slid off the bed.

"Mustn't keep the fine lady waiting," I teased as I slid off the bed and went into the washroom.

I followed closely behind her as she began preparing a bath for herself. I had bathed the night before, but that didn't stop me from watching. She moved differently, with more grace and less of a pip in her step. She stripped her dress, unashamed of my prying eyes as she slid into the water. Her eyes closed in relaxation as she settled beneath the bubbling surface. As she reopened her eyes, they fell upon me, and I saw a glimpse of what

I could only pinpoint as mistrust. I couldn't blame her. I had planted that seed. There was just so much that I couldn't share with her as the King.

"Can you have Lira bring some of my dresses from my room here?" her soft voice finally said.

"Of course." I nodded and slipped from the washroom.

As I opened the door, I commanded the guards to have Lira bring Alethea's clothes to my room. I didn't wait for her as I went back into the washroom. Alethea was scrubbing her body with one of the bars of soap. Her brows were pulled down in concentration as she splashed water across her skin and then began scrubbing at her hair. It had grown since she'd been taken. It reached her waist now.

She leaned forward as she tugged out the tub stopper, and the water gurgled as it wound down the drain. Alethea patted herself dry and wrapped the towel around herself. I perked up as the door closed in my bedroom, and as I stepped out into the space, Lira was hobbling into the room with her arms full of dresses.

"Lira!" Alethea exclaimed.

She was a blur as she rushed past me. She grabbed the dresses from the elderly woman's arms and tossed them onto the ground. She threw her arms around the woman's shoulders, and the woman's bony arms wrapped around her.

"I missed you, girl," she mumbled.

"I missed you!" she breathed back and pulled away.

The woman offered her a wobbly smile before Alethea turned towards me.

"You can leave us," Alethea smiled at me, the light finally reaching her eyes. "I'll be at breakfast once I dress."

I bowed my head to Lira before leaving the room. I stalked through the halls as I thought of the look she had cast at me when she had been in the bath and the smile she had given Lira - the maid. It was like her whole world had brightened when she had walked into the room. My hands fisted at my sides as I recalled the film of distrust she had peered through when she had glanced at me. I knew she was still upset over me not wanting her to train. I had given her space yesterday, and she had spent the entire day outside. I didn't check on her, not wanting to impede on her space. Guards checked on her regularly and reported back to me.

The guards bowed to me as I stalked past them into the dining room. Cadmus and Mykill were already seated at the table. Cadmus was seated at my left, and Mykill was at the seat besides where Alethea would sit. I resisted the urge to force him to move to the far opposite end of the table.

"Good morning," Cadmus said as he dragged a jam coated knife across his biscuit.

I grunted in response as I plopped ungracefully down in my seat. A maid scurried forward and placed an empty plate in front of me. The spread this morning was an egg scramble with peppers, sausage with a side of biscuits, and roasted potatoes. It smelled heavenly, but I found my appetite had already vanished. Leaning forward, I grabbed the pitcher of wine and poured myself a tall glass.

"Someone must have had a bad night," Mykill teased as he cut at the sausage before he bit the small piece.

He always moved so fucking gracefully, and it was grating on my nerves. I fisted my hands and ignored him as I took a large gulp.

I perked up as Alethea passed through the doors in a soft peach colored gown. Her light hair was braided in a crown around her skull, and Lira had adorned her ears with pearl earrings.

"Cadmus," Alethea bowed her head to him as she took her seat on my right side. "Mykill," she greeted.

I resisted the urge to tell her to ignore him, but I knew that would open a box of questions I wasn't ready to answer yet. She leaned forward slowly as she loaded her plate with eggs and doubled up on the potatoes. She reached for the biscuits but came up short, and my entire body stiffened as a biscuit lifted off the plate on its own and floated over to her. She glanced at me, but then she quickly noticed it wasn't me.

Mykill didn't look at me or her as the biscuit settled on her plate.

"Thank you," she said softly before she picked up her fork.

I didn't miss the way her hand trembled before she picked up the fork or her slight pause as she stared down at the food. It was like she was double checking it. My vision tinted red. I desperately wanted to know what that prick had done to her so I could do it to him a hundred times over.

"Medrina offered an herb tonic to help you recall everything the King said and did." Cadmus broke the silence as his fork scraped off his plate.

"What are you looking for?" Alethea asked as she wiped at her mouth and placed her napkin in her lap.

Mykill didn't interject, only watched, as she frowned at Cadmus and me.

"Just as a precaution." I cut in and folded my hands beneath my chin. "Just to see if he hinted at anything that you can recall from your memories. Do you think you'll be able to help us with that?"

Alethea's expression remained blank for several beats, and a far off look gleamed in her eyes, like she wasn't here anymore. Guilt tugged at my chest, but I knew we needed to see her memories to gain further insight as to why he wanted her and how her blood turned those ordinary men into mages.

"I think it's quite unjust to make her relive her horrors," Mykill spoke up.

I glared at him, but he wasn't watching me. He was watching her. Something tightened in my chest at the concern written across his face. He shouldn't be concerned for her or her wellbeing, she was my mate.

"Sure," she finally said, but her voice was small. "After breakfast."

She didn't speak again for the remainder of breakfast. Cadmus tried to engage us all in small talk but slowly realized that we were all in too foul of moods. Mykill didn't say anything as he cleared his plate and exited the room. His body was stiff, angry almost, before he disappeared. Cadmus finally finished his food and rose.

"I will bring the herbs to your bedroom." He bowed his head to me.

Alethea had finished her food, but she merely stared down at her plate. Her body was stiff as a board as she pushed her chair out.

"I'll wait in your room."

"I'll go with you," I offered as I shoved up from the table.

I caught up to her and intertwined our fingers as we strolled towards the stairs. My thumb moved in slow strokes across the back of her palm as I tried to ease some tension. Guilt gnawed at me, and I nearly backed out, but a part of me knew we needed to do this. We needed to see if the High Priest had hinted at how her blood had been changing the men or why he knew he needed her in the first place.

We entered the bedroom, and she wordlessly walked over to the armchair beside the table before sitting down. Her eyes were almost vacant as she stared at the empty fireplace. A knock on the door drew me away.

I opened the door, and Cadmus offered me a small burgundy pouch in his hand.

"Thank you," I said to Cadmus as I took the small pouch from him.

"Just put a pinch in her tea," he instructed before I closed the door.

Stalking over to the table, I poured a glass of tea and dropped a pinch of the dried purple flower. The herb dissolved, turning the water a deep purple, and a sweet aroma drifted up to my nose.

"Here," I said as I offered her the teacup and saucer.

Her hands shook slightly as she took the teacup from me. She stared at the now dark purple liquid before she closed her eyes, tilted her head back, and downed the tea in one swift gulp.

"How long till it takes effect?" she asked as she handed the teacup back to me.

The teacup clicked off the saucer as I placed them both on the table. "It will be ready as soon as you take it."

She blew out a long breath and stood. "I'm ready," she said as she shook out her hands.

Stepping closer to her, I cupped her face in my hands and leaned down, kissing each closed eyelid as my own slid closed. I slid in effortlessly. "Now, recall from the beginning," I said quietly.

She breathed out a shaky breath, but I felt her nod. At first, all I saw was all encompassing black. Then, the black was ripped away, and I saw her. She was lying with her hands bound behind her back and the bag over her head. The creaky old carriage bumped along the road, but she never stirred. The image shifted to her hanging by her wrists in the dungeons. Rage rose in the back of my throat, and I growled. A man wearing elaborate purple robes stepped towards her - the High Priest.

They squabbled for a moment before she took in the room around her. Then, he slapped her, drawing her attention back to him. To my surprise, she let out a hoarse laugh. I kept my rage on a strict tether as I watched. The scene changed to her in a fine bedroom bathing. After she bathes, she's dried, dressed, and led to a vanity. She stiffened as she senses him entering the room, and then he runs a finger up her shoulder. I hear him command the guards, and she's dragged off the stool and onto the bed where they chain both her hands to the headboard.

My heart sped up in my chest as he pounced on the bed. I couldn't hear his words over the rush of blood in my ears as he lifted her skirts. She thrashed, trying her best to fight him as she threw herself back against the headboard and pulled against the shackles. He gripped her ankle, ignoring her cries, and I watched as she turned her face away as he placed his lips to the inside of her ankle.

I wanted to reach out and drag him off of her by his throat.

His hands moved up the outside of her thighs as his mouth moved higher. Something in me died at the sight of the first tear that streaked down her cheek, then the second, as she begged him to stop.

That's when he bit into her thigh.

She bucked forward, then back, as she let out a cry of pain, but he didn't relent. Then he moved his face level with hers and gripped her cheeks roughly before ripping open the front of her dress. Her eyes were wild with fear as she turned her face away again as he lowered his mouth to the delicate arch in her neck.

I wanted to pull away. I wanted to ask her to move on to a different memory, but I needed to see. I needed to see what he'd done to her, so I knew exactly how to make him pay. There would be nowhere the High Priest would be able to hide from me. He was a dead man walking, and his soul was hell bound.

My jaw clenched as he bit down on her breast and covered her mouth roughly as she screamed. Her scream pierced my ears, my heart, and then my soul. I'd never forget the sound. It would haunt my every waking moment. The things I would do to ensure she'd never experience that sort of pain again were unspeakable.

The scene changed. She was seated at a dining table and was trying to eat, but she was eating with her hands. My jaw clenched as he rose from his seat and began shoveling food into her mouth until she choked. She lurched forward as she coughed up the food, and then he dragged her out of the chair. He shoved her face to the floor as he commanded her to lick the food off of his boot. Her body trembled as she lowered herself.

Then, I saw her standing before his throne, and a single man was on his knees between two guards. He waved her forward, threatening her. Her feet moved up the steps as he brandished a dagger. He took her arm and slit her wrist open. I nearly choked in revulsion as he licked the wound, her blood. This was something only mates do, sacred to them and them alone. She didn't know that, but he was throwing it in her face. I growled as I watched the man take her blood and paled. His body fought her blood before his body fractured on itself. The High Priest had her dragged to his bedroom and chained to the floor. He knelt over her, and his rage was evident on his face as he stepped away from her.

Disbelief filled me as a shadowy finger melted from his back and materialized behind him. It stalked around her, and her terror filled eyes followed its movements until it pounced on her. Her shrill scream pierced right through me, causing my heart and breath to stutter.

"Alethea," I whispered as I opened my eyes at the feeling of her shaking body. "We can be done," I said as I pulled her against me.

My fingers cradled the back of her head as I guided her face into my chest, and she let out a sob. Her fingers curled into my shirt as she melded to me. Each cry was like a knife to the chest. I wanted to fix this. I needed to fix this, but I didn't know how. How does one mend someone's soul? There was no herb Medrina could give her to take this pain away. Even the High Priest's death couldn't do that.

"I'm so sorry," I whispered as I smoothed a hand down her hair while her body shook against mine. "My Alethea, words are not enough, but I love you. I love you more than anything in this life and the next." Her cries sounded louder as I spoke.

This had been a mistake. I couldn't make her live through these memories over and over again. There had to be a better way to find what we needed. I would find another way. Carrying her over to the bed, I pulled her into my lap as she molded herself to me. She clutched to my shirt as if it was a lifeline, and maybe it was to her. But I held her through every tear until her they finally dried, and her heavy breaths followed. I knew she hadn't slept well, and sleep had come back to claim her.

Tucking her beneath the blanket, I pressed a kiss to her forehead. I didn't want to leave her, but I needed to speak with Cadmus.

"Get me Lira," I said to one of the guards outside my door.

Minutes later, the door slowly opened, and the elderly maid slipped into my room.

"Watch over her," I merely commanded, and she bowed her head as I hurried past her into the hall.

My powers thrummed beneath my skin, begging to pounce on anything that walked towards her. My feet faltered as I debated turning back towards her. I needed to protect her, to watch over her, but I knew Lira wouldn't let anything happen to her either. The old woman was torn up when she was taken.

I blew out another breath as my feet halted at the sight of Mykill strolling through the halls. His hands were stuffed in his pockets, and his boots didn't make a noise off the tile as he paused with a knowing expression.

"It didn't go as well as you hoped." It wasn't a question.

"Shut up," I growled in response as I stalked past him.

"I would just like to know if you would have put her through that if your mating bond was still intact?"

His voice sent guilt spiraling through me as my steps faltered, but I didn't stop. I didn't answer him as I stormed down the halls. I shoved his question to the back of my mind, as far out of sight as I could make it, because I already knew the answer.

Cadmus was already waiting for me in my office as I threw the door open.

"How did it go?" Cadmus jumped to his feet as I slammed the door behind me

"We're done with the herbs," I growled as I stalked past Cadmus and dropped myself into my chair.

"Done?" he asked as he slowly lowered himself back into his seat. "Did you find what we needed?"

I shook my head.

"We need to keep searching," he argued as he leaned over my desk.

"Then we will find another way," I growled again.

"There isn't another way," he continued as he slammed his hand down.

"Then we will figure something else out!" I roared as I launched to my feet. My vision flashed red as I gripped the edge of my desk.

Cadmus fell back a step as his mouth dropped open. I had never spoken to him like that.

I breathed out a sigh, and let my head drop.

"I'm sorry, but I can't. I can't make her relive the things that he did to her over and over," I whispered as I sagged back into my chair. "I can't do that to her. I won't," I corrected as I raised my head and met his bewildered stare.

We held each other's gaze before his shoulders sagged, and he nodded. "I understand. I don't want her to have to go through that either." He sighed as he sat down across from me.

I reached for the amber liquid in the canister and poured us both a glass. He took the drink in his hands and downed it in one gulp. I took a deep drink and poured myself another.

"He really hurt her," Cadmus said, but it wasn't a question.

I knew he could tell how badly Alethea had been affected. I also knew he valued their friendship and had been just as torn up as I was when she had been taken. I merely nodded. I didn't have the words to describe the ways he had hurt her. I also didn't have words to describe all the ways I needed to make it up to her for failing her.

Chapter 11

Alethea

"Stay away from me!" I screamed as the shadow figure circled me.

It made a sound like clacking teeth before it lunged at me. I screamed as I covered my face with my arms, but I felt the tendrils of shadows shift around me. When I opened my eyes, the shadow figure was gone. The High Priest stood in his place with a sinister smile on his face.

"I would've thought you would have looked more rested." He crossed his hands behind his back as he began to stroll around me.

I gritted my teeth. I didn't know if this was some sort of bad dream or if he was communicating with me somehow, but I didn't want to give him anything.

"It's not a dream." He laughed as if he read my thoughts. "Your blood runs in my veins. Blood Bonds create a special connection between the people that shared the blood. My blood runs in your veins too."

Flashes of when he'd forced his blood down my throat danced across my mind, but I did my best to keep my face blank.

"War is coming," he warned. "We have buckets of your blood being administered to our men as we speak. Maybe you should ask your mate how strong a fae is in comparison to a mage."

"What do you want?" I tried to keep the tremble out of my voice, but I knew I failed miserably as he smiled even wider.

"I want all of you to burn," he growled in a menacing whisper.

Gasping, I startled awake. My chest heaved as I shoved myself up. Sweat slicked my brow and beaded down my spine. The only sound in the room was my quick breaths.

"Are you alright, girl?" Lira asked as she jumped from the armchair on the other side of the room.

"Yes," I said as I shoved myself off the bed. "Can you get me something simpler, please? Fighting clothes," I clarified.

"Fighting clothes?" She raised an eyebrow at me. "The King will not be pleased."

"I don't care," I answered as I began to undo the strings of my dress.

She didn't say anything else as she left the room. Surprisingly, she returned minutes later with a simple pair of tight leather pants with sheaths and pockets up and down each leg. The top she gave me was a snug black long sleeve corset top. She placed a pair of knee high boots on the ground beside my feet, and I slid them on.

"Thank you, Lira," I said as I bowed my head and threw the door open.

Anxiety pounded through me as I stalked through the halls. I knew if Eryx caught me, he'd stop me, so I slunk through the halls like a snake. I double checked around every corner until I finally made it to the War

Room. For some reason, I knew that Mykill would be in here.

"I want you to train me," I said as a way of greeting and propped my hands on my hips.

"And what does your mate have to say about that?" he asked as he hunched over the map on the table, not sparing me a glance.

"I'm my own person. He is not in control of me," I countered as I stepped up to the table. Mykill didn't even look at me. It was like I wasn't worth the time of day to him.

I huffed and blew out my chest. I was so tired of fae not giving me the time of day. I deserved their attention. My eyes darted to the dagger resting on the table beside my hand. Recklessly, I picked up the dagger and stabbed into the table between his pointer finger and thumb. "I said, I want you to train me."

My arm almost immediately throbbed from the impact, but I shoved it down. I couldn't show weakness now. The only sound in the room was the sound of our breaths as he stared at the knife between his fingers.

"I can't decide whether you're brave or stupid," he growled before he gripped the hilt and yanked it out of the wood.

His icy eyes clashed with mine, and it took every ounce of determination in me not to back down from him. I would not.

Mykill moved around the table and gripped my arm. I gasped as he spun me around and shoved me into the table. The cool blade touched the skin of my exposed throat as his hand snaked out and gripped my jaw.

"I recommend not doing that again, especially to someone less forgiving than me," he whispered as he tilted my face up.

His fingers bit into my skin, and I bared my teeth at him.

"Let go of me," I growled and shoved at his chest.

"Let's go." He dropped his hands and angled his head towards the door.

"Where are we going?"

Mykill didn't answer as he led me outside and through the gardens. We passed through them and into the fields beyond. He led me beneath the line of trees. The trees became more congested the further we went, but he still didn't answer me.

His brows furrowed as he looked around us, like he was searching for something.

"What are you looking for?" I whispered as I stepped closer to him.

"Shh." I rolled my eyes at him. "Over here."

I followed closely behind him, his ocean scent hitting me again, but I shoved it down. I grunted as I slammed into his back as he halted.

"There." He pointed to the clearing before us.

There was a sunset orange flower at least double Mykill's size, but the edges of each petal were adorned with rows of razor-like teeth. It opened and closed, almost like a mouth preparing to devour whatever touched the petals.

"What the hell is that?" I demanded as I stepped away from the vine unfurling from the plant. "Some sort of plant monster?"

"It's called a Vine Viper. They're scattered throughout the fae kingdoms and can be deadly if you come across one," Mykill said as he leaned against the tree. "Now fight it."

The vine was long, thick, and a deep green. At the end was a maroon bulb almost identical to a stuffed glove.

"What?" I gasped as I took a step back. "What do I do?"

"Let your gut tell you what to do," he said and held out his hand.

A fighting stick appeared in his hand, and he tossed it towards me. As it fell into my hands, an invisible force shoved me forward, leaving me in perfect striking range of the Vine Viper.

I planted my feet shoulder width apart like Cadmus had taught me and raised the stick up, but the viper moved quicker than my eyes could track. I cried out as the bulb knocked into my stomach. I flew backwards, and the vine followed. I tried to slash at it, but it dodged my every move. It got close enough to my face that the bulb opened like a flower, and a powdery substance was released.

I unwillingly inhaled and immediately choked on it. Instantly, a numbing sensation spread over my entire body, and I collapsed backwards. My eyes widened as the vine raised much like a snake ready to strike. As it reared its head back, an invisible wind threw it back. It let out a heinous hiss and screeched as a bolt of lightning slammed into it. If I could move my mouth, it would have fallen open. I had never seen Mykill's powers before.

Mykill sighed, and I heard the crunching of his boots. "Well, you lasted longer than I thought you would've. It'll wear off." He stooped down, and without warning, tossed me over his shoulder.

I couldn't talk or move. My arms hung down, slapping at his back as he strode through the forest.

Mykill laughed, and the sound vibrated through my body. "Vine Vipers are vicious. After they paralyze you, they will coil around you, drag you towards them, and eat you."

I managed to move my fingers, but I still couldn't respond to him. He didn't speak again as he continued through the trees. I had no idea how he found his way back to the castle.

"Put me down," I finally managed to croak as I fisted my hand.

"You won't be able to walk."

"I said, put me down," I grumbled again and shoved against his lower back to raise myself up.

"Fine," he quipped.

He released the hold around my thighs, and I crumbled to the ground like a sack. All my breath left me as my back hit the ground. Leaves stirred up around me as I cried out. Pain shot up my spine as the feeling slowly resumed to my body. The trees above me whirled and then stilled.

"You're an ass," I muttered as I pushed myself up onto my elbows.

Mykill shrugged as he leaned against the trunk of a tree and crossed his arms. "You requested that I put you down. Try standing."

Resisting the urge to kick him, I shoved myself up. My joints felt like I had never used them as I sat up fully.

"The poison will be out of your system entirely in a few minutes. It'll feel like you've never walked before, but it'll go away quickly." He strode towards me and outstretched a hand to me.

With more difficulty that I wanted to admit, I managed to get to my feet and yelped as my knees buckled. Mykill laughed as he caught me with an arm around the waist. He lifted me up and helped steady me. Once he was sure I wouldn't crumble, he released me.

"That was your idea of training?" I gasped. "Take a human who's never fought in their life to face some sort of plant monster? Wow, what a great trainer you are." I rolled my eyes as I turned away from him and walked back towards the castle.

"Wait." There was no room for negotiation in his voice. My feet instantly froze, and I turned towards him against my will. "Come here." My feet moved on their own accord.

"What?" I snapped as I propped a hand on my hip.

"Stand with your feet apart."

Doing what he said, I planted my feet apart.

"Stand with your feet *apart*," he corrected and waved his hand.

My eyes widened as my foot moved until they were shoulder width apart. "How did you do that?"

"Now, come at me." He didn't answer my previous question as he stood straighter.

I raised an eyebrow at him. "Come at you? Like, just charge?"

He rolled his eyes. "Exactly." He squared his shoulders and waved for me to come forward.

Taking a deep breath, I willed strength into my muscles and launched at him. I expected him to maybe block me with an arm or shove me back. I didn't expect him to lower his shoulder into my stomach and flip me over his shoulder. I let out all my breath as pain shot up my spine.

"Get up." He nudged my foot, and I could practically hear him rolling his eyes.

"Hold on," I groaned as I held up a hand. "I think you broke all my bones.

Mykill groaned as he stooped down. "You're fine," he said as he gripped my hands and yanked me to my feet. "I didn't throw you hard enough to break anything."

"What was the point of that? To embarrass me?" I snapped as I gripped my side.

He laughed darkly. "Maybe partly. You have no strength. I would suggest starting with strength training at least once a day."

Strength training? My favorite.

"Well, this has been utterly useless. Thank you for nothing." I turned from him and started back towards the palace.

"If you start strength training, then I'll train you. But you still need to strength train outside of training."

Stopping in my tracks, I turned back towards him. His face was clear, revealing nothing of what he thought as he stared back at me. He was like a blank canvas.

"Okay. Thank you," I said softly.

Mykill strolled up beside me. "I believe it's time for lunch."

My entire body stiffened, and my cheeks heated as my stomach roared in response. He laughed but didn't say anything as he stepped aside, allowing me to head inside first. I was aware of his body behind mine as I stalked towards the dining room. I expected to see Eryx, but he never showed. Cadmus was already seated.

"Where's Eryx?" I frowned as I took my seat.

"He was working on some things in his office," Cadmus answered.

His gaze bounced between Mykill and I, and his spoon paused midair.

"What were the two of you doing? Why are you dressed like that?" Cadmus raised a brow at me as he set his spoon down and leaned back in his chair. "Please tell me you weren't -"

"I was training," I cut him off as I picked up my spoon and draped my napkin across my lap.

"The King has requested you all meet him in the War Room," the guard's deep, timbery voice spoke, interrupting our banter.

My stomach growled in response. Mykill and Cadmus both shoved out of their seats. Glancing once at my soup, I shoveled three quick bites into my mouth before following after them. I glared and fisted my hands as I stomped after them. Oh, Eryx was so going to hear it from me for cutting into my lunch time.

Mykill pushed open the door and stepped back, allowing Cadmus and I to pass through before he closed the door behind him.

"I need to sit down," I groaned as I made my way over to the table.

"What happened to you?" Eryx demanded.

"Training," I said as I placed a hand on my ribcage and groaned at the ache already working its way through my muscles.

"Training?" he repeated, and his voice dripped with disdain. "I already told you it's too dangerous."

"I was in no danger. I was with Mykill," I countered as I slid down on the stool.

"You're hurt." Eryx dropped to his knees before me and gripped my face. "Tell me where you're hurt."

"She's not hurt; she's just sore," Mykill quipped as he leaned against the doorframe. "She got thrown on her ass by a Vine Viper."

"A Vine Viper?" Eryx's voice rose an octave as he glanced back over to Mykill. "What were you thinking?" He glanced back at me.

"She'll be fine in the morning," Mykill said.

"You will not do that again," Eryx commanded as he rose.

"And you do not command me," Mykill growled as he pushed off the door frame.

Eryx's hands fisted as he stepped up to Mykill. Mykill was over a whole head taller than Eryx. His wings opened behind him almost like a threat, a warning, to show who was more powerful.

"You are in my kingdom." Eryx's voice was a menacing growl.

"I could just as easily leave you and your people defenseless if you're attacked," Mykill quipped. He didn't growl. His voice dripped with dominance and authority. If they fought, I knew who'd win.

Eryx glared up at Mykill before he finally blew out a breath. He stepped away and turned back towards me. "You will not do that again." Instead of commanding Mykill, he was commanding me.

"But -"

"No!" He cut me off. "I've already said no. Now, down to why I've called you in here."

I fisted my hands in my lap and glared. I tuned him out. I didn't care why he called us in here. He had never cared to keep me in the loop of things, and I didn't see a point in keeping me in the loop of things if he wasn't going to let me learn how to defend myself. I had always been weak. I couldn't fight off the guards as they dragged me to Kirin's castle when they plucked me from the village. I wasn't able to fight them off when they dragged me through the halls.

Without saying another word, I jumped to my feet and stormed from the room. I slammed the door but didn't regret it. I hope the sound of it slamming made him realize how overbearing he was. I knew it came from a good place, but it didn't excuse the behavior. He wasn't in control of me. He couldn't just tell me not to do something. He didn't realize that he was controlling my life in almost the same way the High Priest had.

Chapter 12

Eryx

I stretched out across my throne, staring at the ground. The room was silent except for the sound of my breathing. I had cleared everyone out. I needed time to myself, time to think.

She didn't understand that I was only trying to protect her. She was human - she didn't have the strength to fight off a full grown fae. She also didn't have anything to prove. I needed to care for her after I had failed her so miserably. The pain the High Priest inflicted upon her was no one's fault but my own. Even if she had accepted responsibility when she had trusted my sister, I should've been able to protect her.

Groaning, I reached into my pocket and pulled out the large ruby the size of my fist. Medrina's voice echoed in my skull.

"How do I restore our mating bond?" I demanded.

Medrina seated herself at the wooden bench and let out a deep sigh. "There's nothing you can do, my King. I'm sorry, but the bond is gone. It's something that's woven by the Fates. It can't be made, and it can't be remade."

"Can I call upon the Fates?"

She laughed darkly. "You can, but they're not too privy to being called upon like dogs. You need to offer them something. They're rather fond of jewels. They'll be able to sense your longing, and if they think your gift is worthy, then they will reveal themselves. But don't get your hopes too high. They rarely reveal themselves."

I frowned. "Why?"

She laughed again. "They're self-conscious."

"Why?" I asked again like a whiny child.

"If you meet them, then you'll see why."

I glared at the ruby that glimmered beneath the sunlight leaking in through the glass ceiling. Medrina said they would sense that I was calling upon them. So, I sat and waited. Minutes passed, and the sound of a hawk screech sounded above me. Another minute passed, and I sighed.

I felt the shift in the air around me before they showed themselves.

"Why have we been summoned?" a chorus of voices boomed as mist exploded before me.

A being draped in a tattered black robe with shadows leaking around them appeared from the mist. It was at least triple my height, nearly the size of a giant as it stopped several feet from my throne.

"I summoned the three fates," I argued.

"We are the fates, King," the being said as they reached up with their taloned fingers and lowered their hood. As it dropped back, it revealed a face with ghoulish gray sagging skin. Its lips were a faint blue that covered a mouthful of rotting teeth.

My mouth dropped open.

"They're self-conscious." Medrina's voice echoed in my mind as I stared at the single empty eye socket in the center of their forehead.

"Now, tell us, King. Why have you summoned us?" the voices demanded as the ruby floated from my hand.

They snatched it out of the air. Even without an eye, they had perfect accuracy. Their taloned fingers wrapped around the ruby and pet it, almost as if it were a dog.

"Let me be mated to her again," I stammered.

"It cannot be done," their voices echoed, all blending together.

"Just redo it!" I bellowed.

"You lost your chance. The prophecy could have been you, but you failed her." Their voices didn't hold a hint of sympathy or emotion.

My head dropped in defeat. I knew I failed her. The thought had crossed my mind every day since she'd been taken from me.

"And what does the prophecy say fully?"

They ticked their tongue. "It hasn't been fully revealed yet."

"But you know it?"

"Of course," their voices chided at once. "All prophecies are products of us."

"So, you created it, but you don't know what it says?" I growled. My patience was wearing thin.

"If you don't like the answers to your own questions, then don't ask them."

"What can I do? There must be something I can do to fix this," I begged.

"There is nothing that can be done. Her heart even now grows less fond of you. You must win her affections if you wish to be with her, and even now, you're not sure if it was just the mating bond drawing you two together."

My hand fisted as I dropped it onto the arm of my throne. "You're released." I waved my hand, dismissing them.

"We are not your subjects, King," their voices snapped before their form erupted in shards of light and shadow. I winced as I turned my face away from the explosion of fragments.

There was no way to restore our bond. Part of me had known that was the answer, and part of me knew I was losing her affection. I was trying. I just wanted to protect her. I couldn't lose her again. But the more sure of herself she became, the further she moved away from me.

Growling, I rose from my throne and stormed out the doors. They pounded open and bounced off the walls from the heat of my anger. I stalked down the hall towards my room, but my feet froze as I heard soft steps behind me. Turning at the waist, Alethea stopped dead in her tracks as she saw me. Her breaths were light as she stared at me. She didn't speak; her entire body was frozen. I moved towards her. I needed to touch her, to feel her.

"Eryx," she whispered as I stepped before her.

She yelped sharply against my lips as I grabbed a hold of her face and pushed her up against the wall. Her fingers wrapped around my wrists as I melded my lips to hers. She was utterly still beneath me for a few moments before she molded her front to mine. Moving quickly, I lifted her up against me, and we moved towards my room. My feet moved swiftly up the stairs as she secured her arms around my neck. I managed to get us into my bedroom and slam the door behind us as I took her to the bed.

I laid her down and pulled the leathers down her legs. They hung to every curve of her body, nearly making my mouth water as I peeled off the shirt, and she worked on getting my shirt off. Our breaths were quick as we shed off each other's clothing before coming back together. Our breaths mingled as I wrapped an arm around her waist and pulled her to my chest. I moved us back on the bed, laying her down and adoring every part of her body. I worshiped her body like she was my own personal deity. There wasn't an inch of her flesh my tongue or lips didn't claim. She intoxicated me. Every breath and every moan clawed deeper into my soul, etching herself there, so that no matter what happened, I could never forget her, never let her go. I wanted her today, tomorrow, and forever. I would level mountains for her. I would destroy and claim souls for her and lay them at her feet as an offering for being unworthy as I skimmed my hands up on both sides of her. Her skin felt like the finest silk beneath my hands. Her soft moans were a symphony that my heart beat in harmony to, and when she whispered my name, it felt like I shattered into a million pieces.

***

I ran my fingers in slow, deft circles across her back and watched as she breathed. Her breaths had evened out some time ago, signaling that she was asleep. Her hair had fallen out of its braid crown in loose waves that sprawled out across her back and the bed. I twirled one around my finger, and she breathed a deep sigh before shifting slightly. Leaning over her, I placed a kiss to the side of her head before I managed to finally shove myself off the bed. I slipped my tunic and trousers back on. The sun had set some time ago, and we both had skipped dinner - we had been occupied. I didn't have it in me to wake her; she barely slept as it was. Whether she told me or not, I knew she was plagued by nightmares of what the High Priest had done to her. I knew it would take time for them to fade away and heal, but I would do anything to take them.

After I finished buttoning my tunic, I couldn't help but head back over to the bed and drop a kiss to her forehead. She didn't stir as I pulled away and headed towards the door. As I closed the door behind me, I whistled for two guards and stationed them outside my door.

"She shouldn't wake, but if she does, take her to the dining room and have the cook prepare something for her. Then come find me." They both nodded and took up their post on either side of the door.

After we rescued her, I had informed every one of my men that if anything happened to her under their watch, then they would forfeit their lives. She would think it's too harsh, which is why I didn't tell her.

I stepped silently as I made my way into one of the sitting rooms beside the War Room. Cadmus noticed me as he passed.

"I have something for you," he said as he entered the room.

He outstretched his hand towards me, and I took the envelope.

"What is this?" I gasped as I turned the letter over in my hand. The letter was sealed with a black wax seal with Vestor's insignia.

"It looks like a summons," Cadmus answered as he dropped into the seat across from me.

Ripping off the seal, I opened the letter. Sure enough, he was right. Summons didn't have an explanation; they merely stated that my presence was requested, and then the King signs beneath it.

Mykill's kingdom, Vestor's kingdom, and my kingdom were three out of sixteen kingdoms that had reached an agreement after the Great War. We had made the Treaty, which had a set of standards we all had to uphold as part of the Inner Kingdom, or we would no longer be under the protection of the other fifteen kingdoms. There were ten rules and no ruler was exempt from these laws, which meant that I would have to travel to see Vestor.

"Does the invitation extend to Mykill?" Cadmus asked.

I shook my head and scrubbed a hand down my face. "No," I groaned, though part of me was thankful. "I'll bring you with me."

"And leave Alethea here?"

I nodded.

"She's safe here. I don't know why Vestor summoned me, but I won't put her in danger. I'll double the amount of guards watching over her."

"She won't like that," Cadmus laughed. "The last time you assigned guards to watch over her, she began stripping in front of them to get them to leave."

My hand froze midair as I pictured my mate, sweeter than a cherry, stripping in front of my guards in an attempt to get them to leave her alone. I wanted to say it surprised me, but it didn't. She wasn't as meek as she seemed. My head fell back as I laughed.

"Did it work?"

Cadmus barked out a laugh as he draped his arms on the sides of the chair. "I found them both out in the halls with beet red faces. They thought they were going to lose their lives because they saw her bare shoulder."

I laughed again, needing the release.

Chapter 13

Alethea

"Blossom?" Eryx whispered, stirring me from my restful sleep.

He brushed the hair away from my face and tucked it behind my ear. I groaned as I rolled onto my back. The sound of his laugh stirred me, and I peeked an eye open. "Where are you going?" I asked as I fully sat up in surprise as I noticed the sheaths around his body.

"I have to visit another kingdom. We received a letter, and I've been summoned. Cadmus will come with me." His brows drew down as he pushed my unruly hair over my shoulder. "How did you sleep?"

"Just fine." I frowned as he pulled away and finished getting ready.

He was already dressed. His tunic was unbuttoned and flowed freely, but he had his sheaths at his back already.

"How long will you be gone?" I asked as I slid out of bed and trailed behind him.

He picked up his sword off the small resting table in the center of his room and slid it into the sheath on his back.

"I'll be back by tomorrow evening." I handed him the dagger off the table, and he plucked it from my hands and slid it into its sheath on his thigh.

"Are you sure you have to go? It could be dangerous." Worry filled me at the thought of only him and Cadmus on their own. There was still so much unknown.

"I need to. As part of the Inner Kingdom, it's my responsibility to check in on those surrounding us." I nodded, though I still wasn't sure how any of the courts and kingdoms worked.

"Why can't I come with you?" I grumbled as he turned to me and began buttoning up the remainder of the buttons of his tunic.

I pushed his fingers aside and began unbuttoning them.

He laughed. "Blossom." He tried to shove my hands away, but I slipped my hands beneath the material and along his bare sides. "Blossom," he groaned as his eyes closed.

"Please just stay with me for a little while longer," I pleaded as I pushed up onto my toes and kissed him.

He groaned against my lips and said the same words he had said when he had rescued me. "I can deny you nothing." He shoved his shirt and sheaths off within moments, and I squealed as he gripped my thighs and hoisted me up.

His lips claimed mine aggressively, and I heard him shove aside all the daggers. I heard them clatter to the floor, but I was too occupied to notice as he deposited me on the edge of the table.

His hands grasped my face, and then I felt the light wisp along my skin. I jumped at the contact and yanked my mouth away. "What was that?"

He only smirked in response as I noticed the tendrils of shadows leaching out from around him. I held up my hand to the one nearest to me and gasped as it twisted around my wrist. I had only seen his shadows once, right after Cador had died.

"Do you trust me, Blossom?" His voice had dropped, and another tendril stroked lovingly down my cheek as his hands fell to my thighs. His palms slid up them, pushing the folds of my dress up.

Eryx's lips found mine again as I nodded, and he nudged me down until I was flat on the table. My chest rose quickly as he dropped to his knees and spread my legs, baring me before him. The tendrils moved around me, stroking my body, the feeling new but thrilling. My back arched, and my entire body heaved in anticipation. First, Eryx ran his hands up the outsides of my thighs, then the insides. Then, he placed a kiss to the inside of my knee and slowly moved his way up. He paused above my scar, like he did every time, and placed another kiss on it. But this kiss was different from the rest. It wasn't heavy or seductive. It was an apology and a promise in one.

No matter what I said, he would never take the blame of what happened to me off his shoulders, but he was also promising to never let me experience that pain again. I knew he would go to the ends of the world to keep that promise.

His lips trailed up my body, licking and sucking in perfect tandem. My heart hammered in anticipation as his hands traced across my hips while he settled above me. My legs wrapped around his waist, pulling him to me as I gripped his face and kissed him. He moaned and stroked the tip of his tongue along the roof of my mouth. My entire body shivered in response as he gripped my hips, and there was not a space between our bodies.

We melded together, our bodies working in perfect harmony. His hands found mine, and our fingers interlaced. Our breaths mingled together in a single synchronized beat. Love poured out of his gaze, filling every crack and crevice of my shattered being. Every kiss was a promise of forever. We were free from our burdens, the Summons, the High Priest - we were free from it all, unencumbered by the weight of reality.

We fell over the edge together, leaving our bodies spent. My body sagged against the table as I waited for my breathing to even back out. His breath and heartbeat pounded in my ear as he slowly pushed himself up. A smile tugged at his lips, showing his teeth, and his eyes wrinkled in the corners.

"A good morning indeed," he whispered breathlessly as he leaned back down and kissed me.

I could feel the swell of both of our lips, and I squealed as he gripped my hands and yanked me to my feet.

"Go get ready," he laughed as he pressed another hurried kiss to my lips.

Smiling, I picked up my discarded dress and wrapped it hastily around me as I scurried into the washroom. I leaned over the tub, drawing the water and put the tub stopper in before I dropped the dress and slipped beneath the water. I sighed as my shoulders slightly relaxed. Mykill was right. I could feel the soreness in nearly my entire body. The warm water caressed my tired muscles but didn't fully relieve the tension.

I dropped my head back against the lip of the tub and closed my eyes.

"Blossom," Eryx called a moment before he stepped into the washroom. "I'm going to meet with Cadmus in my office. Go down and eat breakfast, and then come to my office once you're finished."

"Okay." I offered him a smile.

He smiled at me before ducking out of the washroom. I heard the sound of the door closing behind him, and as it did, I felt myself breathing easier. It was sometimes easier when he wasn't around. I could let myself feel the sadness that constantly felt like it was leaching out of my heart and overtaking my entire life. Grief was a fickle thing. One minute it wasn't there, and then the next it felt like it was consuming me, drowning me. If someone cut me open, I was convinced that the grief turning my insides dull was all they'd see. That's how the world around me seemed - duller and duller.

If I wasn't consumed with thoughts of my family every waking moment, then I was plagued by the High Priest. He lingered in every dream. I could hear his laugh, see his face, feel his tongue. I could see and feel it all so clearly. Sometimes it made me want to gag until my tongue came out.

Sighing, I splashed the water around lightly and watched the water ripple after the drops hit the surface, another perfect example of my grief. The droplet may have landed in one place, but the ripple extended far beyond the point of contact. It grew, crashing and colliding with the other ripples from the other droplets. My grief would leak out of me until it consumed everything around me, and part of me felt like I wanted that. I didn't want to be reminded of all the good things. Sometimes I wanted to not see my mother whenever I saw a blooming rose or tulip. I didn't want to hear my sister's laugh with the swaying of the trees or think of my father whenever I saw a biscuit and I was reminded of his nickname for me.

This life had been so unfair to them, downright cruel. From what my father had told me, they had willingly taken me in, knowing they were putting themselves in danger. If it was possible, it made me love them even more. They had chosen me, and they had loved me no differently than they had loved Laney.

The water had gone cold.

Sighing to myself, I pushed myself up and pulled the tub stopper up. The water gurgled as it fought its way down the drain, and I stood, wrapping myself in my towel. I hadn't washed my hair this time and braided it around my skull in a braid crown, but it was nothing as elaborate or clean as Lira's braids. That woman had weaver's fingers and could practically do any braid possible.

I patted my body dry and padded over to the wardrobe to grab a dress. My scarred wrist caught my attention as I gripped the handle, and I inhaled a breath. The sight of the shackle marks around my wrists caught me off guard whenever I saw them - just another reminder of the High Priest. I could hear his laugh in the back of my mind as I grabbed a dress and slammed the wardrobe closed. The door bounced back open, and I merely stared at it before marching back into the bathroom.

I slipped the dress on and made sure the sleeves covered my wrists.

***

My feet faltered as I entered the dining room and noticed a very large set of wings tucked against a hard, straight back. He was sitting next to the seat I always occupied. But without anyone else here, it felt strange to sit right beside him. So I turned and walked around the other side of the table. I ignored his face as it snapped towards me and followed as I stopped directly across from him.

"I don't bite," he spoke up.

I pulled the chair out and sat down. "I know you don't, but you're trying to get under Eryx's skin, and he doesn't need the added stress."

I didn't know where my boldness came from when I was around him, but he gave me the overwhelming urge to slap him across the back of his head all the time, even when he just looked at me. I felt almost in a permanent state of annoyance. Maybe it was the steely exterior or the piercing white eyes that seemed like they could see every hidden secret.

"Are you saying that you're his stressor?" His lips pulled into a small semblance of a smile.

"No," I snapped as I started filling my plate with the array of fruits. "I'm saying you are. He doesn't like you, and I don't know why."

"He doesn't even know why he doesn't like me." I rolled my eyes as he leaned forward, bracing his arms on the table. "I think he's jealous of me."

"Jealous of you?" I raised an eyebrow as I grabbed a biscuit and the knife that was perched on the edge of the jam. "What is there to be jealous of?"

His wings unfolded themselves behind him and stretched out on either side of him.

"I think most women are attracted to this," he teased as he folded and unfolded his wings effortlessly.

I snorted as I dragged the jam-ladened knife across my biscuit. "I think you look like an oversized chicken, and the cook should pluck you and serve you for lunch."

His brows shot into his hairline in shock. Then, his lips stretched out in a massive smile, revealing two perfect dimples in his cheeks and his straight white teeth.

"You have dimples!" I pointed out like a schoolgirl as I cocked my head to the side.

The smile disappeared entirely. He focused his attention on his plate, and my chest heated. He cut into the large chunk of the pale orange fruit before lifting it to his mouth. Every evidence of amusement was gone, and that cold, icy exterior was set in place.

"I didn't mean -"

"We can train in the morning," Mykill said but didn't glance up from his plate as he cut me off.

"Train?" I asked.

"Yes," he said as he placed down his utensils. "We can train in the morning." He shoved his chair out and didn't say a word to me as he exited the dining hall.

I stared at the open doors in mortification. Had I embarrassed him? Angered him? I chided myself as I turned back to my plate and dug into my food. Without anyone here and no distractions, I scarfed down my food. I had slowly managed to keep more and more down without feeling sick. Before, I would feel sick after a single bite of eggs and a biscuit, but now I could keep down much more.

I shoved my chair out as I finished and hurried towards Eryx's office. I rapped softly on the door before turning the handle. The door creaked slightly as I pushed it open and poked my head inside.

"Blossom," Eryx smiled as I opened the door.

"Cadmus." I smiled at him as I passed by.

Eryx stretched out a hand for me, and I placed my hand in his. I squealed as he yanked me into his lap. I heard the door shut promptly, and I smiled.

"I think we made Cadmus uncomfortable," I whispered as I adjusted myself in his lap.

"Nonsense," he said as he tucked a free strand of hair behind my ear. "I told him to leave when you got here."

"Why?" I frowned as I pulled back slightly.

"Because I'm not going to see you." He traced a finger across my collarbone, which made me shiver.

"Oh," I nodded and then frowned again. "I have a question."

"What is it, Blossom?" He twirled the strand that had broken free around his finger.

"Why do you hate Mykill so much?" I couldn't bring myself to look him in the eyes, so I focused on the top button of his tunic and began to fiddle with it.

He sighed deeply, and the expelled breath tickled the sides of my face. "He is what's considered High Fae. All fae with wings are. They're more powerful. They are rumored to be descendants of the Gods, the Divine. So, he already had a piss poor attitude, and his people are not very social with other kingdoms in the Inner Kingdom."

I made a mental note to ask what that was later.

"But, a few hundred years ago, he had been betrothed to my sister." My mouth dropped open at the declaration. Eryx laughed dryly. "And at the time, the purity of each party was significant. If it was found out that either of them were unfaithful, then the engagement would be nullified." He sighed again, and I paused, preparing myself for his next words. "It was found out that he was unfaithful with one of his soldiers - the girl he brought with him."

I didn't know why the news hit me so hard, but I felt myself physically recoiling as I shoved away from Eryx.

"He cheated on Freya?" I gasped as I pushed to my feet. "Why did you even ask him here?"

"Because he's very powerful. One of the most powerful of our kind."

I nodded and felt myself begin to wear a hole in the floor. I had noticed the woman behind him when we had argued the morning of me being trained.

"It doesn't matter anymore," Eryx sighed, drawing my attention back to him.

His brows were drawn down, and his cider eyes were enchanting as I draped myself over his lap again.

Chapter 14

Eryx

"I'll miss you," Alethea whispered as I placed a hand on her cheek.

"I'll miss you too, Blossom. I won't be gone long, I promise."

"Are you sure you don't need to bring more protection?" I smiled as her forehead creased in worry.

I rubbed my thumb between her brows in an attempt to wipe the frown from her face. "We'll be alright, Alethea. Please quit worrying." I leaned in to place a kiss on her forehead, and her arms circled around me. Sighing, I wrapped my arms around her and dropped my cheek to rest on her head. "I love you, and we'll be back soon."

"I love you too." Her voice was soft as she pulled away and offered me a small smile.

I wanted to tell her to keep away from Mykill. I felt a little uneasy leaving him here alone with her. But no matter how much I despised him, he had no reason to hurt her, and I doubted he would. Plus, attacking a King's mate is strictly forbidden and punishable by death.

Pulling away entirely, I glanced back at her once more before mounting Adruis and motioned for him to fly. With a shake of his long neck, he took off into the sky, and Cadmus followed.

I couldn't think of her as I flew, or Cadmus would sense it. I couldn't think of how she looked this morning, arched off the table with her heavy breathing, bare and ready for me. The thought alone was nearly enough to make me turn around and damn this whole trip.

But I couldn't deny a summons. It wasn't the same as an invitation. A summons meant there was something more serious going on, and as a King, I was obligated to go. It had been a couple hundred years since I had received the previous one. They were reserved for more serious matters, and they couldn't be denied, which is why they were so scarcely used.

Thankfully, the trip was quick with the speed of our dragons. We were still the only kingdom that dared tame the dragons. The Inner Kingdom had thought us crazy two hundred years ago when we had proposed the idea. They said that we would be burned to husks if we tried to engage with the beasts, but the dragons had been run out nearly everywhere. They were pushed to the mountains, never engaging with people, and when they went in search of food, they were met with violence.

Now we kept food stocked for them and gave them homes.

The wind ripped my bun out at one point, and my hair flew around my head. Vestor's sleek, black palace below us looked much smaller than my own and others in our kingdom. He was a much more humble King, not daring or adventurous. He stuck to what he knew and loved and cared for his people.

There were truly no fae cities with starving fae, but Vestor's people were thriving. Health and joy radiated from every being before us who dropped their heads back to gaze up at us as we descended. They didn't have the space for our dragons, so we were forced to land them in an outlying field and leave them, but they'd be alright.

Vestor's men were waiting for us besides a carriage that took us to the castle. People gathered as we passed, and I waved to those who waved, but otherwise, I remained impassive. My leg bounced in anticipation. I wanted to get back to Alethea.

My eyes stuck on a woman with identical hair to hers holding a young babe with doe eyes and curly blonde hair. I couldn't think of anything better than Alethea baring my children one day - our children. She said she had never given much thought to wanting to have children, but part of me wished after everything settled to have at least one child. I didn't care for an heir. I just wanted to experience that part of life with her. I couldn't imagine a more beautiful soul as a mother. With her soft smile and gentle nature, she'd make a perfect mother. I'd be sure to tell her that when I saw her again.

"The King waits for you," a guard said as he opened the carriage door, and Cadmus and I ducked as we slid out.

The land here was green but more trimmed and refined, cleaner than ours back home. We preferred to let nature take on its own shape, but here they took a hold of it and molded it to their image. The grass was short and even; not a stray bud could be seen as we walked down the cobblestone path leading to the large double doors. They opened as we approached and revealed a massive great hall.

The walls were adorned with paintings of Vestor and his family. The walls were a soft golden, not overwhelming in the grandness. There were two doors on either side of the back wall that led into more grander hallways. The guards led us to the one on the right, and I took the familiar path to his throne room.

His throne was perched on a golden dais with the ornate carvings of roses along each step. His crown was made of cold rubies that sat nestled on his head.

"Vestor." I bowed my head as we approached his throne. As customary, they had a seat prepared for me beside his dais. It was to signal that even though we were not of equal power in his territory, I was still a King in my right.

"Eryx." He bowed his head towards me as a sign of respect. His golden crown glimmered in the flickering faery lights.

"Hello, dear friend," I greeted. "It certainly hasn't been long," I pointed out. The last time I had seen him was at the ball where I had introduced him to Alethea.

"No," he chuckled. "I heard of the restoration of your mate. I hope she's in good health."

"She's recovering," I said as I took my seat beside the dais.

"I'm assuming your flight here was uneventful?"

"If you count a stray bird flying straight into my face uneventful, then yes," Cadmus answered, and I laughed as I recalled his face as he tried ducking and the bird shrieking as they collided.

Vestor dropped his head back and laughed. "Uneventful indeed." "Should we get on with business, or would you like to chat about the weather? I have a mate I'd like to get back to," I bowed my head, signaling my respect.

"Let's go to my office." He pushed himself up and descended the dais.

I followed behind him with Cadmus at my heels as he trailed through the halls. I could see the tension that rested upon his shoulders and the tired lines beneath his eyes. He carried the worry of the entire kingdom on himself, refusing to let others feel it.

He pushed open a set of double doors that opened into an oversized office. There was a stuffed armchair resting behind the desk covered in books and parchments. Each side of the room was lined with rows of bookcases filled with books. Mine was also filled with books, but his far outnumbered mine; his office was its own library.

"We've received this." He waved to a rolled parchment at the edge of his desk as he plopped down ungracefully.

"What is it?" Cadmus asked as he folded his arms in front of him.

"Just open it." Vastor sighed as he picked up one of the glasses and filled it with wine.

Eyeing him warily, I reached for the parchment. It felt brittle between my fingers, like it was old, but it wasn't discolored in the slightest. As I unrolled it, my eyes scanned the elaborate text in search of a signature. My eyes widened to the point of nearly falling out as I stared at the seal at the bottom.

"This is from the Old Kingdom," I gasped.

Vastor grunted in response.

"But the Old Kingdom doesn't exist anymore."

The Old Kingdom had been a dynasty, the largest kingdom to ever be. It was far larger than all of the territories, even now. The Kingdom was ruled by High Fae with powers that far exceeded any ordinary fae's greatest imagination.

"They're asking about an artifact that has been long thought lost," Vestor spoke, drawing my attention to him.

I frowned. "What artifact?"

"They're searching for the mirror of truth," he answered.

"Why?"

"Just read the damn letter." He waved his glass at me, the wine almost sloshing over the side.

They wanted the mirror of truth because they claimed the Dark Mage wasn't dead and wanted to prove it. The Dark Mage was the one responsible for creating the Barren and would continue to do so until they obliterated the fae in their quest for power. The mages wanted the fae dead.

"How did the Dark Mage survive? I thought he was killed," I asked as I took a seat across from Vestor.

"I don't know," he shrugged.

"Do you know anything?" I snapped.

"The mirror is rumored to be across the ocean beneath a volcano."

"Across the ocean? As in Gild's kingdom?"

Gild was probably one of the oldest and most powerful fae alive. He had been alive long before the Mage War. No one knew how he had survived as long as he had, but he was greatly feared and respected. He wasn't High fae, but he was one of the most powerful fae, gifted in casting his powers.

He wasn't a part of the Inner Kingdom either. He decided to branch out on his own and build his domain over the ocean. There had been rumors of people residing there in constant battle, and he wanted to bring them peace.

"So you're wanting us to go on this mission?" I asked as I dropped the parchment back on his desk.

He nodded and placed his glass down. "Yes. We don't have the strength to pull off something of this caliber. I've already sent a letter to Gild requesting for you and your court to venture out there." I glowered at him. "I thought it may also be useful to your mate."

"My mate?" I raised an eyebrow.

"Yes. You can find out if your bond can be restored."

"It can't."

"As far as you know," he quipped. "We've never experienced a mating bond intentionally being broken and living through it. The situation is peculiar, and you know it. You and I both know that you'll do it."

I sighed and sat back in the overstuffed armchair. He was right and knew he was right. But, it could put Alethea in a lot of danger.

"We can't take our dragons. That would appear too much of a threat." Cadmus spoke from behind me, and I nodded along.

"Yes, we can supply you with a ship and a Captain."

"I would think," I snapped as I leaned forward. "You're the one sending us on this mission."

"Quit your whining," he groaned as he pushed himself up out of his seat. "Come, lunch is being prepared for us."

Cadmus and I followed behind him but kept several paces away. I could see the questions eating at Cadmus by the hard set of his jaw.

"Do you think he could tell us how Alethea's blood changed the men into mages?" Cadmus asked as we made our way towards the dining hall.

I merely shook my head. It seemed there was much to discuss.

Chapter 15

Alethea

"Wake up," a deep voice commanded, stirring me from my sleep.

"Go away, Lira," I waved blindly as I rolled onto my stomach and shoved my face into the pillow.

"You need to train." The door to my wardrobe creaked open, and I heard the slap of leathers on the end of the bed.

The voice sounded like Mykill, but he had never ventured into my room. How did he even know that I slept in here?

"The sun's not even up yet," I whined as I pulled the blanket back over my face.

I shrieked as the blanket was yanked away, the cold morning air hitting my skin. "You said you wanted me to train you," Mykill said, his voice taking on the slightest sound of annoyance. "Now get up. I will be back in five minutes. If you're not dressed by then, I'll throw you in the tub myself."

I heard the door close and forced myself to open my eyes. My eyes burned, and the lack of sleep was already taking its toll on my body. I stared down at the leathers that rested at the foot of my bed in disbelief. I didn't realize that when he said he would train me that he'd wake up so early. I cursed to myself as I forced myself out of bed and threw on the leathers. I braided my hair in two side braids and left them hanging over my shoulders.

"You look awful," Mykill said as I closed the door behind me.

I resisted the urge to roll my eyes at him or hit him as I strolled past him. "Someone decided to wake me up before the rest of the kingdom."

"Waking up early gives you a clear mind." He easily caught up to me.

"That may be true for you," I chided as I looked up at him.

He looked well rested, refreshed. "The guards have a training room you can use when you strength train. Until you are able to build muscle, we'll train with the bow and arrow. Knowing how to use it will at least give you some form of self protection."

"Are you sure that's a good idea?" I scowled as my stomach roared. "Are we even going to eat breakfast first?"

"You're not going to starve," he sighed as he rolled his eyes. Then, much to my surprise, he produced a white cloth and held it out to me.

Frowning down at it, I took the cloth and unwrapped what looked like a flaky crescent shaped biscuit. My eyes widened, and I nearly squealed in delight as I took a massive bite. "Thank you," I said around a mouthful of the buttery bread.

Mykill didn't answer as he pushed open the door to the balcony and allowed me to pass first. We descended the steps out to the garden but ventured further than I'd been. I finished off the bread quickly, losing interest in where he was taking me until we stopped at a large clearing with cobblestone and an assortment of weapons. Another training area.

"I really need to explore more around here," I said to myself as I swung the napkin around my hand. "Alright. Trainee, what shall we do?"

Mykill scoffed and snatched the napkin mid swing. "You are the trainee. I am the trainer."

I frowned and then nodded. "Right."

"First, take this." He turned and picked up a wooden bow and sheath of arrows. "We're going to practice with this."

"This seems like a bad idea. What if I shoot you?" I took the bow and arrow in my unsteady hands.

"Trust me, you couldn't." He chuckled as I threw him a glare.

After spending what felt like an hour of him teaching me how to notch the arrow and pull the string back, I finally shot an arrow. It soared by the target in an arch and disappeared into the trees.

"Bastard," I growled at the damned thing and pulled another arrow from the sheath.

I notched the arrow the way he had taught me and released a second one. It soared over the target and landed on the ground. Cursing, I did that over and over until I made it to eight failed arrows.

"Your body needs to guide the shot," Mykill instructed as he stepped up behind me while I notched the ninth arrow.

I resisted the urge to gasp as he reached around me, almost startling me as his body curled around mine. He demonstrated with his hands over mine before releasing the bow. The arrow shrieked as it whizzed through the air and landed on the board. It hit one of the outer rings, but it was closer than I had been.

"Archery isn't in my array of skills, but I grew up doing it," he explained as he stepped back. "Now you try again."

I rolled my eyes at the command in his voice but did as he said.

He stepped back, taking the coolness of his touch with him. I ignored the race of my heart as I tried to copy the movements he just showed me. I released the arrow, and it hit the very edge of the target. My mouth dropped open, and I gasped in shock as I spun around.

"Did you see that?" I nearly shrieked.

A small smile tugged at his lips. "I did. Now do it again."

Rolling my eyes at his commanding voice, I spun back around and fired again. I shot five more times. Two out of the five hit the target, and the other three got lost in the trees.

Triumph flitted through me as I dropped the bow on the ground at my feet. I slid the empty sheath off of me and placed it on the ground beside the bow.

My body stiffened as I noticed the woman Mykill had brought with him standing beside him. She had moved so silently that I hadn't even noticed that she had arrived.

My gaze moved to Mykill questioningly.

"Well, that went worse than I expected," Mykill said. "Thalia is going to train you for a bit." He nodded his head in her direction and crossed his arms over his chest. I thought about teasing him but refrained.

The woman he brought with him nodded at me and offered me a smile. It wasn't a warm or friendly smile, but it wasn't harsh either. Her cat-like eyes followed me as she stalked towards me. She wore leathers that contoured to her body, and her body was well muscled for a woman.

"We're going to work on your punch," Thalia said as she stopped before me, and I noticed the pads she wore on her hands.

I nodded and followed her instructions as she led me in how to stand and the right breathing techniques.

"Now, why do you want to train?" Thalia asked as I held my hands up in the same position she instructed me too.

"To be able to protect myself," I said as I punched the pad.

"Why else?"

Another punch.

The impact jarred up my arms and through my shoulders.

"Why else, Alethea?" she demanded.

Another punch.

"Because I want to be able to control what happens to me," I bit out.

Another punch.

But this one was stronger.

"Good," Thalia breathed. "Now do it again."

So I did.

Punch after punch, I hit the pad. I imagined it was Kirin or the High Priest that I was punching. I felt my blows getting stronger, but as my body wore out, they got weaker.

"I think she's done for the day," Thalia said as she dropped her hands and turned to Mykill.

Sweat beaded my forehead and dripped down my spine. My chest moved with exhaustion. The sun was finally peeking up behind the trees, and I could hear the morning birds chirping happily. I wanted to lay out in the grass and watch as the sky changed.

"Where are you going?" Mykill called.

Turning towards him, I frowned. "I'm going to watch the sun rise."

"We're not done yet." I noticed the sword he held in each hand as he walked towards me.

"But I'm tired," I whined as he outstretched his hand with one of the swords.

"Take it," he commanded.

Grimacing, I took the damned sword and held it up. My arms felt like jelly, and my legs burned. Mykill held his sword up, extended it towards me, and I did the same. I had never used a sword in my entire life.

His icy eyes bore into mine before he spun and crashed his sword into mine. The metal clanged together, and I shrieked as I ducked the blade.

"What are you doing?" I shrieked again and brought my blade up to meet his.

I let my instinct guide my movements, but I could tell he was much stronger than I was. I would be overpowered in seconds. He spun again, our swords crashed together.

"You seem cranky. Maybe you should crawl after your bed-buddy and find some release," I teased and cried out as the butt of his sword struck my stomach.

I grunted as I stumbled backwards and fell onto my ass. My sword went clattering across the cobblestone.

He was on me immediately. His knees straddled my hips, and I managed to catch him by surprise as I threw myself upwards. We went rolling. I fisted my hands and drove them into his chest repeatedly in an attempt to get him off of me.

Finally, we settled on my back, and I hooked my fingers and went for his eyes, like my father had always taught me. He laughed darkly and deflected both of my hands, so I reverted to slapping him. My hand slapped off his cheek, then his neck and chest before he gripped both of my wrists and slammed them to the ground. I cried out as he stretched them over my head before he took them in one hand.

"Get off of me!" I snarled as I bucked my hips in an attempt to throw him off.

He merely laughed as he lowered his face to mine. "Jealousy is not a good look for you." His voice was like the whisper of a lover, and it crawled down my spine as his hands tightened on my wrists.

I growled and tried maneuvering him off of me, but he weighed too much.

"I'm not jealous in the slightest!" I argued. "Eryx told me what happened between you and his sister."

"Eryx knows nothing of what happened." He nearly snarled as he lowered his face to mine. "I sacrificed my name in an attempt to not tarnish his sister. She would have been made out a slut if they had found out she had been unfaithful. She had no interest in getting married and would have done anything to make sure that never happened."

My mouth dropped open at the admittance and that he would even do something like that for Freya.

"You weren't unfaithful to her?" I gaped up at him.

Something flashed across his gaze and he frowned. "I can't stand the woman but I'd never do that."

"Did you love her?" I brought myself to ask.

Mykill merely laughed as he sat back and released my wrists. "Gods no. She's a drinker and is open to more than one male and sometimes female in her bed." He rose swiftly, and I pushed myself up on my elbows.

"And you don't share?" I found myself teasing, but he didn't laugh or smile.

"No." He shook his head firmly, not realizing that I had been trying to lighten the mood as his icy eyes bore into mine. "You would find that I'm quite a committed lover, much to your shock, Alethea. I'll see you at dinner."

He turned away from me and hurt pierced through my chest.

"His sister betrayed me." I didn't know why I said it, but his shoulders stiffened, and his steps faltered. "She nearly left us for dead, and she was part of why I had been taken."

His head turned ever so slowly back to glance over his shoulder. Then, his body followed.

"I needed to get the Eye, and she agreed to help me get it. But, in the end, she stole it." I pushed myself up off the ground and wiped the back of my leathers.

"Where is she now?"

"Eryx said he doesn't know."

"Do you believe him?" One of his perfectly manicured bows quirked.

"No," I breathed and then felt my eyes widen.

"Good," Mykill answered as my mouth dropped open. "One of the things I think you'll learn soon enough is that love and loyalty are a lot like power. It should never be given blindly or to the wrong person."

"He loves me!" I stuttered in shock as his words crashed into me.

"I didn't say he doesn't." Mykill cocked his head to the side as he studied me. "But, you're no longer his mate. His desire to protect you, to do anything for you, has shifted. It's still there, never doubt that, but without your mating bond, selfishness is allowed to take root. There is no room for selfishness when it comes to your mate."

His words settled over me, prickling into my skin and settling into my very blood.

"I'll see you at dinner," he said again before I could answer and turned away.

I merely watched him walk this time.

He loved me. Eryx loved me. He had rescued me. I couldn't afford to think anything else.

Eryx had taken care of me.

But, Mykill's words kept crashing through me, and a voice in the back of my mind accepted them. He loved me but not in the same way. But, maybe that was true for me too - which is why I felt myself distancing myself from him. I could feel the chasm that was slowly opening between us, but I blamed it on the trauma of what the High Priest did to me. I blamed it on my grief of my family being taken from me. Still, there was a part of me that knew Mykill was right.

I found my way back inside and wandered down the halls until I found myself at Eryx's office. Maybe he had a book on mating bonds that I could read to gain more clarity. Everything I knew about fae and mating bonds had come from the mouths of others. I had never done my own research on it.

My fingers fumbled over the spines of books as I searched the titles. I found books on the history of herbs and the kingdoms. I found the genealogy of the royal family. *Useless,* I thought to myself as I stepped away and placed my hands on my hips.

I blew out a breath as my eyes skimmed the next shelf above when I felt a stab in my chest. My breath leached out of me as another stab followed, and I whipped towards the door.

"Mykill," I gasped as I stumbled back into the bookshelf. I clawed at the shelves as I slid down. Books clattered to the floor around me as I gasped his name again.

I tried crying out his name again, but it felt like my lungs stalled. My mouth fell open, but no sound emitted. My hands caught on the shelves, but they couldn't support me. Books fell around me, clattering to the ground. I slumped against the shelf as I slid fully to the ground. I could hear my heart thundering in my ears and the blood rushing through my veins.

"Alethea?" I heard Mykill ask as the door crashed open. "Alethea! What's the matter?"

I heard him drop to the ground beside me.

"Alethea, can you tell me what's wrong? Are you hurt?" I felt his hands briefly run up and down my body, searching for a wound, but he would find none.

"It's him," I gulped. I didn't know how, but I *knew* it was the High Priest. He was pulling on this connection we shared.

My back bowed off the ground, and a scream erupted out of me. With that scream, I felt power erupt from it. The air around me heated as fire clouded my vision. The power erupted in flames, ashes, and embers. My fingers curled into the carpeted floor beneath me, and I felt my nails ripping it up. I felt magic crawling through my veins like a serpent. Fire followed in its wake. I squirmed, needing to get away from the hellfire.

"Make it stop!" I shrieked as I rolled onto my side and curled in on myself.

Strong hands gripped my shoulders and pushed me onto my back. "Just breathe through it. Medrina!"

My hands fisted. "You need to back away," I warned. "Back away!"

I felt flames consume me. I didn't get the chance to see if he had moved. Fire licked up my entire body, wrapping itself around me in a cocoon. All I could see, hear, and feel was a typhoon of flames. My back arched off the ground again, and I screamed. I screamed so loudly, it felt like my throat was ripping open. My hands drifted over my skin. I needed it off. It was melting off, and once I got it off, then I'd no longer feel the heat.

I cried out in relief as the flames subsided, and the pain dulled. I felt a cold breath wash over me, and I exhaled once, then twice. Relief coursed through me when no pain followed. Pushing myself up, I looked around me and found I was encased in a bubble of smoke. My bare skin scraped off the rough carpet, and as I looked down at myself, I gasped. My clothes had all but melted off. They hung in patches off my body but burned to ash before my eyes.

The smoke finally cleared, and I pulled my legs up to shield my bare body. Mykill was still on his knees, his eyes wide in disbelief as he saw me.

"Can you get me something to cover myself with?" I asked, my voice small.

He averted his eyes immediately as he began to undo his tunic.

"You - you look different," Mykill stuttered. The man I'd only ever seen exhibit ice cold features, stuttered.

"What do you mean?" I asked as he draped his tunic across my shoulders and rose to his feet.

He turned as I buttoned it. My fingers shook as I looked around me where the ring of fire had been. It was charred in almost a perfect circle. I pulled his sleeves down over the shackle marks around my wrists before I stood.

I turned as I examined the fallen books that had all been burned. The edges of the bookshelf were charred, and the smell of burnt paper wafted up to my nose.

"I would find a mirror," Mykill spoke from behind me.

Gasping, I swung back towards him. "Why? What happened?" I placed a hand on my cheek, but my skin felt smooth. "Am I burnt?"

I didn't wait for him to answer as I shoved past him. We were nearly on the other side of the castle, but I took off down the hall. My bare feet slapped off the tile, and I heard Mykill keeping up behind me. I needed to see what he was talking about - what was wrong. I moved differently, gracefully.

My bedroom door opened before I reached it, and I hurried into the washroom. I stilled before the mirror, and my mouth fell open like a snake readying to devour its dinner.

My hair was still light and blonde, but it was tinted with the faintest hint of strawberry, and the hazel color in my eyes was gone. Instead, my eyes were a scarlet red.

"What happened to me?" I demanded. My voice strangled as I whipped back towards Mykill. He stood in the door frame, but his usual calm and collected demeanor was gone as he stared at me. His eyes were wide with a hint of panic. "What did he do to me?" I shouted and fisted my hands in my hair at the scalp.

My hair. *My hair.* The last thing that partially resembled my family, that connected me to them - the High Priest took it.

I collapsed to my knees, and my head fell back as I cried out. He had taken every ounce of them from my life, the only part of me left that had resembled my mother, who hadn't given birth to me but loved me as fiercely as her own. I wanted to yank out every strand. Every strand was a reminder that I wasn't hers. It was a reminder that I no longer had anything of hers.

"He took it all!" I wailed as I burrowed my fists into my closed sockets. "He took every last piece of them!"

"I know," Mykill said softly.

"No, you don't! How could you?" I cried, not looking at him.

I heard him drop to his knees, and then he gripped my chin. I cried out as he snapped my head back, forcing me to look at him. "I know that he has tried to erase them from your life, but he can't take them from your memories or your heart. Hold on to that love you have for them, and let it overshadow the grief."

"I don't know how." My voice caught as I felt the tears wetting my cheeks.

"You just have to breathe through it. In and out, over and over, until you can grab ahold of the grief. Don't let him win. Don't let him take them from you."

I felt strength surge against the sadness as my tears slowly subsided.

"Once you do that, there isn't a chance in hell that he can take them from you." The truth rang through me as I forced myself to take breath after breath and recalled my love for them.

"Good," he breathed as he released my chin.

"Have you ever seen this happen?" I asked.

He shook his head as his white eyes roamed my face. "Never." He gripped my hands and helped me rise. "Can you try using your powers?"

"My powers?" I frowned, and my hands instinctively flew to my ears.

Pointed. Like Mykills. Like Eryx's. Like Cadmus's. Disbelief rendered through me as my eyes shot back up to Mykill.

This couldn't be.

The High Priest had changed me, but I wasn't a mage like him. I was fae.

Chapter 16

Alethea

I laid staring at the sky. The sun had risen fully, and the brief heat of the day was at its peak. A light sweat beaded my forehead and the back of my neck. My stomach growled, but I refused to move. I found it relaxing to merely sit and watch the tufts of clouds move across the sky. Occasionally, I'd see a cluster of birds, but the sky remained clear otherwise.

"What are you doing?" Mykill's deep voice spoke from a few feet away.

I didn't look at him.

I heard his feet shuffle over the grass, and he sighed as he sat down beside me. "I'm not laying in the grass." His voice dripped with disdain, like it was beneath him.

I couldn't bring myself to laugh. I couldn't bring myself to do anything other than recall the strawberry color of my hair and eyes the color of blood. My body felt different, fuller and stronger. Even when I felt tired, I felt like I could rip a mountain to pieces. I felt an energy thrumming beneath my skin, but when Mykill tried to get me to use my powers, nothing happened. It was like they were trapped, locked beneath the surface of my skin, and I didn't have the key. I had no way to access my magic. Which made me just as useless as I was before.

Mykill said he wasn't sure how the High Priest could have changed me. He knew that the High Priest had given me his blood when he broke our mating bond but still wasn't sure as to how he could have changed me into a fae. I didn't tell him about the High Priest haunting my dreams either. I was going to tell Eryx, but I didn't want to worry him once he had been summoned. I planned to tell him when he got back.

"I believe your mate is here," he finally spoke, and sure enough, I heard the blow of a horn to signal his return.

His dragon bellowed next followed by Cadmus's. I hadn't taken the time to learn either of their names like I had Cador's.

"Do you think he'll still like the way I look?" I whispered finally.

Mykill sighed heavily. "If he leaves you over your hair and eyes changing, then I'll castrate him for you."

Surprise flittered over me at his words, and I laughed. I pushed myself up onto my elbows and stared at his salt-colored eyes.

"Thank you for helping me today." My voice was soft, but the words didn't lose any of their meaning. He had been my friend, caring for me in my lowest point and comforting me.

His normal cool exterior faltered for a moment and heated, melting away. His eyes softened. "Of course," he breathed.

The sound of the conch horn sounding behind us snapped my head to the side. I pushed myself up onto my feet and wiped the back of my dress. "Are you coming?"

I glanced back at Mykill as he stood. He unfolded his body like a cat. A panther would be a better description with his long body.

Turning away, I averted my eyes anywhere and everywhere else. I dropped my head back at the sky as I noticed Cadmus' and Eryx lowering towards the ground.

"Come on," I exclaimed. I gripped the hem of my dress and jogged towards the balcony.

I hurried up the steps and through the hall that took us to the sitting room at the entrance of the castle. I shoved open the door; the anticipation and anxiety of Eryx seeing me again ripped through me.

Eryx's orange dragon touched down on the ground, and it trembled beneath my feet for a moment. His hair had been ripped out of its bun, much like it normally did when he was in flight.

"Eryx," I gasped as he hopped down from his dragon.

"Blossom!" he exclaimed as he rushed towards me and then halted. "What happened?"

"She's fae," Mykill's voice sounded behind me. "You're going to want a drink for this, I assure you."

Eryx's gaze snapped to him and then back to me. His gaze was full of bewilderment as he looked me up from my head to toes. I wanted to take a step back, feeling embarrassed. I could feel heat creeping up my neck as he continued to stare at me.

I sensed Mykill step up behind me. His presence was almost comforting. "Doesn't she look magnificent?"

My entire body stiffened, and I resisted the urge to turn to look at him. Eryx's eyebrows shot up, and his gaze slid over to him. "She does indeed. How did this happen?"

"We don't know," I answered as I stepped towards him. I felt small, waiting for him to outstretch his arms to me as he stared at me with almost a look of bafflement.

Eryx stepped up to me and placed a hand on my cheek. His brows were pulled down in a frown, but he leaned forward and placed a kiss on my forehead. "I missed you, Blossom."

"I missed you too." I slid my arms around his waist.

His fingers threaded through my hair, and I imagined that the strawberry blonde shimmered beneath the sunlight.

"Let's get inside," Eryx said as he kissed my temple and pulled away.

"Lunch should be ready," Mykill said from behind me, and as I turned towards him, Eryx gripped my hand and held onto it while we made our way inside.

Eryx led the way to his office, and Mykill and Cadmus followed wordlessly behind. We all settled in various seats around his office, and with a deep breath, Eryx spoke. "So, what happened?"

"I was in here." I waved to the office space around me, and his eyes fell upon the charred bookshelf. "I was looking for a book when a pain started in my chest. I collapsed, and it was like my body was set on fire."

"It was," Mykill confirmed. "When I got here, she was writhing on the floor in pain. Her skin heated, and then her entire body lit on fire. It was like watching a Phoenix."

I recalled my clothes melting, but Mykill left that part out. Eryx would go berserk if he learned that Mykill had seen me nude.

"She was in a cocoon of fire for several seconds before it dispersed, and when it cleared, her hair and eyes had changed color. The change completely transformed her."

"How do you think this happened?" Cadmus asked.

"It was the High Priest," I said, drawing their attention to me.

"How do you know?" Eryx asked as he frowned.

"I just feel it," I responded, and I saw the uncertainty that crept into his gaze, along with a hint of sympathy.

"We need to figure out how he was able to do that." My head snapped to Mykill as he spoke. "You're fae now, but your powers haven't manifested," Mykill said as he stared at me, and his gaze slid to Eryx. "It's confirmation that she is the one the prophecy speaks of."

"What do you mean, prophecy?" I snapped my head towards Eryx.

His entire body stiffened as my gaze landed on him, and his eyes slid to Mykill, whose eyes remained vacant.

His lips curled into a smile. "So, she doesn't know?"

"Know what?" I snapped, annoyance setting in. "Someone better tell me what you're talking about!"

"There's a prophecy that's been predicting the fall of the fae. The fae defeated the mages eons ago. Mages were vicious monsters who killed anything in their path that wasn't of their species. It's been rumored for a long time that they're trying to raise the Black Mage again."

"What does that have to do with me?"

"It's rumored that a human girl born of fae parents with no powers or fae attributes is to mate with a fae King. The prophecy talks about a great war coming that could be the end of ages. I would bet my rule that it's talking about you."

"You knew?" I gasped as I snapped my head towards Eryx.

Shame emanated off him in waves, and his eyes fell as he merely nodded.

"A word," I snapped as I shoved myself up out of the chair and pivoted on my heel, not leaving any room for questions.

Fury roared through my veins as I stormed down the hall and up the stairs to Eryx's room. I could hear his soft footfalls behind me up the stairs. I threw the door open and didn't care as it bounced off the wall. His dragon's head snapped up, startled, and took us in before resting his head over the side of the balcony again.

He had kept another thing from me after telling me that I was his equal. He had broken his promise to me, *again*.

"Why wouldn't you tell me?" I snapped at Eryx as he closed the door behind us.

"Alethea," he sighed.

"No!" I cut him off as I stomped towards him and rammed my finger into his chest. "You said that I was your equal in every way. You don't lie to someone that you claim is your equal!"

"But I didn't lie to you, Blossom."

He stepped towards me and ran his hands down my arms.

"No!" I wrenched away from him. "No! You can't just touch me to make it better! Why didn't you tell me? I deserved to know," I demanded.

"It's dangerous, Blossom," Eryx said as he stepped towards me again. "I wanted to protect you."

"This was about me!" I shouted.

Surprise flickered across his face.

"Mykill is winning," he growled as his cider eyes narrowed.

"Mykill has been the only one to tell me the truth. You can't keep doing this, Eryx. First, you hid our mating bond from me. You still haven't told me what you wanted the Eye for, and now you've kept this from me?" I shook my head. "No, this is too much."

"Alethea, please -"

"No!" I gasped as I shoved at his chest. "We were supposed to be in this together, I thought we were in this together. But you've made it very clear that you're only in this for yourself, so let me make myself clear. I am in this for me."

"Alethea," Eryx said as he gripped my shoulder.

"No!" I yanked my arm from his grasp. "At first I thought that it was fate paying me back for sneaking away with Freya but I haven't lied to you since. I have lost everything, Eryx! I have nothing - no home, no family - all because of a prophecy that I didn't choose. I know that you love me, but you've proved countless times that you're in this for yourself. So, I'm choosing this for myself."

"Please, Blossom," he begged as he reached for my hands.

"No. No, I can't do this, Eryx." I held my hands away from him as I stepped back. "You may not have directly lied to me, but you omitted the truth. You chose not to tell me."

"What are you saying?" he asked as his shoulders fell.

"I'm saying that I can't do this. I can't be with you. I won't be with someone who repeatedly hides things from me, only to promise not to just to do it again. We can't be truly in this together with secrets."

"Please," he breathed. "Please don't do this."

"I'll sleep in my room." I turned away from him and strode towards the door. I threw it open and marched down the hall. Much to my surprise, he didn't follow after me, but I heard the sound of furniture crashing through the bedroom. I resisted the urge to flinch and hurried my steps until I reached my bedroom.

I slammed the door behind me and crashed against the door. The sobs emanated from my chest as I slid down to the ground and brought my knees to my chest. I tightened my arms around my knees and buried my face in them as I cried.

Guilt rocked me as I thought of his face, but I hadn't made the choice to lie to me. He had. I knew I had nothing to feel guilty for. The tears flowed for a whole different reason. I never thought I would tell him that it was over, or I'd leave him. Part of me still couldn't believe it, like if I woke up, it would be one bad dream.

I didn't leave my bedroom for dinner. I couldn't bring myself to face Eryx. Seeing his face at the dinner table would be too much, at least for today.

After the sun had long set, I decided to take a stroll. I yearned for fresh air. My chest felt tight, like it hadn't been able to take a deep enough breath all evening. I made sure to keep my footsteps light and checked around every corner before I rounded it. I breathed a sigh of relief every time I didn't see him.

Finally, I made it to the doors that led out to the gardens. Stepping onto the balcony, I wasn't surprised to find Mykill resting in one of the armchairs.

"I had dinner saved for you since I didn't see you," he said as he snapped his book shut and placed it down beside him.

He waved his hand, and a plate appeared on the small table before him. The plate was brimming with smoking ham, two biscuits, boiled potatoes, and roasted beets. My mouth watered as I sat before the small table and pulled the plate into my lap.

"Thank you." I didn't look up at him as I picked at some of the rolls.

Mykill remained silent while I ate. My stomach had been rolling, but at some point, I had shoved aside the feeling and blocked it out entirely.

"How did you know I would come out here?" I asked as I finally set my plate aside and reclined in the seat.

He shrugged as he propped his feet up on the table. "It was just a guess, but you seem to enjoy the fresh air. I wanted to make sure you got something to eat. I'm sure you wouldn't have wanted me coming to your room."

"You could have had a maid bring it," I countered.

He cocked his head to the side. "I also wanted to make sure you were okay."

I opened my mouth to respond but fell short. I don't know where our annoyance with one another blossomed into a friendship, but my heart clenched.

"Thank you," was all I said.

He nodded at me before dropping his head back to gaze at the stars. "The sky is beautiful tonight."

"It is," I whispered in response as I stared at the chiseled lines of his jaw.

Dropping my head back, I stared back up at the sky. He was right; the sky did look beautiful tonight. There was a cluster of stars that shined particularly brighter than the others, twinkling merrily without a care in the world.

"What I would give to be one of those stars up there," I whispered as I clasped my hands over my lap.

I felt his gaze drop to me, but I didn't look at him and kept my head strained towards the sky.

"I think you'd find being constrained in one place boring." His tone was half joking as I dropped my head to meet his gaze.

I couldn't help the bark of laughter. "You're probably right."

"A life of adventure seems to fit you." He craned his head back and stared up at the sky.

I didn't respond. I had never thought of it. My entire life, I thought that I would die in the same town I was born in. But now, my future was unknown. Whether I wanted to admit it or not, I sensed a change on the horizon - a change that was not only going to rock my world, but also move the worlds of those around me.

We both sat in silence for a while. The silence stretched between us, but there was not an ounce of uncomfortability. I watched as a star shot across the sky, leaving a glimmering trail behind it. It was beautiful.

Mykill rose to his feet, drawing my attention back to him, and stretched his arms over his head. The muscles in his powerful arms strained, and I jerked my head to the side.

"I am heading off to bed," he said. "Good night, Alethea. Rest well."

"Good night," I whispered as he brushed past me.

I remained seated for a while after he went inside. I couldn't bring myself to move. The cool night air and the stillness of the forest below brought peace over my limbs. There wasn't a single chirping bird or insect. Everything was just still. I closed my eyes and let my head fall back as I felt the peace wash over me.

After what seemed like an eternity, I dragged myself to my room, but I tossed and turned all night. Lira had left the small jar of sleeping herbs on the night table beside my bed, but I couldn't bring myself to take it. Either the High Priest or Eryx would haunt my dreams, and I couldn't bring myself to face either of them.

Heartbreak and nightmares were two sides of the same coin. They existed simultaneously and would haunt me till the end of my days. I decided sleep deprivation was a better alternative.

Chapter 17

Alethea

Sleep evaded me most of the night, or I evaded it.

"You look dreadful," Lira chided as she coaxed me out of bed with a steaming cup of lemon water.

I grumbled an inaudible response as she led me into the washroom. She already had a bath drawn, and the scent of lavender wafted up to my nose. I sighed as I breathed it in. She pulled the robe off my shoulders, and I stepped out of it. I got into the water with my dress still on.

Lira hissed in response, but I ignored her and lowered myself into the water.

My eyes felt swollen, and my entire body felt groggy. That didn't include the ache in my muscles from training. Moving my arms had become increasingly difficult this morning.

"Give me this," she hissed as she reached for the bunched gown and pulled it over my head.

I ignored her as I settled beneath the water and closed my eyes to help relieve their burn.

"What has got you in such a foul mood?" Lira asked as she picked up my hand and began scrubbing my fingernails.

"The King and I are no more," I whispered as I traced my finger through the bubbles.

I heard her sharp intake of breath. She dropped my hand, and it splashed in the water.

"He kept lying to me. He was keeping things from me."

"I'm not permitted to speak against the King, but know you have my support, girl," she said softly.

I glanced at her. Her face was sincere and sympathetic, but she offered me a small smile. "Thank you, Lira."

"Now on the account of your hair, we'll need to swap out some of your dresses because they will clash too harshly."

I turned my attention back towards the popping bubbles on the surface and tuned her voice out. Tears rushed to my eyes at the mention of my hair.

"Gods, what is it girl?" Lira gasped and stopped.

I merely stared. "My hair was the last reminder of my mother." My voice broke on the last word, and I turned my face away as the tears managed to fall.

"Let's get you out of the tub," Lira soothed as she gripped my hands and pulled me to my feet.

She wrapped a towel around my body and led me back into my bedroom. She led me to the bench before the vanity and gently laid me on it. She was quiet as she brushed through my wet hair.

"You still look just as beautiful," Lira whispered as she set the brush down. "Let your hair dry during breakfast, and then I'll style it."

"Thank you," I mumbled as she handed me a dress.

"Your hair wasn't the only thing you had from your mother," Lira said as she stooped to my eye level and held my hands in both of hers. "From the stories you've told me, you have the same heart she does. Now, she lives on in your heart. Never forget that."

"I just miss her so much," I whispered as the tears sprang forth in my eyes again.

"I know, girl." Lira's voice was comforting as she stroked the back of my hand. "But, she wouldn't have loved you any less merely over your hair and eyes."

She was right. I knew she was right. I nodded as she patted my cheek before rising to her feet.

"Now, go eat your breakfast," she said quietly as she pulled me from the stool.

I smiled softly as I changed into the dress. I recalled our annoyance with one another when I had first been brought here, but she became a friend. I was thankful for her help and encouragement. I didn't feel nervous to share my true feelings with her, and she sure wasn't either.

My feet padded off the floor as I moved down the halls to the dining room. Eryx didn't come to breakfast. Cadmus said he had work to attend to. I couldn't have been happier.

Breakfast consisted of a bowl of oats heaped with diced apples and sliced almonds. Cream and sugar rested beside my bowl, along with a small plate of three pieces of sausage.

"Good morning," Mykill called as he approached, and I felt my movements halt as I glanced up at him.

He was wearing leathers today that hugged his large form. They contoured every muscle in his chest, arms, and legs. With his wings extended on either side of him, he looked like the God of Death as he stalked towards the table. So much power thrummed from his well-muscled form that I couldn't help but balk. I only wished that I emanated that much strength and power merely by entering a room one day.

"Good morning," I swallowed a lump of oats.

"Let's train after breakfast," Mykill said as he sat down.

Cadmus cleared his throat, and his cutlery clattered to his plate as he shoved his chair out. "Alethea." He bowed his head as he stood. "Mykill."

"General," Mykill greeted. Cadmus turned and headed out of the dining room. "I don't think he likes me," he said when he disappeared beyond the threshold of the door.

"I think it's the arrogant attitude," I bit back as I took a bite of the maple glazed ham.

Mykill snorted but didn't bite back with a response as he focused on his food. Neither of us spoke as we focused on our meals. I welcomed the silence. The reprieve from my raging thoughts all night was comforting. Mykill must have sensed that too since he glanced up at me every now and then but didn't speak.

Mykill's silverware clattered as he placed it down and stood from his seat. "I'll be waiting."

After I rushed through my breakfast, I ran to my room. I pulled my leathers on, and Lira braided my hair down my back in a single braid. I still couldn't bring myself to look in the mirror. The stark difference between how I looked before and now still brought tears to my eyes.

"Did you even sleep last night?" Mykill asked as I stepped out of my bedroom and closed the door behind me.

"Gods," I breathed as I jumped. "You scared me! Could you not wait outside?"

"Did you stay on the balcony all night long?" he questioned, refusing to answer me.

I started the walk down the hall, and he trailed after me. "No. I went back to my room, but I had trouble sleeping."

"Did you try any sleeping herbs?"

My feet faltered as we rounded the corner. Eryx was stalking towards us, and he looked as if steam was about to pour from his ears. I nearly groaned. *Cadmus.*

"Where are you two going?" Eryx asked gruffly as he stopped before us.

"We're going to train," I responded.

"If you're going to train, you're not going to do it on my property," Eryx growled as he stalked past us. "I forbid you from training on my grounds."

I heard Mykill's wings unfold behind him. "You can't forbid us!" I balked at Eryx.

He didn't turn as he said, "I am the King. I can do what I wish."

"As you wish," Mykill's cold voice said as he reached down and gripped my hand. "Come on, Alethea."

"Mykill!" Eryx growled as he followed after us.

I remained silent as Mykill led me outside and down the stairs.

"I said you can't train here!"

"Why are you being such an ass?" I shouted as I whipped towards Eryx and ripped my hand from Mykill's grip.

Eryx's mouth fell open to answer when Mykill's chest brushed my shoulder, and an arm wrapped around my waist.

I opened my mouth to ask what he was doing but came up short as we shot into the sky. I shrieked as the ground fell out from beneath me, and the only thing keeping me from falling was him. I wailed my arms and legs, desperate to clutch onto something. My breakfast lurched into the back of my throat, and I clenched my eyes closed.

He managed to turn me so I could face him, and I wrapped my limbs around him. He laughed as his arms wrapped around me.

"I've got you," Mykill said as he tightened his arms around me. "I'm not going to drop you."

I covered my face in his neck as the air whipped around us. My arms and legs were like bands of steel around him as I tried to not picture how easy it would be for him to drop me.

"I think I'm going to be sick," I groaned.

Mykill laughed, his breath brushing my neck. "I'd rather you didn't."

I didn't say anything as I kept my eyes closed and my arms tight around him. My breath came out as panicked breaths until we finally touched down on land.

"You can let go now," Mykill laughed as he practically pried my arms and legs from around him.

I nodded breathlessly as I dropped my hold from around him, and my feet fell upon the grass covered ground.

"Where are we?" I breathed in amazement as I gazed around us.

We were perched up on a mountain top that was flattened around us like the perfect landing zone. There were trees on one side that led further down the mountain. The other side dropped off at a steep ledge that overlooked miles of rolling hills and trees. I gasped as I stared at the birds flying through the air. I imagined rabbits and squirrels frolicking in the woods below us.

"It's beautiful," I said as I turned to Mykill, who merely watched me. "So, what are we going to be doing today?" I propped both hands on my hips.

Mykill pulled the two swords from his sheath that crossed over his back and thrust one to me.

"No," I argued as I crossed my arms over my chest. "Last time we did that, you kicked me and knocked me to the ground."

"Do you expect me to go easy on you?" He raised a brow as he stepped towards me. "You're fae now, so expect me to push you harder."

I rolled my eyes as I took the sword from him and nearly dropped it. It was heavier than the one we had used before.

"Hold it up straight."

"I'm trying." I clenched my teeth as I held the hilt with both hands and lifted the tip off the ground. "Why is this one so much heavier?"

"It's not a training sword," he said as he extended his arm towards me, raising his sword. "Now, come at me."

I glared up at him as I crossed our swords. My arm was already burning from holding the damned thing. He wanted me to come at him, but I knew nothing about sword fighting. I didn't know any fighting techniques at all. But, I sighed and let my instincts guide me as I calmed my already racing heart. I copied Mykill's stance, his legs wide and planted like tree stumps. I took a deep breath, and I arched my sword towards him. Unsurprisingly, his sword met mine, and I did everything in my power to not fall backwards from the force.

He came at me instantly. I raised my sword to meet him and ducked as his leg spun out to bring me down. I jumped back, but he brought me down anyway.

"That was better. Try again," he said as he stepped up to me and extended his arm.

I growled in response to his command as he lifted me to my feet.

"Become one with your sword," Mykill said as he raised his sword. "Let it become another extension of your body."

With that, he advanced first. I held the hilt with both hands and planted one foot behind me as I moved to meet his thrust. I didn't think about how I moved; I just let my instincts guide me. My body moved much quicker and easier than when I was human. I was still out of breath, but not as badly as I had been before. Even the burn was less noticeable. Fae were fighters - that much I had known since I was a child. I let my fae instinct lead me.

We spun, pried, kicked, and lunged towards each other repeatedly. The sun continued to move above us, getting closer to lunch time. Sweat slithered down my neck and back.

Mykill's chest was starting to heave, and a sheen of sweat coated his forehead.

"Let's go one more time," he said as he spun his sword and moved towards me.

Mykill froze mid step. I felt a slither over my skin. It was a whisper that caused goosebumps to spread over me, like my body was alerting me that there was something in the vicinity. My head swiveled to look over my shoulder. A light breeze had picked up and brushed through the trees, making them dance.

"Mykill?" I whispered.

"Shh."

We both watched as the trees rustled.

"Stay here," Mykill said as he approached the tree line.

"No, please don't leave me!" I gripped his arm and dropped the sword.

"Pick that back up. I'll be right back," he hissed as he shook off my hand and turned back to the tree line.

My stomach fell into my ass as I watched him disappear behind the foliage. I waited several seconds that felt like several years for him to pop back out of the brush. My breath rang heavy in my ears. I closed my eyes and took a deep breath. As I did, one of the trees began to shake.

"Mykill!" I hissed as I watched the tree shake.

I resisted the tremble in my hands as I took a step towards the tree line. The branches shook, alerting me that something large was behind them.

"Mykill?" I asked as I took another step closer.

I paused as an eerie feeling crept over me, and the tree stopped moving. My senses told me that the person on the other side wasn't Mykill.

I yelped as a man lunged out of the trees. My feet tripped over themselves as I stumbled back, but I managed to not fall over. I dodged the man's arms as he ran at me. As he passed, I turned, kicked him in the back, and sent him tumbling forward. I whipped back around. Another man had slipped from the trees and walked towards me. His hair was pulled into a bun on his head, and my heart felt like lead in my chest as realization sunk over me.

He was the mage that had changed when I had been held prisoner.

"We were sent by the King," the mage approaching me said and held out his hands.

He fisted his hands, and it was like bands of steel wrapped around me, pinning my arms to my sides. I cried out as he moved his fist down, and I was forced to my knees.

"I knew I recognized you," I gasped as I struggled against his hold. "You're one of the mages that changed while I was still there."

"If I don't ask you a direct question, then don't speak, bitch," he snarled.

Relief crashed over me as Mykill came crashing through the trees. He already had a gash over his right eyebrow and a bruise forming on his cheek. His chest heaved as his eyes fell on me and then slithered over to the mage.

"Alethea," he rasped.

"Now, we have orders to kill you," the mage said as he turned towards Mykill with a sinister smile.

Fear pounded through my chest, but this time, it wasn't for me. It was for Mykill. He slowly became a calming, steady presence in my life, and I couldn't have another friend's death on my hands.

Hands wrapped around my throat from behind, cutting off my words, and I was pulled back to my feet. My arms remained uselessly pinned to my sides. I was yanked back against a chest and watched as Mykill's attention zeroed in on the mage.

"I'm more powerful than you, *faery*." The mage spit at the ground as he approached Mykill.

Mykill didn't need to try to appear intimidating. He just was. Wrath rolled off of his body in waves. His eyes narrowed, and the sky thundered above him. I watched the sky behind him as it darkened, and my mouth fell open as I marveled at the clouds that swirled behind him, ready to obey their master.

The mage smiled and ducked beneath the bolt Mykill sent towards him. The ground where the lightning had struck was nothing more than a charred spot. The mage growled as he spun on Mykill and launched himself at him. Their bodies collided ad the men went rolling to the ground, and concern for Mykill's wings rushed through me. But, he folded them behind him, tucking them protectively together as the two men rolled. Mykill planted both of his feet in the stomach of the mage and sent him flying backwards with the force of a warrior.

Mykill growled as he pushed himself up on his knees. The mage grunted in response as he shoved himself up. The mage moved around behind Mykill while he was distracted, a cruel smile on his face.

"Watch -" I started to warn him, but one of the men clamped a hand over my mouth.

I snarled as I struggled against their hold.

"I suggest letting the lady go," Mykill warned as he spun on the mage and threw his arm out. I marveled as a whip of lightning shot from his palm and tightened around the mage's neck like a rope.

His eyes bulged, and his skin tinted red as he fought for breath. His body shook as electricity coursed through him. His eyes rolled back in his head, and saliva dripped from his mouth as Mykill stalked towards the mage. I watched in awe as Mykill ripped his arm back, and the lightning whip yanked backwards. The mage's eyes widened as his head was ripped from his shoulders. His head went rolling as it hit the ground, and upon his death, I felt the bands around me loosen. I sighed in relief and spun on the man holding me, my fist hitting him in the jaw.

My punch was more powerful than when I had been human, but I knew it wasn't strong enough when he barely fell back. The second man lunged towards me, but I jumped back. The first man laughed as he gripped his jaw and started back towards me. Suddenly, I felt a shift in the air. If I stared long enough, I could see the wall forming between me and the two men.

Mykill appeared beside me, and as I glanced up at him, the murderous rage in his eyes almost made him unrecognizable. The two men cried out as they were shoved to their knees. Mykill didn't look away from me for another beat before his rage was centered upon the two men.

"Bite off every finger that touched her." Mykill's voice was unbelievably calm as he stared daggers at the men on their knees.

"What?" one of them exclaimed. "I can't do that!"

"You can, and you will," he said coolly. "Bite off every finger that touched her and the rest for my amusement."

The men shuddered. One of them raised his fingers to his lips, and I watched as a dark spot spread across his breaches. His hand shook as he opened his mouth and rested his finger between his teeth.

"Please!" he cried as he ripped his finger from his mouth. "Please. I can't do this!"

Rage flashed behind Mykill's gaze as he lowered to the man's level. "Do it, or the pain *I'll* inflict will make that seem like a mercy."

Tears streamed down the man's face as he brought his finger back between his teeth. I winced as he bit down and blubbered before he cried out again.

I couldn't bring myself to look away. My blood rejoiced as the man screamed and wept. I watched the blood run down his hand. It covered his chin and coated his teeth.

When my eyes met Mykill's, it felt like a trance came over me. His eyes reflected mine, a soul that longed and craved violence and bloodshed. Where Eryx had tried to hide that from me, Mykill flaunted it.

The second man refused, and a chill crept down my spine as Mykill's eyes narrowed much like a predator. His screams were far more agonizing than the other's while Mykill tore him apart limb by limb. Mykill's eyes narrowed as his chest heaved. Blood covered the majority of the front of his leathers, and some had even splattered through his hair.

"Let's go back," Mykill said, his voice still strained and guttural as he looked at me finally.

He stepped up to me. I raised an arm and slipped it around his neck as he secured an arm beneath my shoulders and knees. He lifted me easily, and I watched as his wings extended on either side of him. With one powerful stroke and a push of his knees, he lifted into the air. I resisted the urge to gasp as my stomach lurched into my throat. My arm tightened around his neck until we were high in the sky, and he leveled himself out. We blended in with the clouds, and I yearned to stretch my hand out to touch one of them, just to feel what it was like between my fingers.

After several minutes, I pulled my arm from around his neck and let my hands rest in my lap. I resisted the urge to fidget with them or twist my fingers around.

"Are you alright?" Mykill finally said, stirring me slightly.

I raised my head and stared at his marble-like face. Blood was splattered across his cheek, and I couldn't help but think that it was staining him. Without thinking, I raised my hand and brushed it off with my thumb. I felt his entire body stiffen, and a muscle jumped in his cheek.

"I'm alright," I confirmed as I dropped my hand back in my lap.

My stomach nearly dropped out of my body as we descended back towards the castle. I covered my mouth as my breakfast threatened to jump back up my throat.

"If you throw up, I'll drop you," Mykill said, trying to break the tension, but it was near impossible. It was too thick, threatening to suffocate us.

I shook my head as his feet met the ground. He set me on my feet, and we both made our way inside.

"I need to tell the guards to be on the lookout," he said as he opened the door for me.

I nodded and paused as Eryx came around the corner. He froze. His eyes widened in concern as he took in the blood coating Mykill.

"What happened?" Eryx demanded.

Mykill stalked past him and didn't care to even look in his direction. I could practically feel the anger rolling off of him.

"Tell me what happened!" Eryx's hand snaked out and gripped Mykill's arm.

I could've told him that was a mistake.

Mykill spun on him. His arm reared back, and he slammed his fist into Eryx's jaw. I gasped as Eryx stumbled back.

"You will be the death of her," Mykill growled.

Eryx gripped his jaw as he righted himself. Blood dripped from the corner of his mouth. His eyes were wide, but behind them I saw the fury.

"Because of you and your pride, her life was put in danger. She will be hunted as soon as word spreads that she is the one the prophecy speaks of and no longer human. She has the strength now to protect herself, with or without powers." Mykill slammed his hand into Eryx's chest as he stepped up to him. "So stop treating her like she's a fucking useless piece of china, and give her the respect she deserves." His voice had lowered into a growl. "We will train on the palace grounds from now on, and you're going to shut your damn mouth. If you have a problem, then my men and I will leave."

Eryx only gaped at him, his eyes wide as they bounced between the two of us. I wasn't harmed, but he could still see the blood that marred Mykill's neck, cheek, and most of his leathers. Eryx's gaze slid over to me, his eyes still wide.

"Are you alright?" he asked quietly as Mykill stormed down the hall.

My gaze remained glued on Mykill's back as he moved further down the hall. His hands fisted and unfisted repeatedly at his sides before he turned the corner and disappeared.

"Fine, thank you," I said and spun away towards the direction of my room.

Chapter 18

Alethea

As I closed the door behind me, I stripped my clothes and walked to the tub. Lira would chide me for leaving my clothes on the floor, but I felt like my body was overheating. Sweat poured down the sides of my face, neck, and back. My hair stuck to my skin as I leaned forward and drew a bath. I didn't wait for it to fill before I stepped in. The cold water hissed as it touched my skin. I paused as I balked down at the bubbling water as it came in contact with my skin. Steam hissed and rose around my legs. I reached down, touched the surface of the water, and the same thing happened as my fingers broke the surface.

Sighing, I slid fully into the water and waited for the cold water to cover my body. But as it continued sizzling, the water heated, and I was forced to drain the water. After the water drained, I redrew another bath. The water bubbled but not as intensely as before. I didn't even let the water rise halfway before I sighed and gave up. I leaned back as the water gurgled its way down the drain

As I slid the dress on, a knock sounded on the door. Frowning, I let the strings dangle at my back as I strode towards it and opened it.

"Yes?" I frowned at the guard who stood before me.

I had never seen him before, but by the blank expression on his face, he knew who I was. He didn't even look at me as he spoke. "The King is waiting in the war room."

"The King?" I scoffed as I clutched the edge of the door. "You mean Eryx."

"He's the King to you, human," he spit before spinning on his heel.

I glowered as I watched him make his way down the hall. If I could fry him on the spot, I would have. The door slammed as I threw it closed. I growled and mumbled to myself as I reached for the strings that bounced off my back. After several minutes of trying to tie them, I finally managed and headed over to the vanity.

For one of the first times, I sat on the vanity and merely stared at myself - if I could still even be called me anymore. The moisture from the sweat had caused my hair to scrunch at the root. The rest of my hair flowed down in loose waves around my shoulders. I picked up a chunk and ran my fingers through it. My skin glowed compared to how it looked before. I hadn't realized the stark difference between fae and human until I was changed into one.

I couldn't say that I was happy to be one.

I yearned for my mother to just hold my cheeks as I cried. But the tears fell uninterrupted down my cheeks as I hunched over the table and covered my eyes. If not my mother's soft touch, then I needed Laney's teasing laugh to push me out of my stupor. My shoulders shook beneath the crushing weight of my loneliness.

I may have a friend in Cadmus, Lira, and maybe even Mykill, but no one's friendship could compare to the friendship of my sister. Laney could read me without speaking. We communicated in a blend of glances and giggles. We shared the same thoughts without speaking them aloud, and when we needed to for mischievous purposes, we could move seamlessly and avoid detection. There was something about the blend of two sisters that no one could ever replicate, not even a lover.

I didn't stop the tears. I let them fall until my eyes dried, and when they welled up again, I let them come. I knew I needed to feel the grief of missing my family, or I'd become a shell of a person. Mykill and Lira's words rang true. They would live on in my memories, and I would do anything to keep that memory alive and fresh. But, it would take time for it to not feel like my chest was being flayed open. It felt like a fist was squeezing my ribs, trying to squeeze everything out of me until I popped. By the time my eyes had dried entirely for the final time, my throat felt raw, and my head felt like a spear had been driven through each of my eyes.

I shoved myself from the stool. I left my hair down, refusing to acknowledge the unkept waves.

When I opened the door, the guard was nowhere to be seen, thankfully. I didn't want to worry about him manhandling me like the first guard had when I had first been brought here.

The door clicked shut behind me, and I made my way down the halls to the War Room. I could hear Eryx's deep voice arguing with someone. He sounded like he was about to drive their head through a wall when a voice as cold and dry as a blizzard responded. The chill slithered down my spine as I peeked open the door.

"She's not going with us," Eryx growled. His hands were braced on the table as he hunched over it.

"It's her decision to make," Mykill quipped.

"She's not -"

"What are you talking about?" I frowned as I stepped fully into the room, making my presence known.

Eryx's shoulders tensed as he turned towards me. "We need to travel across the seas. There's a kingdom there -"

"The Old Kingdom," Mykill said.

My head shot towards him as he casually admired his nails, his rings glinting in the light.

"Yes," Eryx confirmed before continuing. "Vestor, one of the other Kings, received a letter from the Old Kingdom."

"What do we need to go there for?" I asked as I made my way over to one of the open seats around the round table.

Eryx glanced at me with annoyance. "If you both would just let me finish," he snapped.

Holding my hands up, I waited for him to continue. He huffed out a breath. "He received a letter requesting assistance. Vestor then requested our help because he doesn't have the means or men to retrieve the artifact that they're searching for. We will be traveling by sea with some of Vestor's men. I will lead the venture. Mykill, I am requesting you and yours to come along as well."

"What are we hunting?" Mykill raised a brow at him.

"The mirror of truth," Eryx answered.

Mykill's brows shot up into his hairline. "The mirror of truth?" he repeated. "That's a myth."

"What does it do?" I asked.

"You could ask it any question, and it will reveal the truth to you."

"It's been reported that it doesn't actually exis-" Mykill started.

"We could use it to find out the truth about my birth parents," I said, interrupting them.

Both of their heads turned towards me. Eryx nodded. "If it is retrieved, then yes."

I didn't even know my birth parents' names. Hope filled me at the possibility that I could find them, and better yet, possibly meet them.

"I want to come." My jaw jutted out, and I straightened. There was no way I was taking no for an answer. I'd hide in someone's pack like a stowaway if I needed to.

Eryx remained stiff as a board as he stared down at the table beneath his hands. But I wasn't going to break the silence, I wanted him to sit in it. I wasn't going to argue with him like a petulant girl anymore.

"Fine," he gritted out before continuing.

We all listened as Eryx hashed out the important details - the amount of men each of them would bring, what the duration of our trip would look like, and how they couldn't bring their dragons because it would be seen as a threat. We were to travel first by horse, then by boat.

"We leave in the morning after breakfast, so rest well." He finally nodded his head towards us and rose from his chair.

I pushed myself up and followed after him. I needed to tell him about the High Priest before we left and lost any semblance of privacy.

"Eryx!" I called as he slipped out of the room. "Eryx, can we talk? Please?"

I heard Mykill, Thalia, and Cadmus slip out of the room behind me as I chased after Eryx.

He paused and looked back at me without saying a word.

"Eryx, please," I begged as he turned away from me. "I have something I need to speak with you about."

His shoulders stiffened, but he angled his head towards me. "Let's talk in my office."

I nodded as he turned back towards me. He remained frozen for a few beats before stalking past me. He kept his eyes averted, never making eye contact with me. I sighed but followed behind him. When we were in his office, we both took up our seats on either side of his desk. His gaze was dark and uninviting, and I nearly decided to tell him nevermind.

"Can someone access your dreams if you've shared blood with them?" I finally asked.

His brows shot up in surprise, and he sat forward. "Yes, if a Blood Bond was formed. But you would both have had to partake in each other's blood." His eyes widened. Realization flashed across his eyes, and his mouth fell open. "The High Priest." It wasn't a question.

I nodded as I clenched my hands in my lap. "Yes."

"How often?"

"At first, it started off slow, maybe once a week, but they've increased since then." I kept my stare angled towards my lap.

"How often?" he repeated.

"Every night," I breathed.

He didn't speak for a moment, taking in what I had revealed. I didn't know anything about Blood Bonds, but the concern that had flashed across his face was enough to tell me it was dangerous and needed to be taken care of.

"How do we get rid of it?" I snapped my head up to look at him.

He shook his head, his cider eyes churning. "I'm not sure. I'll speak with Medrina." He sighed as he leaned back in his chair. "What is he saying? What does he want?"

I couldn't keep my face from heating and glanced towards the bookshelf beside him. My eyes followed the charred marks up the shelves. I didn't realize how many books had been scorched when the High Priest had changed me.

"Alethea?" I stiffened at the sound of him saying my name.

"When I was there, he had the ability to form these *things*." My voice faltered. "These shadow monsters that showed you your worst fears. They plagued me while I was sleeping."

"Why didn't you tell me that he was haunting your dreams?"

"I was going to, but then you had to leave, and I had planned on telling you when you got back."

I left the rest of the sentence unspoken.

He let out a sigh. "I'll speak to Medrina." His voice softened. "You can call on me if you need me. Anytime."

"Thank you." I nodded but still couldn't bring myself to look at him.

"Was there anything else you were wanting to discuss?" he asked, his voice even softer.

This time, he left the rest of his sentence unspoken. I knew what he was referring to. He wanted to talk about us.

I shook my head and pushed myself up from the seat. "No." I bowed my head. "Sleep well."

"You too, Alethea." His soft voice followed me out into the hall as I closed the door behind me.

"Get up, girl," Lira said as she ripped the blanket off of me, yanking me from the short amount of rest I had managed to get. "Everyone is already gathered outside."

I grumbled as I rolled onto my back and stared up at the ceiling. We were traveling to the coast of Lavara today. Vestor was sending a boat and men there to make the journey with us. From there, we would cross the open seas to Gild. I had never heard of the kingdom, but Mykill and Eryx had explained that there was a powerful King who was requesting our presence.

The bath was already drawn by the time I dragged myself into the washroom. Lira remained in the main bedroom readying the rest of my things. I quickly bathed and dried myself before I hobbled back. There was a plate with three sausages and a scramble of eggs with peppers resting on the vanity. There was a second plate beside it with a biscuit and a small jar with fig jam.

"Sit and eat!" Lira waved me over to the table as she hurried past me and began packing a small pile of clothes into the bags.

Plopping down on the stool, I quickly shoved the food down my throat, nearly inhaling it.

"Here, dress," Lira waved to the pile of clothes at the end of the bed as she tied a bag closed.

"Ah, what is this?" I asked as I picked up the pair of boots and thick leggings.

"You need something that's easier to travel in," Lira said as she folded another set of clothing of the exact same style but different colors into the pack.

Dropping the towel, I slid on my undergarments and then the leggings. They were the softest material I had ever worn - much softer than our fur lined winter coats my father had saved up for. I slipped the sage colored top on, and Lira came up behind me as she slid a corset along my stomach. I raised my arms up on either side and straightened as she began to do the strings. The top was layered and flowy, covering my backside, and the long sleeves billowed around my waist.

"They deserve to see you as a woman," Lira said as she pulled the top half of my hair back and began braiding it.

"What?" I frowned as I went to turn my head towards her but winced when she yanked on the braid, reminding me to keep in place.

"They've treated you like you're beneath them for too long," she mumbled as she held a pin between her teeth.

"He's done it to protect me," I whispered partly in shock and partly in defense.

"He has not," she hissed as she dropped the braid. She ran her fingers through the loose locks and draped them over my shoulders. "There."

I turned towards her, and she placed both of her hands on my cheeks. "Thank you, Lira."

"You look stunning, like a warrior." She patted my cheek, reached around me, and produced a sheath. "Prop your leg on the bed for me."

I did as she instructed, and she tightened the sheath around my thigh before she handed me the knife Eryx gave me. The soft pink gems glimmered under the light as I twisted it in my hand before sheathing it.

"Here are your packs." She slid one onto my shoulder and handed me the other. "Be safe, girl."

"I will." Before she could protest, I stepped forward and wrapped an arm around her neck.

She mewled in disbelief, but after a moment, one of her arms hooked around me and hugged me back. "I'll be here when you get back."

After she shoved me out of the bedroom, I ran down the halls. She said that they were waiting on me. More guards than usual were posted throughout the halls as I passed quickly through them. I burst out the front doors and made my way down the stairs. Eryx and Cadmus were standing near the bottom of the steps with their heads huddled together. Everyone else was huddled around a group of horses.

"Alethea!" Cadmus gasped as he spun towards me. "Finally! Let's get moving." Cadmus called out as he turned to the men behind them.

My feet froze on the last couple steps as my eyes clashed with Eryx's. His gaze narrowed as they took me in, and his eyes trailed down the front of me. Part of me wanted to blush and hide while the other part of me wanted to jut my chin out and stride past him. I wanted him to see me for who I was, my own person and not just one of his subjects that he could control in any way.

That was the side that won in me. I strode past him with.a pip in my step and fought the urge to smirk at him. I could tell by the dumfounded expression on his face, much like the one he had donned when Freya and I had gone dancing, that he liked what he saw.

I turned towards the men traveling with us. Some of them were winged like Mykill, but others were Eryx's soldiers. Their armor was vastly different. Eryx's soldiers armor was a stone gray with lions embellished on the chest plate, and Mykill's was pitch black, designed to look like snake skin. It molded to their bodies perfectly, and their leathers matched their armor. I couldn't tell where the armor started and ended.

There were horses for everyone - including me, thank the Gods. I didn't want to share a horse with Eryx.

"This one's for you," Cadmus said as he placed a hand on my elbow and steered me towards a chocolate brown steed with braids down its mane.

"Beautiful," I gasped as I reached out and stroked a hand down the steed's neck.

He huffed in response and clicked his hooves off the cobblestone. Cadmus offered me his hand as I mounted. I took the reins and waited as everyone readied themselves.

The air around me suddenly whooshed, and feet thudded off the ground. "These are for you."

I slung around to find Mykill with a quiver of arrows and a bow in his hands. "What?" My mouth fell open as I reached numbly for the quiver.

"These are yours," he said again as he shoved the sheath into my extended hand. My fingers traced the leather. There were clouds engraved in the sheath's brown material, and below them were crashing waves at the end of the quiver. The bow was equally as beautiful with a deep mahogany colored wood and gold metal on the ends.

"Thank you," I said as I slung the quiver over my shoulder. "They're beautiful."

He handed me the bow without saying another word. I frowned as he swung around and strode towards Eryx, who's gaze was already trained on us. His hands were fisted at his sides, and his shoulders were drawn up. Tension lined his entire body. His brows were drawn down as his eyes slid to Mykill. He stopped before Eryx, cutting him off from my line of sight.

"That's a cock fight if I've ever seen one," a feminine voice said.

My head swung to the side as Thalia stood beside my steed. Her maroon wings were tucked behind her back and were much smaller than the men's behind her.

Her sleek black hair was pulled back into a slick back ponytail, and a sweep of kohl lined her eyes, darkening them.

"A what?" I flubbered.

"A cock fight?" She raised an eyebrow at me. "Do you not know what that is?"

I shook my head. She crossed her arms over her chest while she laughed before scoffing.

"Let's move out!" Cadmus shouted again, and her head whipped towards him. Her wings extended behind her, and with a push of her legs, she lifted off the ground. The air moved with her wings as she hovered above me, watching the men behind me.

I glanced back and paused as Eryx mounted the horse beside me. He glanced over at me once before focusing ahead of him. He slapped the reins, and his horse began trotting. I followed suit behind him, as did the rest of his guards. We rode to the gates, and the gatekeepers bowed to him as we exited.

Mykill and his men flew above us, almost like we had our own cloud. People stopped and marveled in the streets. A little girl's head dropped back, and she laughed as she pointed at one of Mykill's soldiers. The young girl beside her, who had to be around the age of four, focused on me. She tugged on her sister's arm, and both of their mouths dropped open as their gazes fell on me. My cheeks heated, and I dropped my face to stare into my lap.

"Ignore them," Cadmus said as he cut off my view of the girls. "They're probably just amazed."

"Amazed at my hair and eyes?" I snapped as I tightened my hands around the reins.

"It's rare that someone's hair is colored like yours with eyes that nearly match," Cadmus said softer this time. "It signifies that you're powerful."

"I don't have any powers."

"You do have powers. We just have to figure out how you access them. We need to figure out how you were turned and go from there."

I didn't respond as we continued through the city. Anger burned inside of me the entire way. I didn't wave at anyone. I wasn't going to. I was merely a spectacle to them, a joke. I wouldn't engage with them because, like Lira said, they did treat me like I was beneath them. But if Cadmus was right, then once I finally got a hold of my powers, then I'd show them I was their equal.

After we rode through the city, we crested the hills and into the forests in the opposite direction of the human lands. These forests were thicker but more upkept, most likely because travel between the kingdoms was more normal than travel to the human lands.

I couldn't explain it, but I could feel the eyes watching me from the trees in my gut as we moved down the path. It was like every branch leaned in closer to me as we passed. Maybe they were just as fascinated by my hair as the rest of the world.

Chapter 19

Alethea

After night fell and my stomach growled, we reached the outskirts of a city. The streets weren't made of cobblestone like Linterfame. The buildings weren't as upkept as Eryx's city either. We had passed an old wooden swinging sign a while back that read *Presparia*, but I didn't know if it was one of Eryx's outskirting cities or if we were in another kingdom entirely.

We continued riding since the streets were mostly empty. We passed a few stragglers who didn't glance our way once. As we rode further into the city, the traffic picked up. We passed by bustling taverns with people pouring out of them and music wafting from the insides. We finally stopped at a tavern named *The Busty Beaver*. My nose wrinkled at the name and an image I'd surely never forget.

"They have a stable around the back," Eryx called, and we all followed down a dark alley until we came to the stables. They were mainly empty except for two stable boys, whom Eryx paid handsomely. They took the reins of our horses and led them into the stables one by one. I shouldered my pack and held the other in my free hand as we made our way back down the alley towards the double swinging doors.

"We'll be staying here tonight. If they don't have enough space for us, then we'll be staying in the stables," Eryx said, and I nearly cringed.

The thought of sleeping in dirty stables with horses made my nose scrunch, and my lip curled.

"Don't worry about the rooms," Cadmus said as he brushed his shoulder against mine. "You will have a room no matter how many they have. The rest of us will figure it out."

"Thank you." I nodded to him as we brushed past a loud drunken man twirling one of the barmaids.

We stopped at a round table most of the men had taken up. Eryx sat on one side with an empty chair beside him. My heart stopped as our gazes clashed, and his arm draped across the back of it. He watched me, his expression unreadable. But when I dropped my bag at the back of the chair beside me and sat down, his eyes darkened. Gathering his composure, he glanced towards the other men seating themselves around us.

"The barmaids said that they'll bring out bowls of soup and bread for everyone," a guard said as he pushed his way to the other side of the table.

He took the empty seat beside Eryx. Cadmus sat at my right. Whether it was a coincidence or Eryx had told him to, I wasn't sure, but it was still comforting to sit beside someone I knew instead of total strangers who all looked down on me.

A few minutes passed until two barmaids came out of the kitchen with trays of steaming bowls. They passed them out and set out three baskets of rolls for the table. All of their hands shot for the bread baskets, but they all froze when someone cleared their throat. They looked at the figure behind me that I wasn't going to acknowledge.

"Ladies first," the icy voice behind me spoke and all their eyes darted up once and then back down to the table.

I gritted my teeth as a burn made its way up my neck and face, but I quickly reached for a roll and placed it beside my bowl. "Thank you," I whispered.

After I took my roll, the hands shot back out, fighting to claim a roll. There had definitely been enough for everyone to have one, but several had scooped up two or three in their haste and refused to give them up. I merely paid attention to my bowl, ignoring the eyes that bore into me from across the table. I wanted to kick Eryx under the table. He was acting like a love crazed stalker. I wasn't in danger here. I was surrounded by almost two dozen highly trained men, and I wasn't as weak as I was when I was human.

After I finished, I pushed my empty bowl away and leaned back. I still ignored Eryx and averted my eyes away from his direction. Glazing over my shoulder, I watched as the people dancing all shouted and laughed. Either the music had gotten louder, or the people had. As the night got older, they seemed to be having more fun. I could see several of them dancing around with glasses in their hands that splashed onto the floor, but their smiles were so big it was infectious.

"Will you dance with me?" I asked as I flipped towards Cadmus. I'd rather do anything but sit at this damned table with Eryx watching me like a hawk.

Cadmus's eyes widened in surprise and slowly slid over to Eryx before he nodded. "Of course."

I jumped from my seat, and Cadmus followed as he moved towards the ever-growing crowd. I noticed several of Mykill's men had already joined the group, but I didn't see Mykill himself. He didn't seem like the dancing type.

"I couldn't sit at the same table with him anymore," I groaned as I gripped Cadmus's hand and spun towards him.

Cadmus gripped my hand and spun me away from him.

"He's my best friend," Cadmus said as he spun me back to him. "I know he's hurting, and I know he cares for you, even if he has a shitty way of showing it."

"That still doesn't make the way he's acting okay."

"I know, Alethea." He sighed. "Just give him time. I'll work on him."

"Let's just dance," I said as I grabbed both of his hands and spun him. He laughed as he faced me again, and we danced. One of Mykill's men brought us both a large pint of a frothy drink, and Cadmus dropped his head back as he chugged it. I didn't know what the drink was, but I dropped my head back and followed suit.

It tasted disgusting, but the burn that chased down my throat was numbing.

"Look at her!" one of the guards who had been dancing beside me exclaimed. "She's catching up to you, Cadmus!"

"Shut up, Fern!" someone else shouted, but I didn't look. I was determined to finish the entire thing, even if it did taste like cat piss.

With one final gulp, I stretched my hand with the cup up towards the ceiling, and the crowd around me cheered. Cadmus finished a moment later and laughed as the men behind him shook him by the shoulders, teasing him.

"That's awful!" I exclaimed as someone took my empty glass.

"It'll help you sleep tonight!" Cadmus laughed as he grabbed my hands, and we began to dance again.

We all moved together, clapping, twirling and stomping our feet as the time passed. Sweat beaded my forehead and spine, but all I could do was laugh as Cadmus and I hooked elbows and jumped in a circle again. For the first time in what felt like a long time, I just let myself breathe and enjoy the night.

I could deal with reality tomorrow.

I danced till it felt like I would wear a hole in my shoes, and my cheeks ached from smiling so much. Cadmus pointed me to my room, and I halted as I opened the door. Eryx sat on one of the chairs facing the fireplace with a stick of wood in one hand and a blade in the other.

"You look like you were enjoying yourself," Eryx said quietly as he continued whittling with the piece of wood.

"You could have come to dance," I said as I stepped into the room fully and closed the door behind me.

He sighed as he placed the wood on the table between the two chairs and stood. His eyes were haunted as he turned towards me. My entire body felt glued to the spot as he moved slowly through the room until he was standing in front of me - against me.

His eyes roamed my face, and there was such sadness, such longing behind his cider eyes, that I wanted to reach out and touch him. I wanted to ask him what was wrong, but I knew what was wrong. Things would continue to stay this way between us until he decided he wanted to be entirely truthful with me.

But that didn't stop the sharp inhale of my breath as he leaned into me. His lips brushed against mine, the touch barely there. He hovered there for a moment, waiting for me to push him away. I remained frozen, but my body felt like it was on fire. I sucked in a breath as he sealed the space between our mouths. His hand swept through my hair, cradling my head as he shoved me against the door. My hands found his cheeks as I groaned.

I forgot how good of a kisser he was.

But this wasn't right. I felt it in my chest. It was like trying to put two pieces of a puzzle together that didn't fit anymore. I had changed, and he wasn't willing to keep up with who I was changing into.

"Wait," I panted as I shoved his chest.

His hands dropped immediately as he stepped away. His face was flushed, and his eyes widened as he stared down at me.

"Alethea." He whispered my name like I was one of his Gods, and he was praying to me. The back of his finger brushed down my cheek. "I'm so sorry."

"Sorry isn't enough. Be truthful with me." I pushed off the door and slipped around him. "Tell me why you were invading Kirin's kingdom in the first place. What were you there for?"

"We were there for the map to the Eye."

I nodded. "What did you want the Eye for?"

His mouth fell open, but it snapped closed a moment later. He shook his head, and his gaze dropped.

My mouth tightened, and I glared. "Fine." My hands clenched at my sides. "Goodnight, Eryx."

I turned away from the door as his head dropped. The door opened behind me, and his footsteps paused before it finally closed behind him. Mumbling angrily to myself, I stomped over to my pack on the ground and yanked out a slip. I stripped down to my undergarments, folded my clothes, and shoved them into the pack before changing.

After I changed, I threw myself into the creaky bed. I pulled the covers up to my chin. I turned onto my side and stared out the window as I waited for sleep to claim me.

I didn't expect to get much sleep, but I didn't expect a blaring voice to wake me up at the butt crack of dawn.

"Alethea!" a voice called, and a fist pounded on the door.

I groaned as I rolled onto my back and stared up at the ceiling. My eyes were bleary and swollen as I rubbed at them to help ease some of the puffiness. I resisted the urge to drive a sword through the door.

"Alethea, it's Cadmus. If you don't answer, I'm opening the door!" he shouted through the door.

"I'm up," I responded hoarsely as I shoved out of the bed.

"We're leaving in a half hour, so get dressed. There's breakfast out here for you," he responded before I heard his boots clop down the hall.

I made my way into the washroom, bathed quickly, and pulled out another outfit Lira had packed for me.

It was another fashion statement.

This one consisted of tight black trousers that I tucked into my boots and a billowy cream v-neck tunic with wispy sleeves that draped off my shoulders. I tucked the shirt into the waist of my trousers and threaded the belt through the loops. Copying Lira's movements, I managed to secure the sheath around my thigh. My fingers threaded through my hair as I braided my hair into a braid crown.

The pins were wet from holding them in my mouth, and it didn't turn out as pristine as Lira's did. There were two strands that had slipped out and framed my face, but I decided to leave them. I shouldered my pack and headed down for breakfast.

Our men were scattered throughout the tables, all grumbling to themselves as they ate what looked like a bowl of porridge and a second bowl of dried oats and berries.

I glanced around the room. Mykill sat beside Thalia and the rest of their men. He seemed to sense me staring as his icy eyes latched onto mine, and it felt like they bore down my throat, cooling my insides. He nodded his head in greeting before bringing his cup to his lips and throwing his head back.

"Alethea!" I turned as Cadmus waved me over to where he was sitting with my bowl beside him.

Turning away from Mykill's icy gaze, I headed over to Cadmus and sat down beside him. One of the men finished up, stood, and grabbed my bag at my feet. "I'll strap this to your steed," he said without looking at me.

"Thank you," I called after him, but he paid me no attention.

Breakfast was quick, and we hurried back to the stables as soon as we were ready.

We continued riding through the hills and valleys, but this time, we rode into the night. We didn't stop much except for brief moments so the horses could drink and everyone could relieve themselves. We weren't long into the trip, but my ass already began to ache, and I became restless.

I watched Mykill's wings beat in the air as he led the group of men above us. His men were spread out around us, alert for any threat.

I still felt like there was a pair of eyes on me at all times, but it couldn't be Eryx because I was staring at his rigid back sitting several people ahead of me. It left a pit in the bottom of my stomach that continued to fester.

The sun had set what seemed like hours ago. The forest was nearly silent around us, and we hadn't stopped in a while either.

There was at least six feet between me and the men around me, and they all were focused ahead. Their faces were set in grim lines. Weariness ate at the edges of their stoic demeanors, but they were soldiers. They didn't have a choice to stop. I wondered if they would have stopped if they weren't under Eryx's command.

As the thoughts bounced around inside of my skull, I felt my eyes slipping closed on their own accord. I didn't notice Mykill as he swooped lower and angled his body towards us.

"We need to stop for the night," he said to Eryx as he lowered near him.

Eryx's back remained rigid, and I saw him shake his head. "No, we're riding through the night. Sunrise will be in a few hours."

"She's about to fall off of her horse," Mykill said, his voice barely audible this time.

Eryx shifted towards me, finally glancing at me for the first time since we had left the tavern. I shook my head. "I feel fine."

I was fine. I would make it through the night. I needed to appear stronger than I felt.

"You're not fine," Mykill said to me. He glanced back down at Eryx, who had turned away from me. "She's not a soldier. If we keep going, she's going to pass out."

Eryx huffed out a long sigh before he finally said, "Alright, we'll stop here for the night."

My mouth dropped open in protest, but Cadmus nudged me with his foot. My head whipped towards him, and he shook his head. I bit down on my lip but remained quiet as everyone trotted off the path and headed into the tree line in an effort to remain hidden. When we reached a spot that Eryx found suitable, everyone dismounted. Cadmus took the reins from my hands and tied them to one of the branches for me. If I had done it, then it was sure my steed would have freed himself.

"Sunrise is in a few hours, so get some rest. Rotate watch." Eryx's voice was gruff as he commanded everyone.

He stalked past me, slid down at the base of a tree, and propped his back off of it. His eyes locked with mine. I could see the open invitation in the way he sat and how he kept his arm propped open.

Whipping away from him, I stomped over to the opposite side and took my place up against a tree. I used my pack as a pillow and nuzzled down into it. I ignored the rocks and roots that jutted out of the ground. This was as good a spot as any. The men arranged themselves around me, and I noticed some took up places on the other side of my chosen tree. I resisted the urge to scoff and roll my eyes at Eryx's obvious command. Rolling towards the tree so I couldn't see anyone, I closed my eyes, and just before sleep consumed me, I felt the weight of a blanket drape over me.

✳✳✳

It didn't feel like we slept for a few minutes, much less a few hours. I could see the tiredness in everyone's eyes, but we knew we needed to keep going if we were going to arrive on time. My ass was surely bruised from sitting on this damned horse. I had never ridden so much in my life. I couldn't believe that Eryx's men rode them as if nothing was wrong. Every bump caused me to wince.

The sky was stunning as the sun slowly rose. It was the perfect distraction. I could hear the sounds of birds awakening and calling out to each other. The branches bounced and swayed as squirrels ran across them in pursuit of one another. The sky turned from pink, to orange, to blue, until the sun finally poked up from behind the mountains from its slumber. At least the sun was well rested.

As we continued riding, the terrain changed from a forest to a very narrow path carved on the side of a mountain, overlooking a glooming cliff that fell into rocks. Surely, I'd be impaled if I fell over the edge. I kept my eyes glued to the horse in front of me to keep me from looking over the edge until we finally trotted through the mountain into miles of rolling hills.

I regretted not putting my hair back in a braid as the day began to heat. It had fallen out while I slept, and I didn't have time to fix it. We didn't have any trees for cover, and there were barely any trees scattered around us throughout the endless fields of grass.

Finally, a large city crested the top of the hill, and I could have cried because I was so relieved. A city meant beds, baths, and most importantly, food.

As we neared the city, the first thing I noticed was the smell. I gagged and covered my face with the hem of my sleeve.

"Gods!" I exclaimed as I coughed. "What is that?"

"Fish," one of the guards beside me laughed. "It smells terrible here, and it's only going to get worse the closer to the docks we get."

I didn't believe him, but he was right. The stench was so bad my eyes were nearly watering as we rode through the streets. We found some stables that we could keep the horses at until we returned and headed to the shores on foot. My stomach was practically roaring, and the sun was at its highest peak. The back of my neck was drenched in sweat because I left my hair down. That was a massive mistake.

I nearly asked Eryx if we could stop for some food because I was starving, but I decided against it. They had already stopped last night because I had been tired. I wasn't going to make them stop for me again.

I hoisted my pack further up my shoulder and apologized as I bumped into one of the guards. People stared at us as we passed, and I ducked my head. I wasn't interested in being a spectacle as we passed by, and I didn't want to see their faces when they saw my eyes.

Someone's shoulder bumped into mine, and I snapped my head up. My eyes were met with a bundled napkin that held a vine of grapes and a buttered biscuit. My eyes moved further up to see Mykill's marbled face staring straight ahead. His icy eyes bore ahead like he wasn't trying to hand me something.

"Thank you," I muttered in disbelief as I took the napkin.

He strode ahead of me without a word, and I carelessly dug into the food. I still wanted a real meal, but it would be enough to hold me off until we sat down for one. My mouth nearly watered as I popped three grapes in my mouth at one time. I was so distracted by the food that I didn't realize we had made it to the docks.

My nose had eventually adjusted to the smell, and my eyes no longer watered. We were overlooking the fresh open sea, and it was stunning. The sun reflected off the waves, making the surface appear like it was crusted with hundreds of glittering diamonds. Waves lapped at the pilings beneath our feet and crashed into the rocky edge. The sound was almost calming. Seagulls called out to one another and swooped down in search of any stray food they could find.

"King Eryx!" a hulking man boomed as we stopped before a massive ship. The wood was stained a deep red, and there were elaborate carvings and borders of thick gold.

The Empress was embroidered in swirly black writing across the hull.

"Were you sent by Vestor?" Eryx asked as we all stopped. The man smiled at us. His smile seemed too big for his face, and his teeth were halfway rotted.

"Aye, I'm Captain!" he exclaimed as he extended his hand and clapped me on the shoulder. I nearly stumbled forward from the blow, but I willed my spine to remain rod-straight and adjusted my pack on my shoulder. "We're ready for you all. There are rooms for the ladies below deck, and we set sail within the hour."

"Thank you, Captain," Eryx said as he turned to the wooden ramp that led up to the deck.

"Welcome to The Empress," the Captain greeted as we all filed into a single line and boarded the ship. It swayed briefly beneath my feet as the waves continued. I had never been on a boat, and Lira had briefly mentioned how she had gotten sea-sick whenever she was on one.

I followed the line of soldiers to a set of stairs that led below deck. The space was large and filled with hammocks throughout the room. The soldiers all dispersed, dropping their belongings at their chosen hammocks. I glanced around and found another set of stairs that led to another level. It looked like a kitchen and dining hall. Through the back, there was a long hall with open doors. I claimed one of the bedrooms. They were cramped and tiny with nothing but a bed and a wardrobe, but it was better than sleeping in a hammock. There was a small door at the foot of the bed that led into a small washroom with nothing but a tub, a bucket, and a pile of washcloths on the ground. I wrinkled my nose and turned.

I dropped my bags at the end of the bed and gasped as a wave rocked the boat. I lurched forward and collapsed on the bed. I did my best to not throw up the small breakfast Mykill gave me. Even after the water calmed, I remained on the bed, eventually rolling onto my side. My eyes felt heavy, and my body was spent. I didn't even bother closing the door as my eyes closed.

Chapter 20

Alethea

My feet moved slowly as I crept silently down the hall. The boat rocked as I clutched onto the wall and door frames as I passed them. A low whistle echoed all around me. It sounded like it was beside me, but whenever I turned, there was no one. A chill crept up my spine, waiting, like it was biding its time until it wound around my neck.

I entered the dining hall. There was not a single soul. The further into the ship I moved, the harder my heart pumped. I made my way up the stairs to the room full of cots, and there was no one. There weren't discarded bags like there had been before; it was like I was on a ghost ship.

I forced my feet to quicken as fear pumped through me, and I ran up the last flight of stairs. As I broke onto the deck, my chest heaved as I spun around in a circle. The ropes all hung from the beams above us, and water sprayed over the side of the boat as it rocked violently. Lightning stuck across the sky, lighting it up, and I cried out as I fell forward.

A wave of water doused me as it crashed onto the deck. I kicked away the fish that had been stolen from the water and shoved myself to my feet.

"Hello?" I called as I spun around. "Is anyone here?"

My cries became more frantic as I ran to the edge of the boat to overlook the storm. My heart dropped into my stomach as I gripped the railing and stared over the side. The water that was supposed to be blue was stained red. Men, winged and wingless, floated throughout the water. Some of their faces were familiar, others were not.

Eryx. Cadmus. Mykill. Even Captain.

"No," I gasped as I covered my mouth. "No, no, no, no," I kept repeating.

A laugh echoed around me, nowhere and everywhere all at once. Spinning around, I froze as a barren stood before me. But he didn't appear as. a normal barren. He was thicker, muscles corded his arms and legs and there was a crown woven along his head with spikes that dug into his skull and rotted berries that hung from it. He laughed as he stepped towards me. and I fell back. a step into the railing.

I spun as the sound of waves crashing sounded and fear pumped through me as a wave a hundred times taller than the boat rose and barreled towards us. I felt tears stinging my eyes as I stumbled back a step and fell backwards. I cried out as my back hit the deck. The wall of water got closer, curling in on itself. I screamed as I covered my face and brought my knees to my chest. I took one last breath before the wave hit the deck, and I was lifted from the boat, thrown into the sea.

My hands clawed at my throat as I wrenched up from the bed. My chest heaved, and my heart beat so loudly in my chest I was sure everyone could hear it. There was a fine sheen of sweat covering nearly my entire body. Pushing myself to my feet, I wiped my hair away from my face as my breathing evened out. I wiped the back of my neck and took a deep breath. I ran my fingers through my hair, needing to feel something to remind myself that I was safe. My eyes scanned around the room. The scent of the sea breeze wafted even all the way down here, and I could hear loud roaring laughter upstairs.

As my nerves began to calm, I made my way back upstairs. There were a few men straggling in the dining hall, but they didn't pay attention to me as I passed by them. I took the stairs up to the level full of cots, and I noticed two of our men lounging on their chosen cots. I tried to keep my footfalls silent as I crept up to the deck. As I stepped above deck, I noticed a group of men who were all circled around a small table with cards. The two men playing had pulled up barrels to sit on, and everyone else gathered around them, gazing over their shoulder.

"Ah, the fair lady," the Captain called and bowed dramatically at the waist.

I smiled at him and waved him off. "Please, just call me Alethea."

"A beautiful name, miss, truly." He beamed as he slipped his arm through mine and began giving me a tour above deck.

"As the sun sets, the men make their way to the common room. There's drinks, cards, and sometimes they play music, so feel free to join them later. We don't have much that we can offer you in terms of elegance. The food merely consists of some soups, beans, and rice -"

He continued his tour, and we strode across the deck. I smiled and patted his arm. He was chivalrous, I'll give him that. "I'm perfectly content, but thank you, Captain."

He offered me a toothy grin before releasing my arm and turning to command his sailors. I watched as they moved around beams and ropes, tossing them to one another, and pulling. They work together in a blend of unity and familiarity.

"Have you ever been over the sea before?" a cold voice said behind me, and a tall figure stepped in front of me.

I paused as I looked up at Mykill. His eyes roamed around me, taking in the ocean.

"No," I answered as I stared up at him.

I frowned and waited for him to continue. He had never been one for small talk, so there had to be a reason why he was prodding me.

"How long is the trip to Gild?" I finally asked when he didn't say anything else.

His eyes slid over to mine as he clasped his hands behind his back. "We should be arriving there tomorrow evening."

"Have you ever been?"

He shook his head. "They've never been open to visitors."

He stepped around me, and I followed. "Why did you agree to come?" I decided to ask as I draped my arms over the railing.

He didn't answer right away, contemplating what to say. "I'm curious."

I frowned as I looked at him. "Curious of what?"

"Why they have kept to themselves for so long," he answered as he turned his head to meet my gaze. His brows were drawn together, and there was a storm brewing in his icy eyes.

I frowned at him and then nodded as I glanced back out at the water. The sun had begun to set, and I could hear the Captain telling some of his men to take a break for the evening.

"It looks like the party that he promised is starting," Mykill said as he pushed off the railing. "I'll see you down there."

I didn't answer him as I watched him retreat below deck. Sighing, I turned back towards the ocean and listened to the slow swaying of the water. The sky had turned a beautiful blend of purple, pink and orange, as the sun made its way to its slumbering place for the night.

Sometimes I'd sit and wonder what the sun did when it went to sleep. I had always been told the stories about how the sun and moon had been forbidden lovers, sentenced to an eternity of never being able to touch. Maybe it wept when it was alone.

My sister and I would sometimes sneak out early in the morning to watch the sunrise. There was an old oak tree we would find with the perfect branches at the top for us to sit on. We would sweat as we pulled ourselves up branch after branch, exerting all our energy. When we got to the top, Laney would pull out the desserts she had snatched, and we would split them as we watched the sun wake up, bringing the forest along with it.

There was nothing more serene.

I sighed as I pushed off the railing. The deck had nearly emptied out with maybe three or four stragglers who were typing up rope or whatnot. I could hear the faint sound of cheering and shouting from below deck.

I headed down to my room and changed into a lighter dress Lira had packed for me, I braided my hair and draped it over my shoulder. The laughter floated down the hall as I stepped out of my bedroom and closed the door behind me. As I entered the dining hall, I smiled as I watched the dance they were doing. It was one that normally the entire crowd joins in on, but it seemed there were only two men who were competing. I laughed as I slipped into the room.

I sensed Eryx before I laid eyes on him. I could feel his eyes burning into me as I made my way around in search of a spot to perch to look upon the festivities.

"Would you like to dance?" I halted and turned as one of the Captain's men asked.

My mouth fell open in shock, and then I smiled. "I'd love to." I took his outstretched hand, and he led me to the middle of the crowd.

The song had changed, and everyone had joined in. It was a dance I learned when I was a girl.

The man laughed as we hooked elbows and danced in a circle. We released each other, spun around, and repeated the action. The fiddle continued to play, and we continued to dance. The music lit me up from the inside. I smiled so widely and laughed so loudly; I wished the night would last forever.

I laughed as we stopped before each other, bowed, and turned to applaud the musicians. The man placed a hand on my back as we moved through the crowd in search of a seat to rest our feet for a few minutes. My blood nearly went cold as I noticed Eryx and Mykill on separate sides of the table, and they both were glaring daggers at the man behind me. My feet halted, and I spun back around.

"Maybe we should keep dancing," I said as I peered up at him.

He offered me a smile and took my hand as we rejoined the group dancing. We spent the remainder of the night dancing. I could get lost in the movements for the remainder of my life and never tire of it. I couldn't think of anything more joyful than becoming one with the music. There was no worry when I was dancing. My thoughts quieted, and my body took over. It was one of the only times I was able to relax. The alcohol made it easier too. The more alcohol I drank, the freer I felt.

I didn't realize how many drinks I had before my feet tumbled one over the other, and I crashed into a hard chest.

"I think that's enough, Alethea," Eryx grumbled down at me as he softly gripped my arm.

Laughter bubbled out of me, and I gripped his hand before I spun myself. "Dance with me!" I exclaimed.

I spun once, but my feet caught on my dress, and I went tumbling again. I couldn't find it in me to feel scared. All I could do was smile. An arm wrapped around my waist to pull me upright, and I giggled.

"Let's get you to your room," Eryx said into my ear and lifted me off my feet.

I laughed as he tossed me over his shoulder. "See you later boys!" I shouted and tried to salute them, but my hands hung limply.

I watched as they swung side to side with his steps. I knew he was tall, but it looked like I was dangling from a tree. After several more minutes, he placed me down on my feet.

"Go to bed, Alethea," he said and went to reach behind me, but I jumped at him.

"Lay with me," I breathed as I gripped his cheeks and raised onto my toes.

He groaned as our lips brushed, but his hands wrapped around my wrists, and he pulled them away from his face. "You need to sleep, Alethea. You've had too much to drink."

"Nonsense," I giggled again. "I feel fine. My head's spinning a little, but it's better that way."

"Go to bed, Alethea," Eryx said as he released me fully and reached behind me to open the door.

I groaned and rolled my eyes at him. "Fine. You never know how to have any fun," I said as I rolled across the wall and into the room. "Good night!" I called as he closed the door behind him.

***

Eryx had been right. I drank entirely too much. When I woke up, my head was pounding so badly that I could only squint as I stepped into the dining hall. The candles lit throughout stabbed my eyes and pierced through to my skull. I groaned as I plopped down next to Cadmus, who was in a less than engaging conversation with the Captain about gutting a fish.

"As enticing as this conversation is, can you quiet down please?" I covered a hand over my eyes and groaned again.

The Captain let out a booming laugh, and I dropped my head on the table. "Someone had too much fun down here, I see?"

"If I had my dagger with me, I'd run it through your throat," I mumbled.

The Captain laughed even louder at that.

"Here," Cadmus said softly as he sat back down beside me.

I forced my eyes open and found a bowl of oats sprinkled with a layer of nuts. There was a basket of biscuits in the center of the table but no butter or jam to go with them.

"Thank you," I grumbled as I picked up the spoon and began picking at the oats.

After breakfast, a group and I circled around one of the crew members as he told us the story of how he lost his eye. The sun beat down on us, causing sweat to trickle down my spine as I leaned forward to hear him better.

"And then the man jumped at me. I told him again that I didn't have any money." He grinned slyly as he looked around at the crowd that had gathered around us. "But I kept it where the sun don't shine, if ya know what I mean?" I cringed as I sat back. "After I told him I didn't have any money again, he lunged at me. The next thing I knew, I was screaming in a puddle of me own blood. He took me eye and me pinky." He held up his right hand, and I cringed again.

"Lotto!" the Captain shouted, drawing our attention towards him. "We're approaching Deadman's Grove!"

"What's Deadman's Grove?" Cadmus asked as he stood up beside me.

"Siren infested waters," the Captain answered as he started shouting orders. "Everyone, assemble around the masts!"

I glanced over at Cadmus and Mykill as they both stepped closer to me. Cadmus placed a hand on the small of my back as he led me to the nearest mast. Eryx was already standing beside it on the other side as I glanced at the chains that hung around the mast. There were shackles on the end of the chains, and some of them had dried layers of blood on them.

"The sirens don't care who you are, man or woman. They will lure you into the water and shred you with their nails," Captain warned. "Get the cotton in your ears, and keep it there. It's enchanted and will block out the sound of their singing."

Mykill locked the shackle beside mine around his wrist and took the balls of cotton Thalia offered. He ripped them into smaller balls and shoved them in his ears before handing me the remaining balls. I secured the shackle around my wrist before I glanced at Cadmus beside me and Eryx on the other side. Five of us were tethered to this mast, and five others were tethered to the second a few feet away. The others seemed to have gone below deck and were tethering themselves down there.

As I glanced back at the sea, I searched for any sign of life among the open waters. But, as far as my eyes could tell, the water just shifted.

Turning back towards the mast, I tested my shackle one more time and went to put the cotton in my ears when my entire body stiffened. A soft melody drifted up to me, and I gasped as I flipped around. The music lured me, wrapping around my joints and muscles. It pulled me towards it, and my body craved to know where that sound was coming from. The music was like the air in my lungs. If I didn't find it, then I would die.

"Alethea," Mykill said as I moved out of his reach and let the cotton slip from my fingers.

I started towards the edge of the ship but was brought up short as the chain stopped me. Glaring down at the shackle around my wrist, I tugged against it. I needed to get to the water. I tugged again, but my wrist wouldn't slip free. I used every ounce of strength until I heard a loud *crack*, and my wrist was free. I felt pain radiate up my wrist and mangled fingers, but I knew with my new fae body, that I'd heal quickly. It was a small pain compared to the bliss I knew I'd feel when I reached the source of the music.

"She broke her own wrist!" a voice shouted. "Someone grab her!"

I ran forward until I hit the edge of the ship. My eyes scanned the surface of the water, looking for the source of the beautiful music.

My eyes narrowed on a brunette woman with only her eyes peeking above the surface of the water. Her eyes were the color of glowing emeralds. Her hair stuck to the sides of her face as she slowly raised up above the surface, uncovering an elegant pointed nose and full pink lips. She was stunning.

"Someone grab her!" a voice shouted again, and without looking back, I gripped the edges and jumped.

Someone screamed my name before I hit the water. I pulled in a breath before I was submerged. I caught sight of a glimmering tail that was longer than my body through the wall of bubbles around me. I moved my arms, pumping them as I searched for the source of the music.

The music seemed louder as I flipped back and forth until I felt fingers skim up the back of my neck. Relief nearly coursed through me as I flipped back around and faced the woman I had seen before. She smiled at me, revealing perfectly white teeth, and then the music stopped. Her glowing eyes darkened, and I screamed as the siren smiled at me, revealing her elongated canines. Water filled my mouth, and I instinctively inhaled. Water rushed down my nose and throat, filling my lungs, as I pushed backwards. She slashed at me, and I threw my arms up to protect myself. Pain flared up my arms as her nails shredded through my skin. I kicked my feet, desperate to get away. My eyes burned, and I didn't have another choice but to close them as I splashed around, uselessly looking for the surface of the water. My lungs burned from lack of oxygen.

Firm hands grasped my face and shook me. My eyes flew open, and Cadmus was pressing his face closer to mine. He slipped an arm around my waist and pulled me to him as he pushed for the surface of the water.

"Mykill!" Cadmus screamed, the cotton making him yell louder.

I felt a hand tighten around my ankle as I coughed up water. Then, the lyrics reached for me again, beckoning me back into the water. I struggled against Cadmus's hold as he yanked on the rope.

"Pull us up!" he shouted up.

"I need to get back!" I shouted.

I screamed, the sound ripping from my throat as nails raked down my arm. My flesh ripped open, and the salt water burned as I thrashed. I wasn't making it easy for Cadmus, and I wasn't going to. I just knew I needed to get back in the water.

"Please, let me go!" I pounded my hands against his arm, desperate for him to let me go.

"Just hold on," he grunted.

"Grab him!" another voice screamed, and I heard the sound of another body hitting the water. "Man overboard!"

"Please," I cried as I threw myself forward, but Cadmus refused to release me. His arm tightened around my waist as our heads were pulled above the side of the ship. Arms reached over the edges and pulled us over.

"Alethea," Eryx gasped as Cadmus dropped me on the deck.

The scratches on my arms seared into my bones, but I wanted to go back into the water. "I need to get back!" I cried as I threw myself forward.

"Alethea, stop!" I shoved Cadmus away from me, sending him tumbling over himself.

Another set of strong arms yanked me backwards and flipped me onto my back.

"Let me go!" I screamed as Mykill pinned my wrists to my chest. I grunted as I tried to bring my knee up to knock him off me.

Mykill grunted and chuckled as he deflected my knee. "Trying to hit me where it hurts, huh?"

I screamed as he circled his arms around me, successfully pinning my arms to my chest, and he rolled. He was rolling us away from the water. He made sure to angle his body just enough to not crush me.

"Get me cotton!" he shouted, and I felt fingers on my head. I kicked my heels into the ground as my head was turned to the side. A ball of cotton was shoved into my ear, my head was turned, and more cotton was shoved in my other ear. The music drowned out, and I heard Mykill whispering to me. My chest heaved as reality crashed into me.

"It's okay. It's okay," Mykill said breathlessly as he held me against him.

My body trembled from the cold, the pain in my wrist, and the fire in my arms. His body heated mine as Captain yelled something in the background.

"It's okay," he whispered again, almost as if he was telling himself, not me. One of his hands cupped my head, keeping me pinned to his chest, and I closed my eyes. "You're alright."

Both of our chests heaved as we laid there. The scent of his breath engulfed me, calming me.

"I'm okay," I finally whispered as I uncurled my fingers from his vest and opened my eyes. I hadn't noticed he had opened his wings, shielding me from the view of everyone else and retaining the warmth.

Mykill pulled away slightly, searching my face before nodding and pushing himself off me. He shoved himself to his feet as the Captain approached us.

"Are you alright, girl?" Captain asked as he frowned down at me. "You gave us all a pretty good scare."

"I'm alright," I said softly as he reached a hand down for me and pulled me to my feet.

I froze as my gaze clashed with Eryx's. His brows were drawn down, and a scowl was written across his face. His cider eyes darkened, and for a moment, I swear hatred flashed across his features before he tucked it away.

"We lost a soul," the Captain said as he stared at the water behind us. "Curiosity got the best of him."

"Who was it?" I demanded as I looked around the group of people looking for the missing person.

"It was Lorne," one of the guards said. His shoulders sagged, and his eyes were filled with unshed tears. "He was my best friend."

"I'm sorry," I whispered to him as sympathy crashed through me. "I know what it's like to lose someone you love. When this is all over, we will give him the burial he deserves."

The guard nodded at me. "Thank you, My Lady." He bowed his head before slipping back into the group of guards.

I turned back towards Mykill, Cadmus, and Eryx, who were all staring at me with concern. "I'm going to go downstairs and change."

Turning from them, I booked it down the stairs to my cabin. I pushed past Thalia and two other people before I threw the door open and slammed it behind me. Tears streamed down my face as I stormed towards the washroom while stripping off my wet clothes. I started a hot bath and slipped in while the water was still filling.

I had almost gotten Cadmus killed. My friend had almost died because of my stupidity.

Grabbing the bar of soap on the ledge, tears streamed down my face as I scrubbed at the already fading cuts. The water turned pink as I scrubbed my blood off of me.

How could I have been so careless? Why did it take me so long to shove the damn cotton in my ears?

I was tired of people risking their lives for me. I shrieked as I threw the bar of soap into the water and fell back. The water splashed around me and spilt over the sides as I stopped. My heart pounded in my ears, but the burn in my skin was slowly disappearing. I closed my eyes and laid in the tub until the water ran cold.

Chapter 21

Alethea

I brushed my fingers through my now dry hair. I knew I needed to leave my room before someone came looking for me to see if I was okay. I changed into another pair of leggings, a flowing tunic with billowing sleeves, and a belt to accent around my waist. My boots were still drying, so I was barefoot as I stepped into the hallway and made my way towards the dining hall.

I paused at the threshold of the doorway to the dining hall as Mykill's gaze clashed with mine. His wings were folded neatly behind him, but he was the only one besides me.

"Hello, Alethea," he said softly as he swirled the drink around in his glass.

"I'm sorry," I said softly as he gazed at me.

"For biting me, punching me, or trying to kick me in the balls?" He quirked an eyebrow at me as he raised the glass to his lips.

"I didn't realize I bit you," I said sheepishly as I slid onto the bench across from him.

The glass thudded off the wooden table as he placed the glass down. A small smile tugged at the corner of his mouth. "You broke my skin in some places, but don't worry. It healed quickly."

"I didn't realize their call could be so alluring." My voice was quiet as I tugged at one of my fingers.

He made a noise of agreement and slid his glass across the table to me. "You seem like you need it more than me."

I looked up at him as I gripped the glass and sniffed it. "What is it?"

"Rum," he answered as he extended his wings on either side of him, stretching them.

Glancing back at the amber liquid, I dropped my head back and drank. I immediately hissed as it burned its way down my esophagus. "That's awful," I croaked as I placed the glass back down.

He laughed lightly. "It is," he agreed.

"Land ho!" a voice shouted from above deck. "Everyone to the deck!"

Mykill frowned and pushed himself up. I followed behind him as we started up the two flights of stairs. As we made our way to the rails, I gasped as I took in the city before us. Parts of the city rested on the shore. A range of mountains nested behind the gray castle. It was beautiful and elegant, but it was much smaller than Eryx's castle.

Men waited for us on the shore. There was a single carriage and a dozen empty horses accompanied by another dozen horses with men on them.

"Welcome to Gild," a man in yellow and green robes said as he extended his arms on either side of him. "I am the royal advisor, Nikolai. We will escort you to the palace."

The crew hustled around us as they prepared for us to deboard. They threw ropes around, secured them, and laid out a wooden plank with rope handles that rested in the sand.

"We'll be waiting here for you when you're ready to depart," the Captain said as we began to deboard in a file.

The sand shifted beneath my feet as I stopped and waited for instructions. Nikolai smiled as Eryx and Mykill both stopped beside me.

"A carriage for the Kings," Nikolai bowed at the waist as Eryx and Mykill passed him.

"I'll fly, thank you," Mykill said as he pushed off the ground. His men and Thalia followed suit.

I went to brush past Eryx to head towards one of the horses, but his hand grabbed mine. I paused as his fingers wrapped around my wrist and frowned at him.

"You come with us in the carriage," he said firmly.

I opened my mouth to argue, but Cadmus nudged me in the side with his elbow, and I snapped my mouth shut. Eryx dropped his hold of my wrist but kept close to me with a hand placed on my back as his men made their way to their horses. He opened the door to the carriage, and I ducked as I slid onto one of the benches. Eryx shifted as he ducked and slid in across from me. One of the other guards closed the door behind him.

I gripped my arm as I stared out the side window. Unease bloomed in my chest as we hobbled along, bouncing at every rock on the road. Eryx didn't say anything, although I couldn't tell if that made the tension between us worse or better. I could sense the unspoken words on his tongue the entire ride.

The last time we had been in a carriage alone the outcome had been much different.

Once we reached the castle, I didn't wait for a guard to open the door. I sighed as I threw it open and breathed in the fresh air. My eyes landed on Mykill, who seemed to have been waiting for me as he stared at me. His gaze shifted behind me to Eryx, and I could feel the hatred radiating between the two of them. It shocked me that they managed to remain cordial with one another for so long.

"This way," Nikolai called, drawing my attention.

Following down the path behind him, we walked through an outside hall through elaborate columns. His feet clacked off the stone as he stopped and turned on his heel. He held up his hands, and the sound of his bracelets sounded like coils rustling together in a bag. "May I present, King Gild, the king of the Gild Kingdom." He bowed, and I resisted the urge to snicker as he turned towards the door.

"His name is actually Gild? He can't be serious," I whispered to Cadmus as he stepped up beside me.

"He is," he whispered back as we followed Eryx and Mykill through the doors.

"Your Majesty." The man on the throne immediately rose. He ripped the crown off of his own head, and it thudded off the ground as he bowed on one knee.

"There's no reason for that," Eryx said and waved a hand at him.

"I'm not bowing to you," the man said and raised his head, eyes wide in astonishment. "I'm bowing to her."

Eryx's head snapped towards me. I felt Cadmus and Mykill's gazes burn into me from behind. My skin prickled as every set of eyes in the room turned to me.

"I'm not royalty," I said and held up my hands. I resisted the urge to take a step back and run.

"Your Majesty," the king said again as he rose. "I have seen your face on the statue of the Divine. It is one I will not forget."

I shook my head. "You must be mistaken. I'm -" I paused before I stuttered. "I was a human but was turned fae. I can promise you that I am no royal."

"You're the one the prophecy speaks of?" he gasped, and his mouth fell open. His eyes widened, and a flush spread across his face. "Goddess," he whispered in what seemed like awe.

"She is. We should discuss this in your personal office," Eryx said as he stepped forward and blocked my view of him.

"What's your name?" the King asked, ignoring Eryx.

I poked my head around Eryx's shoulder. "Alethea."

"All hail, Alethea, the gift from the Divine." He didn't even finish his sentence before he lowered to one knee and bowed his head. The subjects and guards around him all bowed, following suit.

Eryx glanced back at me, his eyes wide in shock and disbelief. He reluctantly stooped to his knees and bowed his head. But I wasn't seeing him anymore. Mykill was the first to kneel, without question. His head bowed, and he placed a fisted hand over his heart. When he finally raised his head to meet my gaze, he winked at me. My mouth fell open, but I had no words as I stared around to every bowed head. This was wrong - so, so wrong.

"The one to purify us all," the King finished before rising. "Please, dinner is prepared for you all. Follow Nikolai. I will join you in a moment."

Gild's dining room was set up much differently than Eryx's. There were two tables decorated simply with a white runner and vines that twisted around simple white candles with wax pooling around them. There was a third table that overlooked the two with more elaborate place settings. The table cloth was a deep green, and Gild's crest was printed on it in bright gold.

The crest was nothing more than what appeared to be a silhouette of a crow resting on the branch of a thorn bush.

"Come here, King Eryx, King Mykill, and Alethea Divine," Nikolai waved towards us.

My face flushed at the name, but I followed. They seated us at the table overlooking the other two tables. I sat between Mykill and Eryx, both of them so close to me our arms brushed.

Maids poured out from a side door with plates in their hands. I gave thanks as a maid placed a plated bowl that brimmed with a creamy soup. My stomach growled in response, and I stiffened as I heard Mykill chuckle beside me. My gaze became murderous as my eyes slid to him, and he was hiding his laugh behind his napkin like a coward.

"If you keep laughing at me," I threatened as I pointed a finger at him and stiffened even more as my stomach roared as the scent of the food hit my nose.

"Please," Mykill waved to his plate. "Eat mine if you need. I think you've starved the beast for entirely too long."

I clenched my teeth and whipped my head away from him. "You're not funny."

Mykill's answer was only a laugh, and I ignored him as Gild took his seat on the other side of Eryx.

He picked up the goblet that the maid filled and took a deep drink before rising back to his feet.

"Tomorrow we will host a ball!" Gild cheered as he raised his golden goblet.

His wine spilled onto his hand, but he didn't seem to notice as he laughed. The subjects cheered and laughed as they all toasted.

"To Alethea Divine!" he cheered.

They all smiled at me as if I was a savior, but I wasn't the savior of anything. I hadn't been able to save my family, the most important people in my life, so I had no clue how I was supposed to save these people. I didn't even know what I was saving them from. No one was truthful with me as to what was going on. I knew there was a storm brewing, but I didn't know what side of it we would fall on.

The next morning, King Gild had seamstresses sent up to my room for a dress fitting. The seamstresses said he wanted something more elaborate than anything they had ever sown.

The dress truly was marvelous. It was something a queen would wear. The dress was strapless with a simple a-line bust, but the bottom half of the dress puffed out at least two feet on all sides of me. It was as black as night, but the overlayers of black tulle shimmered golden beneath the light.

After they took my measurements, they helped me out of the gown, and I slid on a silk robe. I cinched it around my waist and didn't care about putting on clothes beneath it as I made my way outside. I had seen a small sitting space that had called to me the moment I passed it. After searching for the wine cellar, I managed to find a bottle of wine and held it to my chest as I lounged in one of the chairs.

Ducking my head back, I took a deep swig and welcomed the sting in the back of my throat. Cadmus had been right. The alcohol had been helping me sleep.

"Are you sure that's necessary?" a cold voice asked behind me, drawing me from my thoughts.

I didn't need to look to know who it was.

"I have been standing, poked, and prodded at with needles all morning, I feel it's justified," I snapped as Mykill sat across from me.

He didn't say anything as he propped his feet up on the small center table adorned with a glass apple resting on two books. I glanced up at Mykill over the rim of my bottle and dropped my head back as I drank. I hissed and sat forward. The glass thudded off the small wooden table, and I sat back.

"If you have something you want to say, then say it."

Mykill sighed in response. "The stress seems to be getting to you."

I laughed harshly. "Stress? What stress? Do you think being told that I'm the kingdom's savior when I have no idea who they're talking about is stressful? No." I waved a hand towards him.

"You don't have to hide it," Mykill said.

I couldn't help but laugh again. "Don't I? No one seems to want to tell me what's going on anyway, so why does it matter?"

"What would you like to know?" He raised an eyebrow at me.

My mouth fell open, but my mind drew blank. I didn't know what I wanted to ask first.

"What does this prophecy have to do with me?"

"I don't know much about it other than the part about a human girl born of fae blood."

"So you don't know the full prophecy?"

He shook his head. "No. I've only heard whispers about it. It's been rumored for thousands of years. Our realm has always teetered on the verge of war, but this is the closest we have been."

"What's pushing you so close now?"

"Barren attacks are increasing. There have been reports about it across the entire Inner Kingdom."

"What's the Inner Kingdom?" I frowned.

"It's a collection of Kings who decided to sign a treaty of peace. Each King would rule over their own land, but the laws were the same for each."

"And you're a part of the Inner Kingdom?" He nodded at my question. "Why have you stayed and helped Eryx for so long?"

"Because I'm bound by the Treaty." He sighed as he stretched his arms over his head. "Whenever a King's mate is endangered, we are obligated to help."

I nodded. My focus shifted to the tree above us, swaying in the wind as it dropped its leaves on us.

"Are you coming to the ball tonight?" I asked as I leaned forward and reached for the wine bottle.

Mykill didn't move. He didn't even speak as the bottle drifted away from my grasp. I hissed as my gaze snapped up to him as the bottle floated to his hands.

"Stop trying to drown your sorrows," he said, and the bottle disappeared entirely.

I jumped to my feet and almost screamed in frustration. "Why did you do that?"

"Because you're using it as a crutch. You're using it as a way to avoid feeling, and I won't allow that."

I opened my mouth to respond but snapped it closed. He was right. I knew he was right, but I wasn't going to tell him that. I didn't say anything as I spun away from him. Hot tears streamed down my face as I stormed towards my room. Thankfully, there were no lady's maids when I slammed the door behind me and threw myself beneath the covers.

After some hours, the lady's maids returned and lured me out of bed. The ball started in a few hours, and they needed to help me get ready.

I stood like a statue as they slid on the dress. It formed against my body, hugging my breasts and hips. My arms were on display, but the back was high enough that my scars wouldn't be seen. They used their magic to curl my hair. They would simply hold a piece of hair in their hands, run their fingers through it, and it would curl as they went. I only hoped I could do the same one day.

After doing my hair, they moved onto my face. I begged them to leave the majority of my face clear, and thankfully, they obliged. They merely swept the black paste on my eyelashes to lengthen them and added a pink powder to my cheeks.

I spun in the mirror, taking in my reflection. I paused as one of the ladies stepped up beside me with a dagger and sheath.

"What's that?" I asked.

"It's a gift from King Gild," she said softly as she began to strap the sheath to my arm and slid the dagger in place.

It was a gold dagger with a pitch black jewel embedded at the base of the hilt. A dragon was carved into the gold metal. It was menacing.

As she finished strapping the dagger to my arm, she stepped back and admired her work.

"Thank you," I said lightly, and they both bowed.

They escorted me down the halls, where the ball was being hosted. Mykill and Eryx were both standing beside Gild before a set of closed double doors.

"Ah, stunning," Gild said as he spun towards me. Mykill and Eryx followed.

Both of them froze mid step as they took me in. I felt the blush creep up my neck as I stopped between them. "Thank you." I bowed my head to Gild. "Thank you for the blade. It's stunning."

"It was the least I could do." He bowed his head back and looked at the three of us. "I will introduce you to my subjects."

They both nodded, not daring to speak a word. Gild paused as he glanced over at us over his shoulder.

"Go on, clasp arms." He waved sporadically at us before turning back towards the door.

I glanced at Mykill first, and he offered his arm to me. I paused as I sucked in a breath. There was a storm brewing behind his eyes again as he took me in. I slid one arm into his grasp and turned to Eryx, sliding my other arm in his. He was wearing a black suit with gold embellishments, similar to what he wore when he had hosted his ball in Linterfame. Mykill's outfit was the exact opposite. He wore matching storm gray trousers and jacket, a black sash around his waist, and the same rings he always wore.

Gild pushed open the doors and stepped through them. The men and women below all cheered as he greeted them and then turned towards us.

"Introducing our most beloved guests from LinterFame and Asgaith, King Eryx and King Mykill." Everyone clapped lightly and bowed their heads in respect. "And with them, Alethea Divine, daughter of the Gods."

My head snapped in his direction at his words, and everyone clapped again. My cheeks heated again, but I forced myself to curtsy and bow my head towards him. Together, the three of us descended the steps as everyone watched us.

"You can breathe," Mykill whispered just loud enough for me to hear.

"They're all staring," I responded back quietly.

"Because you look stunning." I inhaled another breath at his words as we continued our descent.

Only six more stairs.
Five.
Four.
Three.
Two.
One.

I breathed out a sigh of relief as we reached the bottom steps, and the attention seemed to shift away from us. I slid my arm from theirs, and Mykill disappeared into the crowd without a word.

"You look beautiful." Eryx's voice was soft.

I snapped my head in his direction and offered a small smile. "Thank you."

He bowed his head to me, and I offered a small curtsy. He lingered for a few moments, shifting uncomfortably on his feet before he disappeared into the crowd too.

"You look stunning," Gild said as he stopped before me and bowed his head.

"Thank you," I smiled as I curtsied. "May I ask what Goddess you say I resemble?"

"Petria," he said as he slipped his arm through mine and led me through the crowd.

I had briefly heard her name before. "And what is she Goddess of?"

"Purification." He released my arm and turned towards me.

"Does she have a temple here?"

He shook his head. "No," he chuckled. "The temples have all been abandoned during the Great War. They're back on your side of the sea."

I frowned as disappointment filled me.

"Enjoy yourself," Gild said as he bowed and placed a kiss on my knuckles. He disappeared into the crowd a moment later, leaving me on my own. I turned, taking in the space around me. The room was beautiful. The beauty of the fae world would always marvel me.

"Would you like to dance?" I turned in surprise as Mykill came up behind me.

I raised my eyebrows at him as I fully faced him, and he reached for me. "You're not going to ask Thalia for a dance?"

"Careful. I've already said before that jealousy is not a good look for you," Mykill whispered as he placed a hand on my hip.

I snorted and rolled my eyes. "Please."

I placed a hand on his shoulder as we began to sway to the music. Being this close to him should've made me feel uncomfortable. I should have felt disgusted that I was dancing with him while Eryx was somewhere in the same room as us.

"Do you like to dance?" I asked and stepped back as he spun me gracefully.

"Not at all," he said as I came back to him.

He caught me with an arm around my waist and lowered me into a dip. My arm around his neck tightened, and we paused. Our faces were so close, our noses nearly touched. I could feel his breath on my cheeks. It was like everything around me drowned out as Mykill's eyes beheld mine. Slowly, he dipped me backwards, and this time, he followed. I sucked in a breath as the world around me fell away. His eyes stormed as our gazes remained locked. I felt like I couldn't breathe. Warmth cascaded through my entire body, even though his hands chilled my heated skin. He breathed in deeply and slowly raised me upright again. His hand lowered on my back, and he pulled me closer as the music softened.

"Do you?" He paused. "Like to dance, that is?"

"I love it," I whispered.

"What does this song remind you of?"

I paused, contemplating my words. I closed my eyes and focused on the violin.

One single violin stood out more than the others. The notes were drawn out, fuller than the others. Nothing but true emotion could change the way a single note sounded. I imagined the violinist's face as they played, pinched together in focus. It was like they poured themself into every note.

"Heartbreak," I whispered.

"If I didn't know better, I'd say you're a hopeless romantic."

His words were teasingly light, but I laughed harshly. "I don't know what I am anymore."

I gasped as he pulled away abruptly and spun me away from him. My grip on his hand tightened as he pulled me back to him again.

"Have you not found your mate?" I asked as I dropped my head back, and his eyebrows shot up. "I mean, I'm sorry - Eryx had said that it's very uncommon for fae to find their mate in their lifetime."

He kept his gaze at something behind me. "It is rare, but it's not that rare."

"That's not an answer," I retorted.

"Do you see me with a queen?" he threw back.

"Maybe you keep her in your pocket." I raised a playful brow at him.

Surprise flitted across his face, and his mouth fell open. His lips moved to form words but faltered, and a surprised grin pulled at his lips. A low laugh rumbled out of him, and I felt my entire body freeze. His laugh coated every frayed nerve in my body. That was the first time I'd ever heard him laugh in a truly amused way.

I yelped as he pulled away, gripped my hand, and spun me. As I twirled, my hair flew around me like a halo. His fingers dug gently into my hip as he pulled me back to him. Our chests pressed together as a sense of security washed over me. The room became a blur of dancing, mingling, and colors as I gazed up at him. His eyes were piercing as our stares met.

The music paused, and a moment later, Mykill's grip loosened, then disappeared entirely. He stepped away, and my arms fell limply to my sides.

"Good night, Alethea." He draped his arm across his waist and bowed.

I bowed my head and lowered myself into a curtsy. He was gone before I had even risen, leaving behind the scent of the churning ocean.

Chapter 22

Alethea

After I had danced with Mykill, I hung around the ball for a little while but snuck out with a bottle of wine. I drank it in my bed until I passed out. I woke up in a puddle of it. The alcohol made my limbs move slower.

I moved groggily down the halls as I rubbed my eyes. Eryx had told us to meet him in the front courtyard where horses would be waiting for us. By the time I arrived, everyone had already mounted, only waiting for me.

We rode well into the afternoon, only stopping once for the horses to drink and everyone to relieve themselves. We rode in silence. Eryx hadn't spoken to me this morning. He hadn't even glanced in my direction. It felt like he was trying to punish me for being upset with him, but I was perfectly content with him ignoring me. It helped keep my emotions clear. I didn't have to worry about his cider eyes clouding my judgment.

We finally came upon the volcano that they had referred to. It towered high into the clouds, and at the top, I could see the lava lighting the sky around it red. We dismounted our horses and tied them beneath the cover of the trees before we stopped at a crevice in the side of the mountain that didn't even look like an entrance.

"We move in quickly. The tunnels are sure to be lined with traps. Be alert at all times." Eryx's voice was firm as he addressed each one of us. His gaze lingered on me before sliding over to Cadmus beside me.

One of Mykill's men, Kerrigan, led the way. It took my eyes several minutes to adjust to the darkness. I ignored the webs that clung to my skin as we moved. My insides felt like they were crawling, but I needed to appear as unfazed by them as everyone else was. The tunnel never widened, but large scones appeared on the wall, and a fire roared to life at the tip of each one. They continued down the hall, lighting one after the other, and revealed a tunnel that seemed unending.

"Be alert everyone," Eryx said, his voice echoing down the tunnel.

Kerrigan paused as a click sounded around us, and he froze with his arms outstretched on either side of him. He cursed lightly.

"What was that?" Thalia asked as we all froze in place, not a single one of us daring to move.

"It's a pressure plate," Kerrigan said as he extended his arms on either side of him.

"This isn't good," Thalia breathed. "No one move."

"Everyone, get to the ground," Kerrigan said. To my shock, his voice didn't waver once.

"Do not move," Mykill commanded. "I am commanding you to not move!"

"We don't know what it will trigger," Eryx said.

"I know that!" Mykill snapped in his direction. "We can send people back to get rocks to pile on it."

"You're not going to find rocks heavy enough to replicate my weight," Kerrigan said. "Besides, you won't have time. The plate is timed."

"How do you know?" Mykill asked.

"it's slowly pushing me back up. Once it gets back in place, the trap will spring. You need to get away from me."

"We'll figure this out, Kerrigan. Do not move!" Mykill shouted.

Another click sounded, and we all held our breath as we waited for what would happen next.

"Go!" Kerrigan billowed as he flared out his wings, blocking us off, as a whistling sounded through the air.

I gasped, covering my mouth as sharp spikes embedded themselves in his wings and body, poking out the other side. Blood dripped down the feathers, and his body collapsed backwards.

"Is he?" I choked on my voice as I stepped towards him.

Mykill stuck his arm out, blocking me from going any further, and stepped in front of me. "He's dead," he confirmed, his voice laced with sadness.

I turned away from Kerrigan's prone form as I noticed the spikes embedded in his torso and neck. Blood covered his entire front side, nearly making me choke as tears filled my eyes.

"Let's move quickly," Eryx commanded as he waved everyone forward.

My hands shook as I turned back towards the group. One by one, they stepped over Kerrigan's mutilated form, but I couldn't walk over him.

"Alethea," Eryx prodded as he stepped up beside me and gripped my upper arms. "We need to keep moving."

I nodded, turning my face away as Eryx lifted me up and over Kerrigan. We continued down the hall. The shake in my hands didn't stop as we moved deeper into the mountain. Every once in a while, the mountain would tremble, and dust would rain down. It was the lava shifting above us. I wasn't sure how it remained above us without melting through the rock, but I was thankful.

I gasped as my foot hit a rock on the floor that wasn't a rock at all. As my foot moved, it was more like a lever.

"Eryx," I whispered as my head snapped towards him.

"Alethea!" Eryx roared before strong arms circled around me, and we spun. He dropped to a knee and covered my body with his as the smell of flames hit my nose. The hairs on my body prickled as one of his wards shielded us as flames roared around us. The flames only lasted a few moments before dispersing, and he rose to his feet.

"Thank you," I breathed as he released me, and I stumbled back a step.

He nodded at me, his eyes not meeting mine as he turned back down the hall. "We need to proceed with caution."

As we walked, I reached my hand out to him. Much to my surprise, he didn't push me away, and his strong fingers intertwined with mine. I needed his strength to help ground me as the fear pounded in my ears. My heart was thumping so quickly it nearly hurt as anxiety of what would happen around every turn plagued me.

Finally, we came upon a doorway with inscriptions engraved along the frame. Eryx paused as he tried to read them. "I don't know what language this is." His voice was quiet as he stepped towards the frame and traced his fingers along the inscriptions.

"They're the language of the Old Kingdom." Mykill answered.

I glanced at him and noticed how his gaze dipped to mine and Eryx's intertwined hands. My breath quickened as I quickly dropped Eryx's hand and brushed my hands on my thighs.

Eryx glanced at me with a frown. "Let's move inside," he said.

The room wasn't much bigger than my washroom back at Eryx's kingdom, and the only thing inside of it was a pedestal in the center of the room. I expected there to be a mirror resting on the pedestal, but I was wrong.

"They're scrolls," Thalia breathed as she stood before the pedestal. Her mouth parted, and she stepped closer, examining them. She reached out for them and shrieked as a tiny bolt shocked her. She rubbed her hand. "Someone else try and get them."

Eryx stepped forward and extended his hand, but a tiny bolt of lightning struck the back of his palm too. He tried to hide his wince but failed and stepped away. One after the other, Mykill tried, Cadmus tried, and even a few guards tried, but the scrolls refused all of them.

"You try," Mykill said as he stepped behind me and nudged me forward.

I glanced at him and then back at the circle that had formed around the glowing pedestal. I noticed Eryx tense across from me, but he knew that even if I was shocked, I wouldn't die.

My hand began to tremble as I reached for the scrolls. I steeled a breath and wrapped my fingers around them. They were warm to the touch, but nothing zapped me. I held my breath and gasped as something stabbed into my palm and wiggled beneath my skin, pulling my blood from my body. I hissed and tried to yank my hand away, but it was like the scrolls were glued to my hand.

I gasped with wide eyes in amazement as my blood that was being pulled from my body inked itself upon the scrolls, changing the letters from black to red as the scrolls glowed. My mouth fell open as the glow died down, and I snatched them to my chest.

"I don't even know what just happened," Thalia gaped.

Her lips were parted when I met her gaze, and her eyes were wide. "The scrolls chose her," someone behind her said.

"They weren't supposed to be scrolls in the first place," Eryx said gruffly.

The walls around us rumbled, raining dust down on our heads, and we all looked up. Fissures began making their way across the ceiling.

"Move!" Eryx commanded.

Cadmus reached for my arm and yanked me behind him as we made our way back the way we came. No one spoke as we all ran. The ground trembled, and I imagined the lava chasing after us, nipping at our heels.

"Move quickly!" Thalia shouted from behind us.

The walls around us rumbled again, and I clutched the scrolls to my chest as my feet moved. I pushed myself to move faster, praying to the Gods that if they would let me live through this, I'd run more.

"It's collapsing!" someone shouted, and I couldn't help but look over my shoulder. Dust flew from the end of the tunnel, and the sound of rock tumbling echoed around us.

"Go!" Cadmus shouted.

"Thalia!" Mykill roared as the tunnel behind us collapsed entirely.

I glanced back over my shoulder as she disappeared behind the rubble. Her hand outstretched towards us with wide eyes, and I knew that would be the image that would replay in my mind. Disbelief washed over me as I stared at the wall of rubble. This was the only entrance. The tremble beneath us caused my feet to stumble, and I hit my knees. Arms hooked beneath my armpits and lifted me to my feet.

"Go!" Cadmus shouted in my ear as I was shoved forward.

Pushing my tired body to move, I sprinted towards the light at the end of the tunnel. First, Eryx burst through the cave, then Cadmus, then Krina, and finally Jay. Dirt kicked up around me, making me cough and sputter. I covered my mouth with my arm in an attempt to keep from inhaling more dirt. A hand on my back pushed me to the exit faster.

"Go!" Mykill hissed.

I heard the sound of rock collapsing behind me, but we were so close. The dirt was clearing as someone rammed into my back, and I was launched forward. We broke through the tunnel just as it collapsed behind me.

Pushing up, I coughed as I fell back on my ass. The entrance to the tunnel was gone entirely, and the lives lost in it were gone forever. Glancing around us, I counted the rest of us, and sadness filled me. We had gone in with fifteen and came out with eight. Five men disappeared behind the rubble with Thalia. Three of Mykill's men and four of Eryx's men, left for dead.

"We need -" Eryx said, but he was cut off as the mountain exploded above us.

Fingers wrapped around my elbow as I stepped back in shock. Lava and rocks flew upwards in streams and then arched above us. The flaming chunks of rock sailed over us and careened into the forest. The impact shook the ground. My mouth fell open as large, mighty wings broke free of the mountain, and the body that followed after was at least the size of half the mountain. A roar echoed all around us and shook the ground beneath our feet.

"It's a dragon," Cadmus gasped in astonishment.

"You need to get out of here," Eryx said as he stomped over to me and gripped my shoulders.

"What?" I gasped as I stumbled back a step.

"Take her," Eryx commanded, but he wasn't looking at me as he shoved me towards Mykill. "Get her out of here, now."

Mykill nodded as he wrapped his arms around my midsection and shot towards the sky. I clutched his body as we soared through the tree line. A dragon's roar pierced the air, and I cringed as I resisted the urge to slam my hands over my ears.

"Where are we going?" I shouted. "We can't just leave them!"

How would they protect themselves against a dragon?

The dragon must have sensed the scrolls because he sailed right over our group of men on the ground and came straight for us.

"Thieves!" the dragon roared as he chased after us.

Mykill hissed as we dropped into the canopy of trees. Branches tore at my skin, and I curled into him, hiding my face in his neck. He finally landed on a large branch and shoved my back until it was flat against the trunk of the tree. The dragon's shadow passed overhead as my breath trembled in fear.

"Shh," Mykill whispered, his lips brushing my ear as he covered my body with his.

"I can smell you, girl," the dragon's voice said. The timber of his voice was so deep, it felt like it rattled my bones.

I clutched the scrolls to my chest and squeezed my eyes shut as I pressed closer to Mykill.

"I can smell you both," he said again and laughed. "Thieves. Give it back." He drew out the words as he hissed them.

My bottom lip quivered, and I bit down on it in an attempt to not cry. Mykill placed a hand over my mouth and placed a finger over his lips. I didn't feel shame or embarrassment as a tear slipped down my cheek. His white eyes softened, a crack in his cold exterior, as my tear hit the side of his palm. He pressed closer to me, shielding my body with his wings flared on either side of him.

I screamed as the tree erupted around us. Mykill was thrown backwards, and the branch beneath my feet disappeared. I was free falling. I screamed but didn't lose my grip on the scrolls. Branches tore at my body as I fell through them. They gave way beneath me and splintered until I hit the ground with a resounding thud. All the breath left my body as I gasped.

I groaned as I rolled onto my side. Pain radiated up my arm and shoulder. I had definitely broken something. Nausea threatened to consume me as I sat up.

I glanced over just as the dragon was launching towards Mykill, who threw a bolt of lightning at him. The dragon laughed as it struck him and left a small burn on his glittering scales. Mykill ran for me, dodging the stream of fire the dragon threw his way. His arms pumped faster, and his wings extended on either side of him. Right before he reached me, he pushed off the ground. He swooped low, slipping his arms beneath mine, and took to the sky.

"I can't be killed by powers. You may think you're powerful, boy, but I was here when this world was formed. I've seen magic your kind has never seen!" The dragon roared and reared his head back as he shot another tunnel of fire at us.

I curled my fists into his leather and tightened my legs around Mykill as he evaded the stream of fire. The heat singed our bodies, burning his back and my brows.

Mykill shouted as flame hit his back, and we went tumbling to the ground. He angled his body upwards as we collided with the ground, shielding me from the blow. I heard the breath expel from his body, but his arms remained like bands around me, securing me to him.

"Mykill," I gasped as I strained against his arms. "Mykill, are you okay?"

I managed to break free of his hold as I rolled off of him. He groaned as he rolled onto his side, and I slapped my hand over my mouth as I gasped. His skin looked molten and black. His beautiful feathers had almost disintegrated, and I patted the remainder that were still on fire with my uninjured arm.

"Alethea, get behind me," he groaned as he pushed himself onto his hands.

"Alethea!" Eryx screamed.

My eyes were locked on Mykill as he tried and failed to push himself up. His arms strained, and I could see the tremor working its way up his arms.

"Be prepared to die." The dragon's laugh rumbled through the ground.

My head whipped back towards the dragon as he reared his head back.

"Stop!" I screamed as I gripped one of Mykill's swords and unsheathed it. My hand didn't shake as I pointed it at the dragon.

I wasn't going to die like this. I wasn't going to let this dragon kill Mykill without fighting for him.

He laughed mightily and continued to rear his head back. I heard Mykill roar my name, but my feet were glued to the ground. I couldn't move as the flames curled from his open mouth. The heat of them hit my skin and surrounded me. It singed my skin and filled my nostrils, but the heat never grew; it simply existed. My body became one with the flames, and the flames ran through my blood. My skin absorbed the flames. It invigorated me, and as I breathed, the scent of the flames filled my lungs.

The heat got so hot that the flames turned blue before finally, the flames died, and the blue sky became visible again as the heat dispersed. My eyes shot up to the dragon first, then to Eryx and Cadmus who had fully stepped out of their cover. Their eyes were wide with shock.

"What are you?" the dragon's voice thundered as he raised above me.

"I was human," I responded as I raised my head toward him. I couldn't find it in me to fear him as he gazed down at me in amazement.

His nostrils flared, and hot steam poured out of them. His eyes closed as he breathed in deep.

"Goddess," he breathed as he bowed his head. "You're the woman the prophecy speaks of."

He was the first being to call me a woman, not a girl.

"*A mortal born of fae-blood will be a harbinger of destruction, her existence a crack in the veil of fate. A bond forged by the Fates will be broken by betrayal. The tears of a shattered heart shall bring about an era of sorrow and despair. With the threads of destiny torn asunder, she will find herself torn between two identities of herself."*

My mouth fell open. "The prophecy?" I asked.

"Only the beginning," the dragon answered as he raised his head.

My mouth and throat were too dry for me to gulp as I struggled to come up with words. I glanced back at Mykill. His eyes were wide and trained on me. Not a hair on his body had been frayed.

"That's about me?" I asked as I whipped back towards the dragon.

His throat vibrated as he nodded. His massive talons scraped the dirt beneath his feet as he reared back. Steam poured out from his mouth as his body began to shift. I stepped closer to Mykill, who placed a hand on my shoulder. I jumped as I glanced back at him, now fully standing.

"You are the great defender of the fae, the salvation of our lands," the dragon said.

"Against what?"

He didn't answer as the smoke disappeared from around him, and he stood as tall as Mykill. He had glowing amber hair with matching amber eyes and skin bronzed by the sun. His hair fell around his shoulders in waves. Although he looked human, his eyes were still slitted like a serpent's as he strolled towards me.

"The scrolls are yours. They belong to you. Your blood is now inked in these scrolls." He placed a hand on my shoulder and bowed his head. "May the Fates be by your side."

"Thank you," I muttered as I tightened my hold on the scrolls. I didn't know if it was because of my fae blood or the flames, but my shoulder was fully healed. It didn't even ache when I moved it.

He raised his head to meet mine, and as he did, his body erupted into flames. I yelped as I jumped back into a hard chest that gripped my upper arms as they turned me. Eryx's cider eyes bore into mine. "Let me have the scrolls."

"What?" I gasped as I tried to step back, but he held onto my arms firmly. "He said they were mine."

"I'll keep them safe, Alethea," Eryx prodded.

"Let go of my arms," I snapped.

"Give me the scrolls."

"Let go!" I tried yanking away from him, but he refused to let go.

"She said to let her go." Mykill's cold voice slithered over the two of us, and I shivered as Eryx's eyes slid up. He glowered.

"Stay out of this." Eryx's jaw clenched, and a muscle popped in his cheek.

"Let go of me, Eryx," I said again, firmer this time.

His gaze slid back to mine, and slowly, one by one, he lifted his fingers off of me. I stepped back from him, ignoring the ache in my arms from his grasp, and bumped into Mykill's chest.

"Give me the scrolls," Eryx demanded again, but he forced his voice to sound softer.

I tensed as I glanced around him. His soldiers had assembled behind him. Their hands rested on their swords, and I'm sure if I turned around, I would find Mykill's men doing the same.

I couldn't let anyone get hurt because I refused to give him the scrolls. I sighed and stepped towards him. "Here." I clenched my teeth and rammed them into his chest. I didn't wait for him to grab them before I stepped away and turned towards Mykill. "Can you take me back?"

He obliged.

Chapter 23

Alethea

My feet ached as I took the stairs up to my bedroom. I desperately longed for a bath. I couldn't recall a time in my life when I had run as quickly as I had today. Even running through the woods with Laney had been different. We weren't running from danger; we were running for enjoyment. It wore my body out differently.

The magic in the room must have sensed that I needed a bath because an oil infused bath was already waiting for me when I got to my room. I stripped and dunked into the tub, nearly groaning as the warm water caressed my aching joints. I scrubbed the dirt off my skin and out of my hair before I closed my eyes and lounged back on the lip of the tub.

My stomach growled, and I groaned in response as my hunger sucked the joy from my bath. I grumbled to myself as I drained the water and quickly dressed into a simple dress that had been left for me. I hurried back down the hall, desperate for something to eat. I knew everyone would already be down there.

Turning the corner before I reached the stairs, I immediately gasped as I collided with a body. There was a sharp tug in my abdomen, and my eyes widened as fire lit up my torso.

I stared into familiar eyes as my body went numb. My mouth moved, though no words came out, leaving me gulping like a fish. My fingers curled around the hilt of the blade now protruding from my stomach. I could feel the slickness of blood as it pooled at the wound and spilled down my dress. A fire moved through my veins, painful and painless at the same time.

"No," I whispered breathlessly and fell back a step.

Familiar eyes peered into mine, the carbon copy of her brother. She smiled, her red lips pulling back to reveal white teeth.

My back pressed into the wall as I slowly slid down. "I told Eryx what would happen. Now, he must reap the consequences." Freya smiled as she knelt to my eye level. "Goodbye, Alethea."

I opened my mouth to say her name, but all I managed to do was to blow out another breath. *Eryx knew what would happen? What was she talking about?* I thought as I tried not to focus on the pain. *He had told me he hadn't heard a word from her.*

I couldn't die like this, so helplessly. I had so many unanswered questions. I still didn't understand this world and wanted to learn more. I needed to train. There were so many things left to do, and I was running out of time to do them.

I willed someone to walk down these halls. Someone must come looking for me when I don't show up for supper. The numbness spread across my body, and my arms fell to the sides of me uselessly as I slumped further down the wall until I slid to my side. I needed to staunch the flow of blood, to slow it down, but I couldn't bring my arms to move. My eyelids grew heavier by the moment, threatening to pull me under, but I refused the pull.

I wasn't ready to die yet.

"Alethea," I heard Mykill, but I couldn't turn my head towards him. I couldn't do anything. "Gods, Alethea."

The sound of his knees hitting the floor beside me echoed in my head to the point of near pounding. He scooped me up in his arms, drawing me to him. My head lolled backwards, and my hands fell limp.

"Eryx!" he roared. "We'll find who did this, I swear it, Alethea. Just keep your damn eyes open!"

My lips moved numbly, and I tried to nod but failed. I needed to tell him to be careful, that Freya was still on the loose and on a killing spree.

"Eryx!" Mykill's voice thundered through my skull.

Mykill stood carrying me, and my arms dangled behind me as he ran. I didn't know where he was going, but he needed to be fast. I don't know how I could tell, but I knew I was almost out of time.

"Alethea, please, can you talk to me?" Cider eyes appeared above mine. "Blossom, can you tell me who did this to you?"

"It's poisoned," Mykill said, his hand still holding my wound. "Who would do this?" I heard him roar for Cadmus and the healers, but they wouldn't make it in time. I knew that my time was up. My eyes closed on their own accord, and I heard Mykill or Eryx roar my name. My hearing had gone fuzzy, and I couldn't tell who it was. I felt the ground beneath me tremble, and then, there was nothing.

***

My body felt nothing and everything all at once. I shivered through an overwhelming chill but also an all consuming fire. There was serene, and then there was chaos, like I was teetering between the two.

"Alethea," a familiar voice sang, calling for me to open my eyes. "Alethea, dear."

A breath of cold air washed over me, and I forced my eyes open. The space around me was all consuming white.

"Alethea."

My head snapped to the side and disbelief rocked through me as I sat up.

"Mama?" I gasped as she leaned towards me.

Tears blurred her face as she touched my cheek with her fingers. I closed my eyes, savoring the warmth.

"Mama," I cried as I threw myself forward and wrapped my arms around her neck.

"My girl," she said as she tightened her arms around me. "My sweet, sweet girl."

"Laney? Papa?" I asked. My lips trembled as I breathed in her scent.

"They're at peace," she whispered. "Don't worry about us."

"I'm so sorry!" I couldn't help but sob. "It's all my fault. I ran, and whenever I ran, one of you died! It's all my fault. Please forgive me!" My body shook as she ran a soothing hand down the back of my hair.

"It's not your fault, dear. We knew what the consequences would be when we took you in."

"Why would you do it?" I sniffled as I wiped at my nose.

My mother ran her palm down my cheek. "You were only a child, and your parents would have done anything to protect you."

I didn't have words. I had always thought my parents were kind, generous people, but I had never realized how truly selfless they were. They sacrificed everything for me. They put their entire family's safety on the line to protect me.

"Alethea, we don't have much time. Be careful. There are many secrets stirring," she warned. "Things are not as they seem. You must get those scrolls."

"Eryx has them."

"I know who has them, but you must get them. He has ulterior motives for the mirror. You can only ask the mirror three questions before it disappears for another thousand years."

My mouth fell open as I realized what she was saying. "He's not going to let me ask about my birth parents?"

Her eyes were sad as she shook her head. She stretched her hand out to me again and placed it on my cheek. "There are not many you can trust in this world, unfortunately. Do not give your love blindly."

I sucked in a breath at the words that sounded too familiar.

"Love and loyalty is a lot like power, it should never be given blindly."

My mouth fell open in shock as Mykill's words crashed over me. He had warned me. He must have known.

"I love you, Alethea. It looks like we've run out of time." Her voice was soft as she stroked my cheek. "Be strong."

"I love you, mama," I whispered.

I gasped as I shot up. My chest heaved as I took in my surroundings. I was laying in my bed. The healer sat at my feet, and Mykill, Eryx, and Cadmus were all huddled around a table at the end of the bed.

"Alethea," Eryx gasped as they all swung towards me.

"You lied to me!" I shouted as I slid out of the bed. "You told me you hadn't heard from Freya!"

Eryx winced slightly as he started towards me. Mykill watched us, but Cadmus and the healer ducked out of the room.

"I wanted to protect you," he said as I threw the blanket off of me.

"Is that your only answer? You wanted to protect me?" My voice rose an octave as I stormed towards him and poked my finger into his chest. "I almost died!"

"I know that!" He roared back. "Damn it, Alethea. I know that! I felt you die in my arms!"

"I would suggest lowering your tone towards her," Mykill said, cool as ice, as he admired one of the rings on his fingers and twisted it around. "So where is your traitorous bitch of a sister now?"

"I don't know!" Eryx exclaimed, his eyes wide, desperately trying to convince us to believe him. "I didn't know she was even here."

"Get out," I snapped as I turned away from him and stared out the window.

"Alethea - "

"Get out!" I screamed as I whipped back towards him.

Eryx's mouth dropped open, and he stumbled back in shock. He shook his head. His mouth shut and opened again.

"You heard her." The words floated through the room - the only warning Mykill would give.

Eryx's eyes shot to him, and they instantly hardened. His hands fisted at his sides, and I thought he was going to charge Mykill, but he merely dropped his head and pivoted towards the door. I didn't wait to watch him go.

I turned to Mykill, who still remained on the loveseat with his arms outstretched across the back of it. His brows were drawn, and a storm swirled in his eyes.

"How are you feeling?"

I nodded as I began pacing. "I feel fine. No one saw her? She just slipped free?"

"I didn't go after her. No one was there when I found you. I just needed to make sure you lived."

"How am I supposed to just walk around like I wasn't almost just murdered?" My breath hitched.

"We will find her." Mykill left no room for negotiation.

"How? The one person who should've warned me didn't. How am I supposed to trust that?" I nearly wailed as I thrust out my arms.

I gasped as Mykill caught my arm and yanked me towards him. "Have I ever broken your trust?"

My mouth fell open before snapping shut.

No, he hadn't.

I sucked in a breath, and as I did, I realized how close we were. Our chests brushed, and I felt him shift closer to me. I didn't stop him.

My entire body froze as the tip of his finger stroked across my bottom lip.

"You scared me." His voice was so quiet. I was sure I misheard him.

My eyes snapped to him. His pupils had narrowed, and his eyes had darkened. The storm still brewed in them. He leaned down. Our noses brushed, and my eyes closed as he sealed the space between our mouths. His lips were shockingly warm compared to the rest of him. One of his arms slid around my waist and pulled me into his chest, forcing me onto my toes.

Something that resembled a moan slipped from his mouth, and I felt a surge of confidence as I slid my tongue into his mouth. Our tongues clashed, and our teeth clanged together as our kiss went from sweet to fervent in a matter of seconds. Heat washed over my entire body, threatening to consume us both as my hands ravaged his hair.

We stumbled back a step, and one of his hands slid up the back of my neck to cup my head as he tilted it back. His fingers were delicately sweet as they twirled in the strands at the base of my skull.

Then, a single face popped into my mind. A single face who would burn the world down if he were to witness what we were doing.

"Wait," I gasped as I shoved at his chest and fell backwards into the bed.

We couldn't do this.

Eryx and I had barely ended things, and I wasn't even sure what I felt towards him, much less Mykill.

"We can't do this." My fingers flew up to my mouth as my lips tingled. "We can't do this," I repeated.

HIs cold mask settled back over his face as he nodded once. "You're right. I'm sorry."

"You need to go, now."

No sooner than the words left my lips was he heading towards the door. My eyes remained glued on his back as the door closed softly behind him, and he didn't spare a glance back at me.

**

I didn't sleep that night. I was wide awake by the time everyone had prepared to leave. I had gotten to the boat so early that the Captain and I had breakfast together, and I waited on the deck for everyone else to arrive. He had been chatty like he always was, which helped my mood a little, but not by much.

"We're ready," Mykill said as he and the remainder of his men stepped up to the dock.

My head snapped in his direction as I heard his voice.

My cheeks immediately heated as his eyes fell on me. But much to my surprise, there wasn't a single emotion in them. He turned away, and his gaze shifted over me as quickly as it had landed on me. I expelled the breath I was holding and made my way up the ramp to the deck. I didn't wait to watch for Mykill and his men to follow. I perched over the rail and stared at the churning waters below us.

"A storm's coming," the Captain said as he draped his arms over the rail beside me. "But we'll be ahead of it, so we shouldn't get hit too hard."

"That's good to hear. Is there a way around the sirens?"

"No, lass. It would take up too much time and leave us susceptible to the storm. We can't risk that."

I nodded at his words as he left to command the others for our departure. I remained by myself as I gazed out at the water.

I didn't look at Eryx as he stopped beside me and leaned into the rail. "How are you feeling?"

"Betrayed."

Eryx sighed. "I mean, are you healed?"

I nodded. "Physically, yes."

"That's good." His voice was quiet as he remained there for a few minutes.

When he realized that I wasn't going to strike up a conversation with him, he sighed and pushed away. His heavy footsteps disappeared behind me, and I was left alone. We sailed across the waters. The waves were lighter this time, which meant the ship swayed less. I didn't move for what felt like hours, even when my feet began to ache from standing. I could hear some men behind me playing cards and shouting at one another, but I merely watched the endless roll of water.

The light reflected off of it, making me wince and look away at certain angles, but if I watched long enough I could sometimes see a dolphin jump out of the water. I smiled every time I saw one. I had never seen a dolphin in real life. I'd only read about them and seen drawings. Nothing would compare to how they looked in real life, even if I only saw them for a split second at a time.

"We're approaching the siren infested waters!" the Captain shouted, pulling me from my haze.

Glancing back at the water, I listened as the Captain instructed everyone around the mast as they shackled themselves to it again. My eyes remained glued to the water, fear spiking in my throat, as I waited for a head to break the surface. The only thing I could hear was the pounding of my heart as I stepped back. Flashes of the siren's teeth and the feel of her nails emerged, and I couldn't push them back down.

"Alethea, come on." Eryx reached for me with cotton already in his hands.

"No, I don't want to." I shook my head as I stepped away from Eryx's hands.

"Alethea, you don't have a choice. If you don't, you could go overboard again," Eryx demanded.

"Let me go below deck. I want to go below deck." My voice was frantic, near hysterical, as I stepped back and tried pulling my arm from his hand. "Let go of me! Stop grabbing me!"

I heard a thump behind me, and Eryx's eyes turned hateful as he glanced behind me. I sensed it was Mykill before he spoke. "I'll take her."

"She's not an object," Eryx snapped.

I yanked my arm from his grasp and turned towards Mykill. "Take me to the sky, please. Let's just fly above."

"You can't do that!" Eryx said.

I ignored him as I stared at Mykill. "Please." My voice nearly broke as it shook.

He didn't say another word as his wings opened behind him. The black feathers almost looked brown with streaks of mahogany in the sunlight. I could have marveled at the beauty of them all day.

He stepped towards me and secured an arm around my waist before he shot towards the sky. My stomach dropped out from beneath me, and I screamed as I tightened my arms and legs around his body. His laugh sounded in my ear as I clenched onto him with a death grip.

"Gods, you're shaking," he gasped as he leveled himself out. "It's alright, Alethea. We should be safe up here." His arms tightened reassuringly around me.

I breathed deeply, and a sense of calm washed over me.

He smiled wickedly as he pried my leg off his hip. "As much as I like feeling the length of you pressed against me, it's rather difficult to hold you like this."

I felt a blush creep down my cheeks, neck, and chest, but I growled at him. "How do you want to hold me then?" I snapped.

"Just keep your arms around my neck, and let your legs go," he instructed.

"But you're going to drop me."

He laughed. "I'd never drop you, Alethea."

Doing what he said, I let my legs dangle momentarily and resisted the urge to squeal. I kept my arms tight around his neck as he slipped an arm beneath my waist and then another beneath my knees.

"See?" He raised an eyebrow at me. "I didn't drop you."

"You wanted to," I threw back at him.

"That wasn't what you said. Wanting to and doing it are two different things." His voice was teasing.

"You're distracting me." It wasn't a question. He was distracting me to help calm me down.

"Yes," was all he said.

"You didn't want me to lose it like I did in the dining room?" I said only half jokingly.

He didn't answer for a few moments. The silence stretched between us, and I fiddled with my fingers in my lap. "I don't like it when you're upset, and he manhandles you."

My mouth fell open in response as I stared at him. I could hear the sincerity in his voice as he stared below, searching for the ship.

"He only does it to protect me." My voice came out barely above a whisper.

"He does it to control you," he snarled. I instinctively flinched and swore I saw a strike of lightning out of the corner of my eye.

I turned away from him to look over the clouds and ocean. I didn't know what to say. Part of me didn't want to accept his words.

"I'm sorry." His voice softened. "It just upsets me when he manhandles you like you're his property."

I opened my mouth to respond, but my words died off as I realized that I didn't have anything to say. His arms tightened around me as we continued to fly. The boat disappeared beneath the clouds before reappearing moments later. Words evaded me as he continued flying.

"They should be out of reach now," he finally said as he tucked in his wings and shot down.

I squealed and dug my fingers into his neck as we dropped. My stomach felt like it came up my throat before his boots landed on the deck.

"We're all good. No casualties," the Captain said.

I slipped from Mykill's arms and stepped away from him. My teeth clenched as I glanced at Eryx and then whipped around. I only had one thought in my head as I crossed my arms over my chest. I couldn't wait to get off this damned boat.

Chapter 24

Alethea

We got back a week ago. I ignored Eryx the entire time, and he must have taken the hint because he was never at any meals. I barely even spoke to Mykill unless he was training me. I felt angrier as I stalked through the halls and spent the majority of my time in my bedroom. I had accumulated a pile of books that Lira brought me every few days. I couldn't bring myself to visit the library, not when it had been Eryx's mother's and he had, in a sense, gifted it to me. It was just a slap in the face of his betrayal and lies.

Thankfully, I had gotten much better at shooting the bow and arrow. It was like my fae blood was picking it up quicker than if I was still human. Sometimes I was still so shocked that I was fae that I would just stare at my ears in the mirror. I would poke and prod at the pointed end of my ear.

Today was different. The silence was eating me alive, but I couldn't see Eryx, and Cadmus acted like an awkward school child whenever he was around me. He had told me he would work on Eryx, but I had made it abundantly clear to him after we got back that I wanted nothing to do with him. I knew Cadmus felt awkward because he was Eryx's best friend. I also had asked Cadmus if he had known about Freya, and he couldn't answer me.

That was answer enough.

I stalked down the halls to the only person who didn't make me want to pull my eyes out. Thankfully, he hadn't brought up our kiss, and neither had I. I didn't trust that Eryx didn't have ears listening to everything that went on in the castle. At least things weren't tense between Mykill and I since our kiss. He didn't push me to talk about anything, and he respected my silence.

I paused as I came upon his door and took a deep breath as I raised my hand. I knocked softly and waited for a response.

"Come in," Mykill answered on the other side.

Nudging open the door, I stepped into the room. Mykill was lounging across a sofa beside a crackling fireplace. He had a book resting in his lap, and a glass filled with amber liquid rested on the small table in between the sofa and set of armchairs.

"Alethea," he drawled as he waved a hand at the set of chairs. "This is certainly a surprise. Please, sit."

My feet faltered, and I paused as I took in his calm demeanor. I opened my mouth to respond, but no words formed on my tongue.

"Not in the mood to speak?" he answered as he picked his book back up and looked away. "If you're needing a quiet space with company, then feel free to lounge. Grab a book if you'd like."

I glanced at the bookshelf behind him, but I didn't see anything immediately grabbing my attention. I looked back at Mykill, but he was already immersed in his book again. So I closed the door behind me and strode towards the bookshelf. I ran the tip of my finger across a selection of golden spines. They appeared to be historical romance, and I chose the first. I cracked it open and took a seat across from him. Surprisingly, the silence that spanned out between us wasn't uncomfortable. It was almost comforting and relaxing. It gave me the perfect energy to dive into my book.

The story immersed me. I pictured myself running alongside the main character as she explained her life. Hours passed, and I eventually got about a quarter into my book when a knock sounded on the door, cutting through the harmonious silence. Glancing up from my book, Mykill called for them to enter without sparing a glance. He turned the page, the rustling echoing through the room.

The door was shoved open, and one of his men strode in. His steps faltered as his gaze fell on me. I could see the disgust disguised as shock behind his eyes. It used to sting, but all the guards in Eryx's kingdom had all done the same. They thought that I was below them.

"Sir -" the guard started.

"I would suggest that you reevaluate the way you're looking at her, or I'll pluck your eyes from your skull." Mykill's voice was cool and calm. He hadn't even glanced up at the guard.

"Ye-yes, Your Majesty," the guard stuttered. He glanced at Mykill, then me.

"Yes?" he asked as his eyes slid over to the guard.

Mykill's gaze was cold as he snapped the book shut. He dropped his feet to the floor and placed the book beside him. He raised an eyebrow at the guard.

Annoyance flitted across Mykill's face. "You have three seconds to state your business -"

"You told me you wanted me to inform you if there's been an intrusion."

"There are barren here," Mykill interrupted as his entire body stiffened.

"What?" I gasped as I snapped my book closed and dropped my feet onto the floor. "How do you know?"

"Get the men ready," he commanded his guard. The guard bowed his head and rushed from the room.

"How do you know there are barren here?" I asked as Mykill checked his sheaths for his swords.

"I can feel it," he said.

"Take me there," I said as I stopped in front of him. I fisted my hands at my sides as I glared up at him.

"No," he said as he dismissed me and went to brush by.

"No!" I shouted as I placed both of my hands on his chest and shoved him backwards. At least, I tried to. His feet remained rooted to the spot, and he raised an amused brow at me.

"Shove me again," he dared.

I grunted in frustration but stepped away from him. "Fine. I'll go on my own."

"You will do no such thing," his firm voice commanded.

"You don't get to tell me what to do!" I exclaimed as I gripped the door handle.

"I wouldn't do that," he drawled.

I ignored him as I turned the handle. Yanking back the door, I fell backwards as my hand slipped from the door handle. The door remained closed, like it was glued shut. Anger tasted in the back of my throat as I slowly raised my head towards him. He had the gall to laugh as he lowered himself in front of me.

Surprisingly, he extended a hand towards me. "I don't think you'll like what you find out there," he warned.

Glancing down at his hand, I looked back at him, but he just watched, waiting. Reaching towards him, I took his hand and shrieked as he jerked me to my feet.

He waved his hand, and my bow and sheath of arrows dropped by my feet. "Pick them up."

Obeying, I picked up the full quiver and slung it onto my back. I held the bow in my hand. He gripped my hand, and without warning, the ground fell from beneath my feet. I resisted the urge to shriek, and we materialized moments later. We were in the throne room, perched on a beam overlooking what was unfolding beneath us.

Cadmus was between two barren with his hands bound by barbed chains. Blood pooled beneath his joined hands. Eryx glared at a barren male that appeared to be larger than any of the others.

"Let's play a game, shall we?" the barren man said.

Eryx's hands fisted at his sides, and I could see the muscles in his jaw clench.

"We will slaughter everyone in your kingdom, or you can hand over the girl." The barren man turned to the men holding Cadmus.

My breath hitched, and Mykill's arm settled around my waist, securing me to him. His heavy hand rested on my stomach. I inhaled a breath, ignoring the feeling in my stomach.

"We can't find her," one of the barren said.

The barren man growled before settling his gaze back on Eryx. "Fine. Your other option is to send your men and beasts to lay waste to the human lands."

I gasped. Humans couldn't defend themselves against dragons and fae. They would be slaughtered. The High Priest had made it clear he didn't care for the people in his kingdom. He'd let them burn.

Mykill slammed his hand over my mouth, smashing my lips together and silencing my protest. "They will try to take you if they discover us," he whispered in my ear. "Ready your bow."

With his hand still covering my mouth, I obliged, notching an arrow.

"Aim it at the Barren King."

This was the King of the Barren? Those vicious monsters had a king?

I pulled the bow taunt, aiming for his heart. "Good girl." Mykill's low voice sent shivers through my body.

"What?" Eryx gasped.

"Your mate would love that, wouldn't she? Slaughtering everyone where she grew up. Erasing every last bit of her life and killing everyone she ever knew."

"Never," Eryx growled in response.

The Barren King laughed. "I should tell you that we've already got your military on their knees." He glanced at Cadmus. "Isn't that right, General?"

Cadmus glared at him before his gaze slid back to Eryx. His chest heaved, and the more I looked at him, I noticed more of the cuts and bruises that covered his skin. Reluctantly, he nodded, confirming what the Barren King said. Mykill cursed in my ear.

"What will it be?" The Barren King laughed as he extended a hand to Cadmus.

Cadmus growled as he yanked on the king's grip. The barren growled in response and shoved the tip of the dagger into his skin, just enough to draw a slight dribble of blood.

Eryx's eyes widened as he took in his friend. I could see the war waging in him. But the fae were gifted. They were stronger than humans. That was the only logical choice.

My heart plummeted as he spoke. "Send everyone to the human lands. Destroy it."

My mouth fell open, and shock radiated through me. He couldn't. The humans wouldn't be able to defend themselves. They weren't granted powers and unique strengths like the fae were.

"Aim for the barren holding Cadmus," Mykill whispered. I obeyed. "Fire."

On command, I let the arrow fly free. It whizzed through the air before embedding itself in the forehead of the barren on his left. Gasps erupted throughout them, and Eryx's head swung in our direction. The ward around us fell away, and his eyes narrowed as he beheld us. I notched another arrow, aiming for the Barren King, who had also swung towards us. Shock radiated through me at the familiarity of his face, he had been the barren I had seen in my dream.

Cadmus managed to break free of their hold. The barren all began to swarm their king. They screeched, and their movements were animalistic as they crawled around him like spiders. I released my arrow anyway, and it landed in the back of one of the barren. It shrieked and shriveled in on itself as it faded away.

"Get them," the Barren King commanded as his head swung our way.

Mykill's arm tightened around my waist as one of the barren who had been holding Cadmus notched an arrow. It aimed the arrow straight for me and released it. Eryx bellowed as he spun on the creature, catching it beneath the jaw. Its eyes bulged as Eryx crushed its neck beneath his fist. Mykill roared, and his wings circled around me, cutting off the view of the room below us. I felt the tingle of the ward settling around us, and then Mykill lowered his wings.

My gaze landed on Eryx, and I couldn't stop the overwhelming feeling of disgust surging in me as we held contact. He called my name, but I didn't want to hear what he had to say. This choice shattered us, and he knew it as his gaze fell. He pleaded with his eyes, desperate for me to understand why he had done it. But I couldn't understand. His shoulders fell as his gaze dropped to Mykill's arm around my waist. Fire brimmed in his eyes.

"Take me to the human lands," I told Mykill without looking at him.

I saw my name on Eryx's lips again, but as the thunder cracked, we were gone. The air screamed around us as the throne room fell away, and the brimming blue sky greeted us. In the distance, I could see dragons mounted by Eryx's men, and they were heading towards the human lands.

"I can't keep up with dragons," Mykill said.

I merely nodded as I slipped my arm around his neck to at least lift some of the burden of my weight. I knew what he didn't say. He couldn't fly as fast carrying me. I watched as his mighty wings beat up and down. His eyebrows were drawn down as he flew through the air. The wind whipped around us, and my stray hairs flew from behind my ears. Anxiety built in my chest to the point where it was nearly exploding out of me as I watched the dragons before us. They seemed like they were lifetimes away.

"I can't summon lightning again. It will give way to our position," he told me.

I nodded in response. If our position was given away, then the barren could find us - or worse, the High Priest.

I held onto him like a vice as we flew. I wasn't sure how long it took, but anxiety bloomed in my chest when the spires of the castle I had been held in peaked above the clouds.

"I have wards around us. He won't be able to sense you," Mykill said into my ear.

I glanced at him and frowned, wondering how he knew, then noticed I had dug my fingers into the bare skin above his collar. I blanched and offered him a sheepish smile. "I'm sorry." I pulled my hand into my lap. "Thank you."

He swooped down, angling his body, and I resisted the urge to scream as my stomach fell. I clenched my eyes closed and curled my fingers into his shoulders. He felt me tense around him and tightened his arms around me, further securing me to him. We finally dropped onto a mountain overlooking the city. I didn't wait for him to release me as I ran to the ledge. I clutched a hand around my throat in fear as I watched.

"We can't help them," Mykill said as he stepped up behind me.

The screams floated up to us as we watched. Fire emanated from the dragon's mouths, engulfing entire roads. Carts and houses went up in flames. Fire-engulfed bodies fell to the ground. I covered my face with both hands and didn't think as I turned into Mykill. He tensed as I dropped my head to his chest

"I'm so sorry," he finally whispered as one arm circled around my shoulders, and the other dropped around my waist.

I didn't cover up my sobs as the screams grew louder and louder until they stopped entirely. I could hear the flames as they devoured the city, and when I finally looked back, Eryx's men were retreating. We watched as the flames ate homes and shops, and the sound of wood collapsing in on itself wafted up to us. I wondered what the High Priest was doing now that his kingdom had been destroyed. Maybe he would flee the castle. He had lost his supply of people to turn into mages.

The deep sorrow that burrowed into my chest couldn't be soothed or healed. This wasn't just one life.

This was hundreds that had spanned from children to the elderly. All the history of families, simply gone - erased, as if none of them had ever existed. No soul could have survived the damage Eryx's men had done.

The flames finally died down, and I whipped towards Mykill. "Take me down there," I said.

His eyes were sad as he nodded and stepped up to me. He slipped his arms beneath me and took off into the sky. I didn't feel anything this time as we flew towards the burning remains of the city. As we passed over burning buildings, I couldn't help but notice the amount of charred bodies we flew over. Some of the bodies were so small, too small.

We touched down in the middle of one of the markets. Carts were indistinguishable. The only thing I could make out were the shapes of the displays, but I couldn't make out what carts were selling what. But I knew one of these carts belonged to the elderly lady who sold my family fruit.

There were people I knew, I had grown up with, littered throughout this city, all murdered because of me. If I wouldn't have been caught in the first place when Kirin had been searching for a wife, then they would probably still be alive. The thought settled heavily on my shoulders, nearly crushing me.

My heart thundered in my ears as I stepped over the charred remains. "They had no way to defend themselves," I rasped. Tears pricked the corners of my eyes again as I kicked away rubble, and a burned skull hit the tip of my boot.

I tasted bile in the back of my throat as I covered my mouth with my palm. A tear managed to slip through as I stumbled backwards.

"Let's go," Mykill said as he gripped my upper arms. "That's enough."

"Take me to Eryx," I demanded. "Now."

Mykill looked down at me, his salty gaze searching my face, before he nodded. Thunder roiled as he reached for the sky, and the bolt came down, swallowing us whole. When the smoke cleared, we were standing in Eryx's throne room.

"What do you want to do?" Mykill asked.

My mind felt blank as I stared up at him. "I need to see him."

Mykill's gaze was uncertain, but he still nodded. He reached his hand towards the sky, and thunder rumbled seconds before a stroke of lightning claimed us. The flashes of light danced behind my closed lids until we were on solid ground again. Glancing around, we were back in Mykill's reading space.

I didn't wait for him to follow me as I barreled through the halls. I knew he'd be able to sense if there were barren here like he had before, and he didn't stop me. I followed the halls past Eryx's office, past the dining hall, and I took the stairs up to his wing two at a time.

"Wait out here," I told Mykill without glancing back at him as I threw open Eryx's bedroom door.

Mykill didn't answer me but flanked on the side of the door.

"Eryx," I said, drawing his attention to me.

He gasped as he swung around. His face was strained as he took me in. "Oh thank gods, Alethea. I've had my men out searching for you."

"I was in the human lands," I said as I shut the door behind me.

His eyes pleaded with me to understand. "I had to do what was best for my people."

I laughed harshly as I leaned back against the door.

"Alethea, you don't understand."

"No, I don't understand. I don't understand how you could send fae and dragons to attack humans."

"There was no other way to keep you safe."

I stepped away from the door and towards the bed we had once shared together. I laughed bitterly as I ran my hand over the edge. "You mean, to keep *you* safe."

"Alethea, please." He tried reaching for me again, but I evaded his hands.

"No!" I shouted as he reached for me. "No. You let them die. They were defenseless. They weren't expecting it!"

"If I didn't do it, then they were going to slaughter my entire military and lay waste to the city! My people would have been just as defenseless."

"Fae are never defenseless." My voice faltered as my heart dipped into my stomach. "Fae are never defenseless," I repeated.

"There were families here too, Alethea!" He tried to argue.

I shook my head as I stepped away from him. My entire body shook. The rage felt like it was going to rip out of me and cleave this room in half. I glanced at the bed again, and as I did, a burst of energy left me. Surprise lit up his face as the entire bed lifted up off the ground and slammed into the wall. The pillows tossed in the air and landed in burnt heaps along the floor.

"Alethea, you need to calm down," Eryx exclaimed as he stepped towards me.

Another burst of energy left me.

"*Calm down?* You want me to *calm down?*" Those words ignited a fire in me as I dropped to my knees. My fingers fisted in my hair as I screamed. Flames ignited across my skin as my powers roiled beneath my skin. They were searching for an outlet. They roared to free themselves. I screamed as it felt like my skin was being flayed open just to give them a hint of fresh air.

"Gods," Eryx muttered as he lowered to the ground beside me.

He reached out to touch me and yelped as he jerked back. The fire continued consuming me. My vision tinted red, and I wailed as the force of my grief hit me.

He had murdered every human in that village. It had been one of the four remaining human kingdoms, and he and his men had burned them to the ground. Not a single person had been spared. Every single person I had ever known was just gone in a swoop of fire.

"Don't touch me!" I screamed as I jerked to my feet, but flames clouded my vision.

"Alethea, I need you to calm down, or you're going to hurt yourself," Eryx said.

The doors burst open. "What's happening?"

"Her powers," Eryx responded. "Alethea, please just calm down."

I heard heavy footsteps, and another voice joined in with the chorus of voices surrounding me. Icy fingers wrapped around my jaw and lifted my head. The cold burned through the heat of my skin.

"Take a breath," the deep voice commanded.

My shoulders and chest moved simultaneously as the command wrapped around me. I drew in a deep breath and exhaled.

"Again," it ordered. I obeyed.

The husky voice instructed me to breathe two more times. The fire slowly subsided, the ice burned into my skin, the sound of flesh sizzled, and I could feel the steam in the air around me.

"Open your eyes," Mykill commanded.

My skin hummed in response to his touch as my eyes fluttered open. My eyes clashed with his icy gaze, chilling the remaining fire beneath my skin.

"Good," Mykill breathed.

I couldn't help but inhale as his breath stirred the hair at my temples. He released his hold on my jaw as I slowly rose to my feet and turned towards Eryx and Cadmus.

"Eryx, she's his -" Cadmus gasped from beside him.

Eryx held up his hand, effectively silencing him, as I slowly turned my gaze towards them. "Alethea." He stepped towards me.

I didn't move as my eyes trained on him. His gaze was pleading, and my eyes narrowed. I felt like a predator ready to devour. His body tensed as he glanced at Mykill beside me.

It was astonishing how fast someone could fall out of love with someone else. The once warm feeling in my chest when I looked at him was replaced by nothing. He had once been the man that provided me sanctuary and rescued me from a horrid fate. But as I looked at him now, my chest felt void of feeling.

"Alethea, we need to go," Mykill said quietly.

He gripped my elbow, but I couldn't tear my eyes from Eryx. His gaze pleaded with me as the doors burst open. Barren flooded around us. My head snapped to the side. Mykill wasn't able to respond quick enough. Everything happened so fast as they trampled him, not paying the slightest bit of attention to me. He did his best to fight them off, but there were too many of them. Mykill grunted as one of the barren landed a blow to the side of his face. Two more latched onto his arms and began dragging him backwards.

"Eryx," I gasped as he stepped up to me and gripped my wrists and yanked me to him. "What have you done?"

"I did it to keep us safe - to keep you safe."

My insides were keenly aware of every cry Mykill made as he was dragged away from us. First Eryx had served up the humans on a silver platter, and now he had turned his back on someone who had helped rescue me. Mykill had helped protect Eryx's kingdom, and in return, he sold him out.

"No," I shook my head. "How could you? You can't do this."

"Please, Alethea. They said they wouldn't touch you if we gave him to them." He inclined his head in Mykill's direction.

Horror settled over my limbs as I slowly turned my face back to Eryx. His eyes were wide, pleading for me to understand. Just like they always were because he was constantly making decisions he knew I'd be against.

Without your mating bond, selfishness is given room to take root.

Mykill's heavy words settled over me, and my mouth fell open as I stared at Eryx. Every one of these decisions he made came from his own selfish desires. He had killed the humans to protect himself, and even now, he was giving up Mykill, our ally - our friend. Shock radiated through me.

"We can't just let them hurt him," I gasped and shoved away from him.

"I need to protect you!" he argued.

"Protect me? You were the one who invited the enemy here!"

"Blossom, please. You don't understand."

"Don't call me that!" I screamed as Eryx reached for me again. "No! Don't touch me!" I heard Mykill shout my name as Eryx wrapped an arm around my waist and lifted me. I shouted for him to put me down as I kicked my legs, trying to give me momentum to launch myself forward.

"No!" I screamed and threw myself forward.

Eryx's arm remained wrapped around my waist. "It's already done, Alethea."

"Let him go!" I screamed as Eryx pulled me backward.

Mykill fought them off the best he could, and his eyes widened as I screamed. Even under attack, his frantic eyes found mine. I knew the feeling in my chest as I watched Mykill. I could feel the terror clawing at my insides of them taking him and torturing him before they kill him. I couldn't let them do it - not only because he had helped us, but because deep down in my chest, I could feel it.

I could see the golden thread emitting from his chest to mine. The thread the fates had woven.

I knew it in my heart as tears pricked at my eyes. If I knew it, then Eryx knew it too. It must have been the manifestation of my powers. The bond radiated through me. The feeling felt familiar, but I had never experienced it as a fae. Now, it was something I couldn't ignore. It moved and breathed the same way I did.

"He's my mate," I gasped as I threw myself forward. "Don't touch him! He's my mate!" I screamed.

Anger soared through me as I spun and landed a punch to Eryx's jaw. Eryx stumbled back in shock, his eyes widening. My hands and knees slapped off the floor as he fully released me.

"He's my mate. Please, I'm begging you!" I cried as I crawled forward.

Mykill had stopped fighting. His eyes were wide and were fully focused on me. I could see the confirmation shining back at me. Confirmation as to why my traitorous body had thought of him whenever I had been with Eryx, and why I had always felt so drawn to him - even if the bond hadn't been there before, or if I just hadn't felt it because my body had been void of magic.

"You're my mate," I whispered as all movement around us stopped.

The barren weren't fae. They couldn't sense mating bonds. Their faces were all slack as they took in the situation before them. I wondered if their minds could even comprehend what was unfolding before them.

"Yes," he answered softly.

Shoving myself to my feet, I glanced over my shoulder just as Eryx reached for me again. I dove forward, away from his grabbing hands, and launched myself towards Mykill. His arms caught me like I knew they would. He pulled me into his chest and turned, shielding my body from the barren.

His chest heaved as he stared down at me, bewilderment in his gaze.

"You're my mate," I whispered again in shock as I placed my hand on his cheek. He nodded, and his breath stirred the hair that had fallen from my braids. A muscle in his cheek popped as his gaze darkened.

"I'm going to get us out of here," he whispered.

Everyone around us moved too slow as they tried reaching for us.

Thunder clapped.

Eryx roared, and as I glanced at him, his cider eyes communicated something I never thought I'd see - hatred, and it was all directed at me.

That was the last thing I saw before we were gone. I had saved my mate, but by doing so, I had severed any remains of a relationship Eryx and I had - my first mate, my first love.

Eryx's roar of anger followed us as I tightened my arms around Mykill. I felt the ground fall out beneath us, and then, we were tumbling.

Chapter 25

Alethea

My eyes flew open as I free fell through the sky. I screamed as the air whipped around me.

I heard a loud beat of wings, and a pair of strong arms circled around me.

"I've got you," Mykill said as he tightened his arms around me and pulled me to his chest. "I've got you." He was breathless as he evened us out.

I still couldn't wrap my mind around what Eryx had done.

"You've known," I accused.

Mykill didn't look at me. "I had my suspicions."

I looked away from him. Anger stirred in my belly as we continued to fly. Mykill's wings beat at the air around us as I sat quietly. The weight of what I had done sat heavily on me.

"I didn't know right away. I'm not sure if it was because your powers hadn't manifested yet, but I always felt drawn to you," he spoke.

"Hmm," was all I said.

I felt the same way, but I wasn't ready to tell him that. I had felt drawn to him when he had stalked towards me back in the human lands when they rescued me. Something about the way he moved and breathed enticed me, pulled me in.

"He'll forgive you," he said, breaking the silence.

"No," I mumbled numbly. "No, he won't."

***

By the time we reached Mykill's kingdom, I was fast asleep on his shoulder. I stirred the moment my stomach dropped out from beneath me, gasping as I clawed at his chest. The second his feet touched the ground, lightning struck, and the ground fell out from beneath my feet. I gasped as we landed on a tiled floor a moment later.

"Are you alright?" Mykill asked as we landed, and he placed me down on my feet.

The shock emanated through me. I didn't have the energy to speak, so I nodded.

The space around me was more extravagant than Eryx's castle. The vast room around me was laid out in an onyx marble from the floor until it reached the ceiling. The walls were bare and cold, like Mykill.

His throne room.

I turned to the massive throne. The oversized marble squared seat rested on a simple dais with three steps leading up to it. The wall behind it was the only thing that wasn't a plain onyx. There was a landscape of a mighty thunderstorm and the boiling ocean below it. The array of grays, light and dark, made out the clouds lining the ceilings. Strokes of lightning struck the surface of the ocean. Waves crashed around the edges of the throne, making it look more majestic.

I sensed Mykill step up beside me. He was silent as he waited for me to point out what I had felt back in Eryx's room. The feeling of it slid over my skin, prickling into every one of my senses. I had briefly experienced that feeling when I was a human, but I'd never experienced it when I was fae. The feeling now was unmistakable.

"You're my mate," I whispered again.

I froze, partly in shock, but also confusion. I couldn't think of how this even happened.

I could feel him intake a sharp breath before he nodded. "Yes."

Astonishment rocked my core, but I remained grounded where I was standing. "How did this happen?" I kept my voice low, barely above a whisper, but I knew he could hear me.

"I don't know," he spoke. His voice was low too, but he kept the lazy, arrogant demeanor that I had come to associate with him.

"I don't want this," I blurted. I knew I couldn't flat out deny the bond. I couldn't say I didn't want the bond, or he'd die. I'd die.

Silence greeted me for a moment before he said, "I don't want this either."

"What do we do?"

"We need to get the scrolls from Eryx," he responded.

"That's not entirely what I meant," I said as I swung towards him.

"I know what you meant, but the only thing that matters is getting the scrolls from him before he hides them."

Frowning, I turned away from him as I nodded. "How are we going to get them?"

"We are going to need to sneak back in."

"Sneak in?" I gasped as I spun back towards him. "How are we supposed to do that?"

"We fly there. You use your powers to ward us. They can sense my powers, but you've never used yours, so they won't be able to sense you."

I frowned as I contemplated his words, then nodded. "Let's do it."

After a quick meal and a stock of weapons, we were flying back to Eryx's kingdom. It had taken a little bit of practice, but I managed to hold the ward for the majority of the flight to keep us hidden. Mykill said that Eryx could sense his powers because he had used them before, and Eryx had been accustomed to him for so long.

Mykill's feet touched the ground, and I let the ward around us drop. He set me down and nodded. My hands shook slightly as I raised them in front of me and turned them over.

"That'll stop once you get used to exerting your energy into your powers," Mykill explained. "Let's go." He placed his hand on the small of my back and led me forward.

We had landed on the balcony just above the gardens, and there wasn't a guard in sight.

"Are there any barren here?" I whispered as Mykill reached in front of me and pulled the door open.

"No," he breathed. "I don't sense anything."

I frowned, but we continued down the halls. Questions spiraled inside of me, but I forced myself to remain focused.

I nearly shrieked as Mykill spun on me. My back slammed off the wall, and he smothered my lips with his hand. My eyes widened as I glared up at him, but he shook his head and pressed a finger above his lips. The air around us shifted as the ward covered us.

"Who goes there?" a voice called, echoing down the hall to us.

I stiffened as a whistling sound cut through the silence. Mykill hissed and slapped at the back of his neck. A dart clattered to the ground.

"What is that?" I gasped as I stared down at the dart.

He growled and glanced behind him. The sound of guards rushing down the halls surrounded us to where I couldn't tell where they were coming from.

"It's faelace," he said between clenched teeth. "It suppresses your powers."

A door at the end of the hall burst open, and a dozen guards stopped as they took us in. "Stop and surrender immediately!"

"You need to go," Mykill said as he turned towards the guards and pulled his two swords from their sheaths. "Go get the scrolls."

"I can't leave you!" I exclaimed.

"You don't have a choice, Alethea. Go."

I stepped back as the guards neared us. I wasn't trained enough to help him in combat.

"Go!" Mykill shouted as his sword clashed with the first guards.

I fell back a step as I watched him move effortlessly. Fear pumped through my veins. What would Eryx do if they apprehended us? Would he execute Mykill? Would he throw me in the dungeons?

"Go, Alethea!" he hissed, and I nodded.

I turned away from him and ran like hounds of hell were nipping at my heels. I tore into Eryx's office. The door pounded off the wall, and I dove for his desk. I ripped open every drawer and dumped its contents on the ground. Cursing, I sat back on my heels as I examined the contents of what had been in the drawers. Pens, parchments, clips, but no scrolls.

They had to be here, I thought.

"Your blood is inked on the scrolls." The dragon's deep voice floated back to me.

Closing my eyes, I took a deep breath and tried to feel where the scrolls were. I closed my eyes and pictured my blood calling to me, luring me towards it. I stiffened as it felt like an invisible hand slipped into mine and began pulling me. It led me to his desk chair. I frowned as I stared at the worn leather chair. Realization burst through me as I dove forward and ripped the cushion up. Underneath was a wooden base, and as I opened the compartment, I found them.

Smiling to myself, I scooped them up and held them to my chest.

"Let's go, Alethea!" Mykill hissed as he erupted into Eryx's office. He glanced down at the bundled scrolls tucked beneath my arms.

"I will be the keeper of these," I told him as I froze.

He nodded, and his eyes gleamed with understanding. He knew I didn't trust him. I didn't trust anyone anymore. "Of course. Only you will know where they are."

I stared back at him, trying to read his face for any tell that he was lying. But his face remained impassive as it always did.

"We don't have much time," Mykill warned.

I nodded again as I stepped towards him. He reached his hand towards me, and I paused. My gaze froze on his extended hand with his arrangement of rings and scars. He was my mate, but why did grabbing his hand cause my heart to spike?

My eyes followed a scar that curved around his thumb and up the back of his palm.

One day I'd ask what it was from.

Grabbing his hand, my head moved back up as he stared down at him. I saw a chip in that icy exterior as his gaze softened, but he covered it just as quickly as he squeezed my hand and yanked me from Eryx's office. We fled down the halls, but he kept a slower pace so I could keep up with him. It was painstakingly obvious that I was not in the same shape as him as my chest heaved and my lungs burned. I nearly groaned in relief when we made it outside to the gardens.

We were free.

"Alethea, what have you done?" Eryx gasped from behind me.

My feet froze, my entire body stiffened, and I couldn't help the dark chuckle that escaped me as I turned back towards Eryx. His hair was ruffled around his face, and he was shirtless. My eyes ran down the front of his torso, taking in the golden skin and tattoos.

"I did what needed to be done," I whispered hoarsely.

"No, Alethea. Please," Eryx said as he stepped towards me, but I stepped back into Mykill's chest. His eyes widened as he looked at Mykill with a heady mix of bewilderment and hatred. "You're doing this for him?" Eryx took another step towards me.

Mykill growled in response. "Do not move towards her."

I shook my head as Eryx's body trembled with fury. "I'm doing this for myself."

I heard Mykill's wings flare behind him as he readied himself.

Eryx stepped towards us again. "Alethea, please. We are just pawns of the fates. Please, don't do this."

I glanced down at my hand that held the bundle of scrolls. "I won't let you hide them. This is the only thing that can help me find my parents."

"We will find another way!" he argued.

"I don't believe you."

His eyes widened. He shook his head, but he didn't speak. There was nothing to be said. He had lied to me over and over again, destroying every ounce of trust I had in him. At one time, I would have trusted him with my life.

"We can fix this. Please Alethea, let me fix this," he begged.

I shook my head. "There's nothing to be fixed."

His eyes widened as he gasped. At first, I saw a glimmer of guilt, but when he composed himself, his expression turned bland. Realization settled over my limbs like a wet blanket. This would rock our relationship. We would never be able to go back to how we were.

"Goodbye, Eryx." I whispered the words I never thought I would say.

My hands trembled as I stepped back into Mykill. He slipped an arm beneath my knees and lifted me. I could have sworn I saw the semblance of a smirk on his face as he shot to the sky. Eryx's roar carried with us into the clouds.

***

Mykill's wings beat at the air around us, the sound calming my racing heart slightly. He hadn't spoken since we had left. I had half expected Eryx to come after us, but I knew better. His pride was damaged. His mate had left with his nemesis.

"He'll forgive you," Mykill finally whispered.

I couldn't help but laugh harshly as I examined my hands. I shook my head. "No. No, he won't."

"Maybe one day," he said in response.

The days had blended together since we had come to Mykill's kingdom. I sat in a window overlooking the city below. It still baffled me how different it looked from Eryx's city. This was a city by the sea. Houses were nestled across the rocky mountains overlooking the water. There were marble staircases to each home, but the occupants didn't use them. As I watched, people flew from their front doors or out the windows and into the sky. If I was a painter, I would have painted it.

But no matter how beautiful the scenery was, I couldn't bring myself out of the slump of self-loathing. I had betrayed Eryx. Mykill let me keep the scrolls, and they were hidden beneath my mattress. There was a voice in the back of my mind that wanted to defend Eryx and his actions. I knew the voice was wrong, but that didn't make the feelings go away. He had lied to me over and over. He had proved he was selfish time and time again. My safety had been his excuse for slaughtering an entire city of humans.

Disgust curled through me at the thought as well as heartbreak. He had been my first love - my first everything. Even with the deceit, there was a piece of my heart that I had given him, and I left it there shattered on the ground the last time I'd seen him.

Mykill had food delivered to my room for breakfast, lunch and dinner, but I couldn't even bring myself to bathe, much less eat.

The door to my room burst open, and as I glanced outside, I knew it wasn't breakfast time yet.

I slowly turned as Mykill barged into my room. "Get out," I snapped at him and turned back towards the window.

"Get up," he retorted and threw a pair of fighting leathers at me. "You need to keep training."

I glanced down at the leathers, then back out towards the morning sky. I didn't say a word.

I didn't look at him as he dropped to his knees in front of my seat and gripped my forearms. I cried out as he wrenched me forward so our faces were only inches apart.

"What are you doing?" I snapped and tried to kick him in the leg, but he remained unmovable.

"You do not get to sit here wallowing in your self-pity and shame. You did nothing wrong, You'll drive yourself mad. Now get up, put on your leathers, and earn your keep just like you said you would."

I glared at him before I yanked my arms from his grasp and shoved at his chest. "I fucking hate you," I growled as he rose.

A smile tipped up the side of his mouth. "The feelings are almost mutual."

I stood and moved around him, gripping the leathers to my chest. "Get out," I said again, and he complied.

He paused at the door and kept his back to me. "He'll forgive you."

He had said that multiple times now, and just like every other time, I said, "No, no, he won't."

Eryx

"My reports have come back, and they're at his kingdom," Cadmus said as he entered the throne room flanked by two guards.

I glowered down at them as they came forward. I hadn't gone back to bed after they had fled from their betrayal.

"How fortified are they?" I asked.

"Stronger than us," Cadmus said as he frowned. "We can't attack them."

Rising from my throne, I brushed past them and out into the hall. My rage tasted in the back of my throat as I stormed down the hall. I heard Cadmus trying to keep up with me as I barreled towards my bedroom.

"Eryx!" he shouted as I started up the stairs. "Please, wait!"

I swung towards him. My chest heaved, and I knew my eyes were wide. I felt murderous.

"We can't attack them. She could get caught in the crossfires."

"I don't care," I growled.

His eyes widened, and he stumbled back a step.

"Tell everyone to be ready at dawn," I said as I turned from him and back up the stairs.

"No," he said firmly.

My feet froze mid step, and I slowly turned towards him. "What did you say?" My eyes narrowed on him.

"I won't do it. I won't risk harming her." His eyes were wide, pleading as he gazed at me. "Please, just rest, and we can discuss this in the morning."

"I will be discussing nothing in the morning. I will burn them. They are traitors. If you won't do it, then you're released from your position as General."

"What?" he gasped. "But we've been friends since we were boys."

"I don't want a friend. I want a General. You heard what I said. If you won't do it, then leave."

I whipped around as I continued up the steps. Cadmus didn't follow. I threw my hand forward, and the doors thudded open as I barreled into my bedroom. I growled as her scent hit me. My vision tinted red as I threw my hands back, and the bed went flying through the air. Adrius jumped as he watched me, his eyes wide as he tried to assess if there was a threat.

I needed her scent gone. I needed every trace of her gone from my castle.

Turning, I fled from my room. Cadmus was no longer on the stairs as I flew down them and down the halls.

My feet flew over the floor, and I threw open her bedroom door. I roared as I gripped the doors to the wardrobe and ripped them from their hinges. I grabbed handfuls of fabric and ripped them from the closets. I threw my hand out. Shadows erupted from my palm and began tearing apart the furniture in its fury - *my* fury. Glass erupted in the bathroom, spraying across the room.

I wanted every trace of both of them gone.

I growled as her scent hit me as I opened his door. Her scent was in his bedroom. My vision tinted red, and my body shook.

Traitors.

I roared as my shadows exploded, ripping everything in their path.

I wanted her to watch as I tore his body limb from limb. I wanted to hear her beg and plead for his life and then see the terror in her eyes as I took her mate's life. Then, I'd force her to live without him. Only then she would feel close to how I felt when she had been taken from me. She had become my entire world, and quicker than a bee whizzing past, she turned on me for *him*. I had done what I needed to protect her, but she wouldn't understand. She wouldn't understand because he had gotten in her head. He had wormed his way into her mind, whispering lies about me and my ways in her ears.

But I knew one thing. I would not stop until they were ashes beneath my feet. I would not stop until I held his still-beating heart in my hands and heard her piercing cries for mercy.

Printed in Great Britain
by Amazon